SONG FOR RIA

Also by Michelle Shine

Mesmerised
The Subtle Art of Healing

SONG FOR RIA

Michelle Shine

Red Door

Published by RedDoor
www.reddoorpress.co.uk

The author and publisher gratefully acknowledge permissions granted to
reproduce the copyright material in this book. Every effort has been made
to trace copyright holders and to obtain their permission for the use of
copyright material. The publisher apologises for any errors or omissions
in the above list and would be grateful if notified of any corrections that
should be incorporated in future reprints or editions of this book

'Trouble's Lament'
Words and Music by Tori Amos
Copyright © 2014 Sword and Stone Publishing Inc.
All Rights Administered by Downtown Music Publishing LLC
All Rights Reserved Used by Permission
Reprinted by Permission of Hal Leonard Europe Ltd.

'All The Love' by Kate Bush © 1982, Reproduced by permission of Noble
& Brite Ltd/ EMI Music Publishing, London W1T 3LP

pp.173 Reprinted by permission of SLL/Sterling Lord Literistic, Inc.
Copyright by Linda Gray Sexton and Loring Conant, Jr. 1981.

ISBN 978-1-913062-99-6

Cover design: Kari Brownlie

Typesetting: Jen Parker, Fuzzy Flamingo
www.fuzzyflamingo.co.uk
Printed in the UK by CPI Group (UK), Croydon

To my parents
Elaine and David Ratner
with love

This is a story about a crime of the heart...

Interview with Alison Connaught

Reproduced with kind permission from Over It *magazine*

In case anybody missed it, something phenomenal happened last year. Three and a half years after Alison's daughter Ria died, she released a self-written, self-produced album of just piano and vocals in an elusive style and it went platinum. The amazing thing is that, although she has written many songs for great artists over a span of thirty years, she has never released a singer-songwriter album before.

I spent a long time tracking her down. The people that I spoke to told me she likes to live a quiet life and is not easy to get hold of these days. Turns out, she wasn't easy to reach even when I managed to get through to her own people. Consequently, I've had to wait a long time for this interview.

We meet in the lobby of a London hotel. She is already there when I arrive, with a glass of red wine before her. She is short, slim, has tons of auburn hair, and doesn't look her age. She gets up as soon as she sees me, shakes my hand enthusiastically and says, 'Hi, so nice to meet you; and after all this time, huh?'

Part of my job is to make people feel comfortable in my company, but Alison immediately makes *me* feel comfortable in hers. She points at her glass and says, 'The irony is that most people have to feel stronger to give up wine, whilst I had to feel stronger to drink it again.'

She spent time with a shaman in North America and after that she couldn't drink wine for 'a very long time'. I ask about her experience with the shaman.

'Greg and my stay with the Hopis changed the way I see life. I couldn't write anything new for two years after Ria died, but not only did they help connect me back to the muses so I could compose again, they also helped me to find the courage and strength I needed to carry on with my life.'

'And to write the album.'

'You know, you don't realise – people don't realise – that sometimes when we are so hurt, it's like we are locked up in a cage with that hurt, and we can't seem to fight it because we don't have the tools to deal with it. We have to hook up with anything we can find that's natural to show us the way, and by that I mean something that resonates with the Earth.'

'But not wine.'

'No' – she laughs – 'you have to keep your head together whilst you're working it all out, at least I did; the truth hurts but the truth also heals.'

'How so?'

'Trust me, you don't want to find out.'

'I've been listening to the album for several months now and it's not like anyone else's music. It's not even like your own music, those songs that brought you hit after hit after hit.'

'No, that's right.'

'Without a history as a singer-songwriter though, how did this album actually come about?'

'I was on a mission to understand what happened to Ria and why she was on opioids; I didn't know she was taking them until after she died. So I went on a journey to find out and these songs are the fruits of that journey.

'Then the publishing division of the record company that I've worked with ever since the start of my career approached me about these songs, and initially set up a meeting between myself and the production company that made the series about Ria's life. They wanted to use old material of mine, no doubt in poignant places, as part of the show. They also wanted a new song for the title theme.

'I wasn't convinced about the integrity of that forthcoming production, so I turned it down.'

'I'm intrigued, so how did the album eventually materialise?'

'Well, that's the maddest thing. You'd think my reaction would have immediately put the whole thing to bed. But within days of my refusal of their offer, I received an email from the record company with a proposition for a one-off deal. They promised me the album would have nothing to do with the television series but, nevertheless, the contract would only exist if I could manage to record and put out the work to coincide with the series being shown on terrestrial television worldwide, so that my work could be advertised in the episode breaks. Part of the contract included my commitment to appear on chat shows and give interviews.'

'So that's why we're here.'

She smiles openly.

'They also said something else, the thing that made me want to do it.'

'What was that?'

'That it would give me the opportunity to have my voice heard amongst the milieu of others about my daughter. Oh, and they wanted me to come back to them with my answer within a week. I had only one condition.'

'What was that?'

'My husband, Harvey, wanted to invest in a project that would keep Ria's memory alive – in the way her family and no doubt her friends and fans would want her to be remembered. So I said I'd do it, but only on the proviso that Harvey could be a fifty per cent partner in the project. Thankfully, they agreed.'

To date, the album *Song for Ria* has sold over ten million copies worldwide and won both a Grammy and a Mercury award. I remark on how this album defies genre and yet, at the same time, the melodies and even the lyrics are incredibly familiar.

How can that be?

'I take that as a compliment.'

'Did you write the album thinking that this body of songs will cross the divide and appeal to people of all ages, all musical

persuasions and political classes? Because it really is quite incredible the way this compilation has taken off.'

'No, I was far more selfish than that. I wrote these songs because they saved me from myself. It was a kind of self-flagellation, blaming myself for Ria's death. You know the kind of thing – if I had done this or that as a parent, things would have turned out differently. I was beating myself up with it.'

'Are you referring to Ria being part of a cult?'

'No, not at all. She was never in a cult. Everyone who was close to her will tell you that. There is absolutely no truth in that assertion.'

'So, why do you think the television show ran with that storyline?'

'I don't know.'

'Do you have any idea, at least, of the motive behind why the makers of the show would want to put that idea out there, if it's not true?'

'Spite. Jealousy, maybe… I don't know.'

'Do you want to say any more about that?'

'No.'

'No?'

'Are you trying to make me get down to their level? I don't want to do that. You asked me earlier about the songs on the album, what inspired them and about my guilt. I understand now it's quite a common feeling when people lose a loved one in such a tragic way. Everyone's experienced loss, guilt and shame. We are very often victims of ourselves but we don't talk about it.

'When was it? Last week, I think. I was approached by a couple through a friend of a friend of a friend. They wanted to give me their feedback on the work. They told me that they both couldn't stop listening to the album, but the woman said it was because of the lyrics, whilst the man said he's not a word man, that it's only the atmosphere of the music that means something to him, and the voice intonation – it's the feeling in the sound that moves him.'

'What about the lyrics? The meaning behind them?'

'Well, the truth is, the songs mean what they mean. I mean they might not mean the same thing to me, intellectually, as they mean to you. We all have our own lives, our own experiences, and come to our own conclusions but feelings are universal.'

'Were you surprised by the success of Song for Ria?'

'Of course, but I was even more surprised at having the opportunity to record the work and then to have the exposure.'

'As you said earlier it was because its release was perfectly timed to coincide with the showing of the series, Lucky Girl: The Story of Ria Connaught, *on television in, pretty much, every country in the world.'*

'That's right.'

'Apart from the cult assertion, did you like the series? I mean…'

'Sally Denoué is amazing. The first time I saw her take on the part of Ria was in her apartment in New York. I was spellbound; I thought my daughter was in the room with me. It was also the moment I first heard that they had started working on the series.'

'And how did you know Sally?'

'Ria and Sally were housemates and budding actresses together. They shared a house in LA when they both found themselves working there.'

'And Ms Denoué was nominated for the same Oscar Ria won.'

Alison smiles.

'I've just realised, you haven't answered one of my questions.'

'I'm sorry, which one was that?'

'Did you like the series?'

'Of course not. What mother would enjoy seeing a screen adaptation of her own daughter's demise, and on top of that, one that wasn't exactly accurate?' But, hey, you can't slander someone who's no longer with us and the truth is, I have a strange relationship with that show. If they hadn't made the box set, I would never have had the opportunity to make the album, which I believe Ria helped me to write, by the way. There are bigger forces at work here, you just have to give into them.'

'Meaning?'

'My shaman and the Hopis taught me how to get back into life when I could no longer be inspired by it. They showed me a path, a route to return to acceptance by opening my eyes to what's important.'

'What's it like, being on that path?'

'It's made me more aware of what goes on in the world and my place within it.'

She waves her arms in the air.

'I'm more open. I understand that my daughter is still here in spirit, living inside me. Sometimes I hear myself responding to something or someone and out of my mouth comes a reply that's uncharacteristic for me, but is something she would have said.'

'Coming back to the album, do you see it as your response to the box set?'

'In a way, yes I do.'

'Can you say any more about that?'

She sits back in her chair with amusement written on her face and I can see her thinking. Finally, she says, 'Leonard Cohen sang, "There is a crack in everything, that's how the light gets in". So, I suppose you can say that I have found the crack in me and I have let a chink of light in. This album is my truth; it's everything I have to say.'

Track list:

Broken
Spirit Hunter
I've Been Prey
Disbelief
All the Heroes
Less than Nothing (that's what I know)
From Afar
To Love Again
The Strange Thing Called Truth
Invisible
Warrior
Song for Ria

PART ONE

Broken

Only tragedy allows the release of love and grief
never normally seen
Kate Bush

1

The day after my daughter died, Harvey – my husband and Ria's stepdad – flew to LA. I just couldn't and went to the top of Parliament Hill instead, thinking the higher I could get, the closer I would be to her.

Sitting on a bench, letting the wind batter me, my hair slashing cat o' nine tails against my cheeks, I allowed myself to put my icy hands in my pockets, just.

I was light years away from feeling the nurturing warmth we shared after her birth, when still tied by an invisible cord, I'd wake with erupting breasts just moments before she cried.

She would have been about three months when I began to need my own space again and had to squeeze myself into stolen moments. Inspiration tugged me towards the sonoluminescence of my piano, a Bechstein – Bechs for short – as Ria clamped my nipple and held me still with her eyes. I was engaged in a tug of war, too often torn away from her by a superstition: that if I didn't kowtow to the muses, I risked them abandoning me for some other, more attentive, composer.

It was even harder when Ria began to move. On her knees, she was fast, but once on her feet she became unstoppable. An idea for a song landed in my head and I was its slave, absent without leave from the real world. It might have only been for a matter of seconds, but I would often find myself with a pulsating heart, yanking her away from curbs, catching her on a hairpin turn, as laughing and teasingly, she tried to dodge my grasp.

Ria was funny and clever and feisty, oh yeah. There was a resilience to her. I didn't see it slip away until one memorable day when we were together on the beach. I'd taken up photography; it was a bit of a phase. The sky was white marble with grey threads and blemishes. I found a large seashell with a smooth metallic blue and pink inner surface. My camera was poised to capture it but something made me look up. Ria was messing around by the sea. She was kicking up sandstorms, twisting her body this way and that as if to avoid hands that were reaching out to grab her. Her head was bowed, shoulders hunched.

She was on the cusp of womanhood and seemed so sad for what she was about to become. It should have been a celebration. I wanted her to have the freedom to find herself, be herself, without shame or guilt. I knew that would set her free of my authority, my loan, but hey.

My heart pleaded for her to blossom for my camera, then in one small moment she thrust her hands into her blazer pockets, turned swiftly around and stared into the lens. The tip of her tongue appeared at the corner of her lips as she lifted her chin and raised her luminous grey eyes.

Click.

★★★

Sixteen years later and I'm crooning over that black and white image of a thirteen-year-old girl, frozen in time. I kiss its glossy surface and place it on the piano stand where she stares back at me with a myriad of what-ifs and if-onlys; I too, want to die.

My fingers extend over cold keys. My voice wails. I'm reaching out, yet unable to connect, not even with a note. Frustration has me slamming down the piano lid.

Where is she?

A white feather will do, or a fleeting intangible, glimpsed out of the corner of my eye. But nothing like that happens and I just want to run away. I stand up and knock over the piano stool then bang my fist against my lips.

I go into the kitchen and turn on the tap. Water cascades over the top of the kettle. I jump backwards but not quickly enough and now I'm soaked all down my front. I hoist the wet and heavy appliance over to its electric tray and it doesn't phut and die but surprises me by heating up, then I go and burn myself on its steam.

Over by the window, I'm blowing and shaking my painful hand.

Harvey comes home. Whilst I'm making him a dish of soulless food, he opens a good bottle of wine. I can't gulp it down fast enough. He asks me what's wrong. I tell him I'm surprised he's even asking. I don't remember him saying anything else.

After dinner, which neither of us manage to eat, he annoys me by taking his glass into the other room. He watches football, sitting on the sofa and propping his feet up on the coffee table. I go upstairs and toss and turn in bed. The aggravating sound of chanting comes up through the floorboards.

The next morning, as Harvey steps out of the shower whilst I'm taking a pee, he says, 'You complain that I'm not hearing you, but have you ever thought that it's *you* who's not listening?'

I don't understand what he's saying at first, or maybe it's just that I don't want to understand. I look up at him quizzically and flush the toilet.

He goes on, 'Sometimes you're so wrapped up in your own thoughts, you don't even know someone else is talking.'

'I don't accept that,' I say. 'When I write songs, I'm constantly tuning into characters and someone else's story.'

'Characters and stories,' he says, grabbing a towel.

'Yes, characters and stories.'

'That's not real life, Alison.'

He hurries into the bedroom. I run after him.

'Did you want to tell me something last night?'

'It doesn't matter.'

'No, it does. I'm sorry. I'm listening… I'm listening.'

He can hardly be dry but he's putting on his clothes, saying he's late for a meeting. Slightly dishevelled, he walks out the door.

Harvey is not a creative man. No, let me rephrase that,

he doesn't work in a creative industry. He's a businessman. He doesn't do tai chi or meditation or any other spiritual pursuit but he's thoughtful, I mean he considers things, and most importantly, he gets me and that is both wondrous and devastating.

I'm not going to try and write a song today. When I go into my piano room the instrument I've made music with for so many years is frowning at me in storm-cloud light.

'What do I have to do, Bechs?' I ask, standing at his side and placing my palms on his shiny veneer. I tell him that even though I don't stay in here permanently, this is my room too. 'In fact,' I say. 'If it wasn't for me, you wouldn't even be here. You'd be dumped in an LA lounge, scratched and damaged by some young upstart who cuts cocaine on your beautiful back.'

I am ignored and turn to stare at Ria's school painting. It hangs on the small piece of wall between two floor-to-ceiling windows so that when I play – correction, when I'm able to play properly, now a distant memory – I will glance over and feel the thrill of our two creative spirits wrapping around each other and rising like steam.

The painting is a swirl of rainbow pastels. I slip inside the endlessly changing colours into a whirling time and no-place. Then I pull myself out of the folds and try to rearrange myself in the bitter present; only I can't. The aura of the past haunts me – that night, eating dinner, sharing a bottle of wine followed by brandy, chatting about our day.

'What are we up to this weekend?' Harvey asked.

'Nothing.'

'I can think of something,' he winked.

When the landline rang the first time, we didn't pick up. We thought it must be a cold caller, as everyone else for years had preferred to reach us on our mobiles, even though mine was rarely switched on. On the third ring, Harvey slumped into the hall. His face was ashen when he returned. I can't remember what we did next; if we hugged, locked eyes, or looked away from each other. I do remember being stunned with disbelief, leaving the half-eaten food and trembling glasses on the table. On the way upstairs, I bumped into the doorway and bruised my hip. I didn't take off my make-up, clean my teeth or even undress. I just threw myself on the bed and closed my eyes.

Harvey shook me out of oblivion just as dawn broke the next day. When I asked why he'd woken me, he told me he couldn't stand my mewling any longer.

Some things, even in sleep, are impossible to forget.

★★★

Ria died in the bath from an overdose of prescribed medication. She was twenty-seven years old. I never even knew she was addicted to opioid painkillers. So much for my motherly instincts. What else did I miss? I didn't realise…what?

I am now left hoping for enlightenment to leap out of her year twelve artwork, and when that doesn't happen, I go over things in my mind. Questioning everything, just everything, on continual repeat.

Ria was a very private person. If I had made a point of studying her every move, would she have hated me for poking around? Would she have secretly loved me more? Would it have saved her?

No matter where I stand in this room, or from what angle I view the swirl, I can only see hope in its brightness; a future unravelling that is now totally unravelled without explanation or goodbye.

A flash of sunlight slips through the clouds; the room smiles, mockingly. Sitting on my hands before Bechs, I don't disturb him. I'm not prising his mouth open or forcing him to collaborate with me. No, I don't do that. I just sit there listening to a couple of pigeons duet, hoarse as chain smokers. They go silent. Rain splatters against the window.

There are things I do to distract myself. Listening helps, a play on the radio or a discussion from which I stand apart. I take myself outside and walk the length of the tree-lined drive leading away from our home. The squelch of my footsteps turns to a plod in the sodden grass. Nearing the road, voices stop me in my tracks. I'd momentarily forgotten that they're still coming and going in a vigil beyond the gate. They've made a shrine for her from photos, flowers, candles and written messages. They scream the lyrics to the soundtrack of the film she won an Oscar for, as best supporting actress, in the same frustrated way I tried to express myself yesterday.

I take a left across the grass and trudge to the other, smaller gate that's almost imperceptible amongst the foliage. As I push, it digs into the ground and I have to wrestle my way around it to go into the woods. I wait for Annie on the bench that Harvey and I put there to honour her late husband, John.

They were neighbours who came with the house, living on our land in a small homemade dwelling next to the public footpath. We allowed them to stay, rent free, as did our predecessors. The Foragers – not their real name – didn't deal in money but offerings of eggs, freshly butchered rabbit, pigeon and hand-picked perennials, all brought to our door with thanks.

As I wait, I think of Ria as a small child in a blue dress, yellow wellies, russet hair, playing a jungle game and violently attacking the grass with a stick. I ask, what were you thinking, Ri? Who were you attacking? Someone bad that you had known when I wasn't around? My head shoved so far up my arse I couldn't see what I should have seen.

I shake my head free of those terrible thoughts and look towards the animal smell, at a hen leading her flock and a sheep with a bell. Annie is coming. She's carrying a crooked stick. I have to shield my eyes from a beam of light that's slipped through the trees. The sun disappears and dim reality takes over. Raindrops plop onto leaves at my feet.

'For a moment there, I thought we were going to have a rainbow,' Annie calls. 'Last week I saw one over in the clearing that went right across the sky.'

She waves her stick and sits down beside me in her raggedy clothes that never look warm enough. Her greying, naturally oiled hair sends its musk my way. The smell doesn't bother me. I find it comforting.

Looking down at her muddy plastic shoes, I ask if her feet aren't cold and how come she's able to wear those things even in winter, which is something I've never thought to ask her before.

'You get used to it,' she says. 'You get used to everything eventually. Whatever life throws at you; you either get used to it or life's going to chew you up and spit you out.'

I think about that and ask, 'What about losing John?' She stares ahead at the tree – its arthritic roots peeping up through the ground, its trunk thick and scarred with keloid lips surrounding a gaping mouth – its head of leaves shielding us from the worst of the rain. 'Have you got used to losing him?'

'Yes,' she says. 'I'm used to it. Doesn't mean I like it but this is my life now and I have to be OK with it.'

'I need to ask you something.'

Her eyes fix on me.

'I know when you and John were very young, you were homeless and met on the streets.'

'That's right, we were a couple of drunks.'

'Then you came here.'

'We did.'

'How did you both get off the booze?'

She smiles, shrugs, says she doesn't really know.

'Was it this place?'

11

'I hear you,' she says, but that's all she says.

The rain stops although there are still drops sliding off the tree's foliage. The sheep stands still. The chickens waddle around. A squirrel comes out of nowhere and speeds up the tree. It feels good to be sitting here beside Annie, in silence. I'm startled when she says, 'I once wanted what other people have.' She looks up at the sky, laughs and says, 'I can't tell her that.'

'What?'

She shakes her head.

'You wouldn't understand.'

'Try me.'

'No.'

'Why not?'

Her cheek twitches. A faint flutter overtakes her lips. 'This has nothing to do with me. You and Harvey have always been kind. I don't want to upset you.'

'You won't upset me.'

She leans forward and stares at the ground. I look down too. A twig is wriggling. There's something small and alive under a rug of brown soggy mulch. Why is it alive whilst my daughter isn't? I could put an end to that life, instantly, with my shoe. I could walk away from that murder, go off and live my life and never think about it again. I shudder and look up.

Annie says, 'You have to accept what's happened. Yes, you have to accept it because if you don't the bitterness will get you.'

Accept it? How is that possible? I need to get away from

this moment, from Annie, and I say what I always say at the end of our conversations.

'Is there anything I can get you, Annie? Anything you need?' But there's an edge to my voice, even I can hear it.

Her response is almost imperceptible; the shake of her head followed by a long blink and a nod. I understand that she understands that I don't understand. What I do understand, is that it saddens her that I made her tell me something she knew I would take in bad part.

She stands and waits for her joints to settle. I watch her walk away from me, followed by her animal brood.

2

Phil Hammond phones. He's the A and R man from the music publishing company. He asks how I'm getting on. I don't tell him that I still don't go out, except to the village if I really need something and for walks on the estate. I've started smoking a little cannabis every day because it helps me to be a nice wife. I don't tell him that either. He's talking at me, I'm not taking in what he says. When he goes quiet, I say, 'No.'

'What does that mean?'

'It means, no, I haven't written anything new yet.'

'Have you thought about getting some help from, I don't know, a counsellor or something?'

'For grieving?'

'Yeah.'

'No.'

'What about going to a doctor and getting something prescribed?'

'Yeah, and we both know where that leads, don't we, Phil?' I can feel his discomfort coming through the line. 'And anyway, grieving isn't an illness, it's part of life.'

He is silent and I suddenly realise that both people I have spoken to, not including Harvey, have really pissed me off. So maybe it's not what Phil said, or what Annie said, maybe it's me.

'Look, I'm sorry, I just need some more time, that's all.'

'Alison, this is very difficult over the phone. Can I come and see you?'

'Sure.'

'When?'

'Next week?'

'I'll be there on Tuesday, probably get there around midday; put the kettle on.'

The screen on my phone goes blank. I go cold. There are noises coming from upstairs. I'm taking two steps at a time, shouting, 'Who's in there?' Flinging the door open to find no one. No one's in there.

When Greta comes an hour later – our surrogate housewife – I take her into Ria's room. She stands and I sit on the bed. When she asks why we're here, it seems stupid and I don't know how to respond.

'Do you want me to dust?'

I just look at her.

'Ah, you want me to help you go through her things.'

'Greta, can you hear something?'

'Like what?'

'I don't know, I thought I heard something in here earlier.'

'I was in a house once when the children thought there was a ghost; turned out their hamster was scrabbling between the ceiling and the floorboards.'

'There's no hamster in this house, Greta.'

'I know, but things aren't always what they seem, are they?'

'What do you mean?'

'Alison, can I tell you something?'

'I don't know, Greta, what is it?'

'Something I've been wanting to tell you.'

'Then why haven't you?'

Her cheeks flush, her face tightens and her chapped lips grow paler.

Maybe it's you who isn't listening.

I pat the space beside me as my body turns to water.

'Come, tell me whatever.'

Gingerly, she sits down.

I touch her arm and tell her it's OK.

***

I am out by the sea; the same beach where I took the photo of Ria. It's too early in the year to be sitting here but I'm sitting here anyway, alone, knees to chest, bum sinking into sand, wind playing with my hair.

It's been a clear day. You can just about see land on the other side of the water. The sun is slow-diving with smoky pinks and blues on its tail. There's a boat on the choppy horizon moving up and down like a cartoon image. I admit it to myself, I am completely lost now.

Greta said something happened to Ria, in year eleven. My first thought was, Yeah, it's called not being an adult and not being a child anymore. Lots of coming to terms:

wearing the new scent of sexuality: the imposition of
periods: the embarrassment of boys. Adolescence is shit.
But I didn't say that. I asked what she knew. She said it
seemed serious, changed Ria.

'Did she talk to you?'

'No, but she knew I knew.'

'What did you know?'

She shrugged.

'What did you think you knew?'

'That something had made her unhappy.'

Was she already gone from me? Fallen for that boy?
Informed by touched-up pictures in magazines of models
and rock stars, internet porn, television and the lure of fame?

I guess she was.

Clothes strewn around her bedroom floor and
thumping vibrations that shook the house and reached me
through walls that confined her. I always hoped she was in
there dancing but once she emerged screaming, 'I can't go
out like this. I just can't. I'm too fucking fat.'

I was surprised.

'You're not fat,' I hit back.

'What do you know, Mum?'

'I know a bit about life.'

Angry tears streamed down her face. I wanted my
baby in my arms where I could croon to her about how
everything was going to be all right. I took a step towards
her; she put her hands up to stop me.

'Don't, Mum.' She stamped her feet to show me she
was serious. 'You don't know anything about *my* life.'

17

'So, let's sit down and talk.'

'It's OK.'

'It's clearly not OK, you need to talk about these things.'

Caught in her own whirlwind, she flew back into her room, the door slamming behind her.

I had lost the key to my daughter.

Devastated, I spoke to Harvey in our pseudo-Victorian bathroom.

'I don't know what to do about Ria,' I said.

'There's nothing you can do.'

'I know but I can't just sit here and do nothing.'

'Well, what can you do?'

'Harvey, you're making me feel so alone in this.'

'You could be around a bit more often,' he said.

'I am around.'

The doorbell rang.

'Bye,' Ria called from downstairs.

Another door slammed. I saw her out the window as she climbed into the taxi – short skirt, clinging top, teased hair, make-up like a mask.

'I'm always around,' I said.

But it's true, I was rarely found in the common parts of our home. Too often, I was with Bechs. Something about his sound, so highly addictive. He made me forget everything other than the music we created. Like a lot of women, I could be absent even when I was at home.

★★★

Phil turns up. I'd forgotten he was coming. When I open the door, I'm shocked to find him standing there. He appears old; a little hunched, a little lined, his hair all dried out. Don't they say, what you see in others is a reflection of yourself?

We hug.

I ask after his wife.

'She's good. Harvey?'

'He's good, too.'

We have tea in the conservatory. I pull the blinds halfway otherwise the sun is too glary. We sit opposite each other at the table. He blows and sips his tea. I do the same. He wears a pained expression as if it's difficult for him to get the words out. Eventually he says, 'Look, Alison, the music business is all about making money out of talent. And…'

'You're not here to present me with a gold watch, are you?'

He bites his lower lip.

'Alison, what about the music in your life?'

The tears come; I blink them away and we drink some more.

He says, 'Yours is a very privileged position within the industry.'

'I know that.'

'You're too good to retire now.' He slides his hand across the table and when I flinch he quickly draws it back again. He clears his throat. 'Arguably the best musical works are inspired by tragedy and loss; *Back to Black. Tears in Heaven…*' He licks his lips and sits back in the chair with his interlocked hands cushioning his head. 'Dave Johnson has asked me to ask you what you need for inspiration. He suggested a stay in his villa in Barbados. Does that sound like a good idea to you?'

I scrape my chair backwards. My eyes dart across the room. I pick up his empty mug and leave him alone in the conservatory whilst I go into the kitchen and watch the kettle bang and suck. When I return, he's playing with the salt and pepper pots. He doesn't look up as I put his refill on the table in front of him.

'I'm not Amy Winehouse and I'm certainly not Clapton.'

There's a strained expression on his face.

'Sorry?' he says.

'No, I'm sorry. My river's dry Phil and before I can write for others I need to write for myself.'

He says nothing.

'The thing is, there are things I need to know – about Ria, about me – that I don't know right now and in order to express myself in the way I so bloody need to, I'm going to have to find these things out. Cancel my contract, if you like. Cancel all my contracts, I really don't care.'

'Alison, you can't do that.'

I think about what he's just said, cover my mouth with my hand and nod.

He opens his mouth to speak but says nothing. Leaving his untouched tea on the table, he gets up, walks out the room towards the front door. I follow him, noticing the bagginess of his corduroy trousers and the round bald patch at the back of his head. I open the door for him. He hugs me briefly, whispers, 'Take care of yourself, Al,' and then he's gone.

I sit down on the bottom stair in this large house with its emptiness of sound. My heart leaps with fear and a tiny wisp of hope now that I have something to contemplate. Except, I don't contemplate. My thoughts drift and in a kind of meditation, I see the face of a fifteen-year-old boy. Dirty blonde hair, full lips, chiselled face, lightly tanned skin, green eyes focused inwards. He wears a grey T-shirt with the word Nirvana stamped across its front. I saw him touch Ria once, lightly on her arm; she shivered.

His name is Joshua Waters. He came to our home a lot, but only once after he broke Ria's heart by sleeping with other girls. Ria's red, Sunday-morning eyes are what I remember. Her mooning through the house with unwashed hair and unwashed skin.

'He's not worth it, Ri.'

That contemptuous look again, so eloquent, she didn't have to say, 'Mum, what do you know?'

Harvey took her aside.

'You know I don't want to put restrictions on you, Ri, but I don't want to ever see that boy here again. He doesn't even deserve to shine your shoes.'

The next time I saw Joshua was at Ria's funeral when I would rather have jumped into that hole in the ground than stand beside it. I didn't notice the many faces around me, except one, leaping out from hundreds in the crowd.

His eyes printing themselves onto mine, so that night all I could see was his face on the screen of my lids as I tossed and turned.

I wouldn't know how to get in touch with Joshua now or whether I would have the guts to do it. Instead, my mind turns to Katie, Ria's best friend, who shadowed her throughout her schooldays ever since they were five years old.

I once stood outside the school gates at playtime and watched as, arm in arm, Ria and Katie confidently cruised between groups of children, happily it seemed. Her teacher said sometimes Ria liked to be alone and would sit on the bench watching the other children at play.

'But even so, she excels in socialising. It is her very best subject,' I was told.

Ria the chameleon, generous to a fault; gathering all her possessions to give away to 'the poor children'. Then selfishly coming home with someone else's pencil case, and telling me, she won't give it back.

'But you have to give it back.'

'He let me have it.'

'His mum just phoned; he can't do his homework without it.'

'No, it's mine now.' She held it close to her chest. 'Once you give you can't take back.'

I mentioned to Harvey, she would make a great mafiosa. She was incredibly strong minded. Not a home-bird at all. At seven years old, she liked to go to Katie's house after school, pretty much every day. The idea that an invitation should come first didn't occur to her and the fact that she didn't have one never made her think twice.

'I want to go to Katie's.'

'But you haven't been invited.'

'Stop outside her house anyway.'

'No, you can't just turn up at someone else's home.'

'Why not?'

'It might not be convenient.'

'Let's see if it's convenient.'

'No, it's an imposition, and they might not like to say if it's not convenient.'

It was a kind of revolution, this idea of entitlement. My childhood was, 'Be quiet, the grown-ups are speaking'. And 'Be a good girl now and give Auntie a kiss'. And even if said auntie was fierce with a wart on her cheek and smelling of air freshener, you still had to give her a kiss. We always had to be something we didn't want to be, do something we didn't want to do; we were Stepford children. You had to be good or you never got out of your room.

I'm not saying that as parents we should have continued to be dictatorial. A little balance would have been a wonderful thing. Half of me was siding with myself, a parent, on getting my own way at some point in my life, but then I baulked and we stopped outside Katie's house. Ria demanded that she go up to the front door alone whilst I wait in the car. She came back to tell me, it's OK, she could go in, and I should pick her up at around 6 p.m.

'But what about your homework?'

'I'll do it,' she said, slamming the car door.

I never learnt what Katie's mum, Belinda, really thought about that and all the other impromptu play dates back then. Whether she had other things planned for those afternoons that she put aside, so that my pushy daughter, and no doubt hers too, could have their own way. She was always too polite to tell me if that was the case. I never even explored my own thoughts on the matter; it was easier not to.

Belinda called me about a year ago, out of the blue, to see how I was getting on. She said, if there's ever anything she could do, I shouldn't hesitate. I'm hesitating now. I've been staring at the phone for quite a while. Eventually, I call and after the usual pleasantries, ask for Katie's number.

'She's here now, I'll pass you over.'

'Hello Alison.'

'Hi Katie, are you well?'

'I'm OK, thanks.'

'I'd like to ask you a few questions about Ria, at some point.'

'Oh, I hadn't seen Ria for a long time before…'

'But you kept in touch?'

'Yes, sort of.'

'Well, would you be open to answering some questions anyway?'

I can hear a baby crying in the background.

'OK, but not now.'

'I could come to you, whenever it's convenient.'

'No, no, not a good idea. Look, I'll ask my mum to babysit and I'll come over to you.'

***

Katie stiffens when I try to hug her by the front door. I don't have great recent memories of being in the conservatory and the kitchen ties my stomach in knots with its reminder of food, so we sit at one end of the living room, by the window. I've put the fire and the heating on. This is such a large room with three suites of furniture, heavy wooden antique tables, a grandfather clock, and some interesting paintings, that all kind of works for a party, but maybe not for two people who haven't seen each other for many years, a big age gap and a friendship once removed.

We face each other. She sits on the edge of her seat. It feels like I'm interviewing a suspect in a crime case. I relax into the sofa in an attempt to change that dynamic. She sits ramrod straight, refusing anything to eat or drink and I'm still not sure what I'm going to say to her.

Ancient memories surface: Ria and Katie laughing and then silence the minute I enter the room. Ria and Katie running downstairs hurriedly as a car hoots outside. Ria and Katie locking eyes when I say something benign. If anyone knew Ria…

'I feel like a piece of Ria has returned to the house with you here. Thank you for coming.'

Katie clears her throat and looks around nervously.

'I didn't know you hadn't seen each other for a while.'

'We had very different lives.'

Her eyes flit over mine. The grandfather clock chimes. I look to the painting above the fireplace, a view from

25

the periphery of a forest at dusk. I start to speak as if I'm speaking to myself. 'You know, I think Ria might have been a bit like that painting: beautiful and seductive but also impenetrable. I always thought, as mother and daughter we were close, but maybe I was just kidding myself. We never saw each other as often as we would have liked – no, that's not true – as often as *I* would have liked. The last time we spoke, she said she was happy, loved being a movie star, got a lot of pleasure and satisfaction from it. She didn't care about not having a "constant man" in her life. I asked her what she meant by that and she said Joshua was still "an inconstant".'

Katie leans back, allows herself to be held by the armchair. I ask if she'd like some wine. 'I'm having one if you'd like to join me.' She accepts, tells me she's not driving but only one glass.

I steal a bottle of red from Harvey's stash in the cellar. It pours with a promise to reveal that which is hidden, but I must be mindful of the coda of oblivion.

I put one of the balloon glasses on the table in front of Katie and take a long sip from the other. Katie's sitting forwards looking into her glass as if for an answer. The wind outside slaps the window next to us making it shudder. It's getting dark, even though it's only 3 p.m. Katie picks up her glass and gulps. She draws the back of her hand across her lips and says, 'I didn't know she was still seeing Joshua.' She swallows hard. 'In some ways, Ria did wear a mask. We all do, but Ria's mask covered her whole body, whereas with other people the mask slips and even though they don't realise it, you know what's behind it, like with Sasha. Do you remember her?'

'Yes, I do.'

'She was so great on the guitar, and she wrote these really witty songs, but her eyes were like brick walls. When she started to lose weight, big time, everyone knew she had these really huge problems. She didn't have to talk about them, we just knew. But with Ria it was different.'

Katie holds her now near empty glass in both hands, looks at me and says, 'Ria was the most interesting person I've ever met. When you say she was impenetrable it's true, but you only half knew it. Most of the time you thought that everything she said and everything she did was coming from her soul and that she had no boundaries and had everything sussed. She had this way about her that sucked you into her aura. She was very special. So pretty and courageous. But then she wouldn't answer her phone for days and you'd learn that she'd been in bed the whole time, and when you finally spoke to her and asked what was wrong, she told you she had a sore throat, or a headache, yet she sounded so down. When that happened, I never knew what to say to her, so she'd quickly change the subject and rant on happily about something she'd been up all night reading.'

The ceiling creaks.

'You OK?' she says.

3

We've started to sleep with the curtains open. I want to see it all: dark clouds, rain trying to invade the window, moon, no moon, the outside lights playing on the ceiling, or like tonight; the lights are turned off and I'm staring at stars in an ebony sky and have been for hours.

Harvey fell asleep ages ago. But not me, I'm mulling over what Katie told me and wondering if it was only boy trouble that was upsetting Ria in her teens. Maybe there was something else she was involved in that I never knew about. Would I have known if she was bulimic, for example?

Without any hope for an answer, I have to let go of that thought and my mind flits over things I don't remember from one second to the next, until it lands on the day that Ria was born, a Thursday, 20 March. I start thinking how, usually, I love to be surrounded by water. I find it destressing. Only then I found it distressing. I opted for a water birth but the slightest touch of anything was excruciating and even the water suffocated my flesh. Cold and naked, on all fours, surrounded by only air was better. I elected to be alone. When I was ready to push, two midwives held me as I squatted. Overcome with pain, thinking I could die, I could actually die, I was desperate to get it over with.

She was born facing forwards, ripping me apart. I pushed and screamed and cried until eventually she slid out, red and slimy like a fish. Slumped on the floor, exhausted, I was overcome by the living, breathing warmth of her in my arms. I used to think I knew the reason why my baby's birth had been so painful; if I can endure that, I can endure anything.

I go downstairs, click on the computer and look up Pisces on the internet. I've never really thought about horoscopes before. I read:

Intuitive. Wise. Artistic. Gentle. Empathetic. Can be a victim or a martyr. Overly trusting. Sadness. Desire to escape reality. These people love to sleep. Their favourite environment is a movie theatre.

I can't go back to bed, I'm restless. Bechs is calling me and I haven't hung out with him since the day of the photo when he last shut me out. Opening the door to our room, I creep over to the side table and turn on the lamp. Then I face him and say, 'Hello.'

I perch on the stool and lift his lid, exposing his keys. I cup his chin with my hand. He invites my two fingers to repeatedly play a couple of notes. I listen to the tone. It excites me and as my fingers inch their way up his keyboard, I close my eyes and revisit the time when Harvey and I first met. It was partly lust, but it was deeper than that – a bubble of affection that encapsulated the two of us. I still feel it, even when I spy him on the loo, or he has food stuck between his teeth – especially then, when he is at his most vulnerable. I so wanted him to be the father of my child. To be able to share myself completely with this man who loves me back. We wanted to make a baby, our baby, but it didn't happen.

The desire returns through my quickening fingers and Bechs is taking me over into a Big Bang crescendo. I pull away, slap his cheek, my heart skipping beats and pumping. Everywhere I look, there's another difficult emotion floating on the resonance.

★★★

Ria left home at eighteen to go to stage school, although it wasn't until she was twenty-three that she permanently moved out. Before that, she came and went like an English summer. She swept through the house, wearing her own idea of fashion, some temporary label, and always a different hair colour and style. She said she felt her independence and maturity was leeched by our walls. She needed her own home but didn't want it given to her; she felt she had to earn it. When I asked her about her acting, or her life, she often responded abruptly as if my question was an invasion. There were nights she came home drunk, maybe even a little high on something, but she was never completely out of her mind. I saw her as motivated, engaged in her own life, capable and very beautiful. I am biased, of course.

Things between us changed after she moved to the States, although she still came home randomly and spent the odd night or two here.

'Are you and Dad home this weekend?'

'Yes, why?'

'I'm catching a plane.'

'Anything wrong?'

'No, Mum, I just need to get away from the madness.'

Our special guest. She loved our home then. She loved me then. We lit candles, chilled in the living room and talked for hours. I can't remember a thing that either of us said. Mostly we were catching up. She liked to know what was going on in our lives. She had a soft spot for Annie. But when I asked about the madness she had to get away from, she'd fob me off. 'No, really, everything's cool. It's just too much, that's all.'

I never probed. I always respected her privacy. She left things here but it never crossed my mind to browse amongst them. Now, on the threshold of her bedroom, as I lean against the door frame and hold myself very still, I'm about to change that.

I switch on the ceiling light exaggerating the darkness outside the window. This room is bleak without her. An owl hoots, bringing with it a sense of dread. I question my fear. Is it stupid fear or Ria's energy warning me off? Death of a loved one belittles everything material. So why am I so pained to be doing this now?

There's a tug in my belly and a voice in my head, screaming, 'Don't!'

To which I reply, 'Ria, I must.'

I look over my shoulder, rub my arms, but there's nothing there. I go over to the cupboard and open its doors. On the floor, a lonely pair of black suede boots fold over themselves. A boxy, scarlet-lined, faux-fur jacket wears

31

a diamanté evening bag like a necklace. The trio floats amongst a jangle of empty hangers. I am reminded of a party we gave in Ria's honour after she starred in that English film. A wonderful film. I can't remember its title and pinch the root of my nose as if that will engage my memory. It was an adaptation of a Julian Barnes novel. The one that made Ria's name and catapulted her to Hollywood.

I try to compose myself on the stool in front of her dressing table. In the mirror, it looks as if I'm sitting in front of Bechs just about to embark on a sonic adventure. It might look that way, but this feels very different; much more daunting. And yet, I manage to pull the crystal knob and have the drawer rumble open. An old lipstick, no lid, slides back and forth. I pick it up and twist its base; it's practically new, bright red. My fingers brush over an old red mobile with its charger lying next to it. I sit for a while with my hand on the phone before picking up a book of matches, black gloss, dripping crimson letters, advertising The Dragon Club. I slam the drawer shut. I refuse to see meaning here. It's just junk, discarded possessions and things she didn't want.

I scan the room.

On the bedside table there's a box of Calms, a small bottle of lavender oil and one of those digital alarm clocks that hasn't aged well. The side lamp is on the floor in the corner because we never did install that plug socket behind the bedside table. On the other side of the bed there's a pile of books. I check out the top three: *The Script Circle,* an introduction to play rehearsals written by some Hollywood actor I've never heard of, *The Story of O* and *Dante's Inferno*.

Ria, the actress, accessed the deepest parts of herself publicly. It made me see her as a stranger both in her guises and as my daughter. There's another cupboard and a number of drawers still to explore, and of course under the bed. But I no longer have the stomach to carry on. I'm done in here. Goodnight.

***

Morning is towing in the light and I'm still awake. I've given up on sleep and that unrecognisable face, screwed up and ugly with pain, faces me in the mirror. I go and sit in the kitchen and watch steam rise off my coffee; another swirl to get lost in. Tight strings in my heart pull down into my belly as I think of Ria's room – forlorn and smelling of dust, her scent long gone. This recurring nightmare comes to mind: Ria standing at one end of a large empty room wearing a Victorian nightgown, her hair unbrushed. She's yelling and although I can't hear what she's saying, it's clear she doesn't want me there.

'Why don't you want me, Ri?'

'Selfish bitch,' ricochets.

But I know they are not Ria's words. I know they are words coming from a piece of myself; the self-hatred piece. In the humming-fridge silence, I try to lock out all thoughts, remaining open only for Ria to come through, although not really sure if or how that works. It doesn't work, for me, anyway. I must have sat there with my eyes closed for quite a while. I'm now thinking, it's me, I'm doing something to keep Ria away. Harvey told me I don't listen. Maybe I should listen.

I'm pacing. A grey phantom is in my midst. I try to brush it away but it's not leaving. I feel as if I'm descending into lunacy and grab Harvey's jacket and beanie from the cupboard by the front door. My bare feet squelch inside his wellingtons. My pyjamas are magnets for the cold. Never mind, I must walk, and as I tread, my heart is pumping up a volcanic spill.

Hey, Ri, is this what red means?

Trying to forget my terrorist within, I march over to the fan encampment. The people there are hugging the memory of my daughter. Their relationship with Ria is so very different from mine. What is it like to have only met her on screen, via movie roles and interviews, through a response to fan mail, or in a short conversation when she signed an autograph? I want to know what they've absorbed from her, what they saw in her, why they are holding onto her with this long, extended vigil.

I usually leave through the side exit in order to avoid them, or if I'm in the car they sidle up onto the grass whilst I flash a quick wave and leave them gawking. Except now I'm on foot, digging my hands deep into my pockets. My heart has calmed down a bit but I'm still having trouble getting a word out. I manage, 'Hi,' whilst slipping through the iron gates. Some of the fans are lying in their sleeping bags, or just sitting cross-legged and smoking. Others are sniffing round me like a pack of dogs. A small crowd of four stand before me with curious eyes.

'How are you doing out here, all right?'

They shrug.

One of them says, 'OK.'

'Would you like to come inside?'

They look to one another.

'I'll make you breakfast in exchange for a chat about Ria. You can tell me what you love about her.'

Four of them, all girls, tramp behind me on my way back to the house.

I fry eggs, sausages from the freezer, tomatoes and mushrooms, which I serve with sweet tea and buttered toast.

'Some things you don't have to think about, you just do them. I guess that's why you're here, away from your real lives; because it feels right.'

At the head of the table overseeing them eat, I can't join in. I've been on The Aggravation Diet for far too long and now I can't get off it. There's a constant lump in my throat; food can't get passed and tears won't dissolve it. Wine seems to go down well but not in the mornings. I drink tea with my guests at this time.

'So, you loved her, too?' I say to four heads bowed to their breakfast.

A tall, slim blonde with startling blue eyes and full lips looks up.

'We all think she was great, yeah,' she says.

The others nod in agreement.

'Yes, she was,' I reply and sip my tea.

They eat, slowly, thoughtfully. I'm not sure what else I can say. Stiff minutes drag across the oven's digital clock.

'I'm Agneta,' the blonde says.

'I'm Tulip.'

'Mandy.'

'Tulip's sister, Green.'

'And I'm Alison.'

'Why now?' Agneta says. 'It's been over one hundred weeks.'

I take my time and think about how to answer truthfully.

'At first, you were all in the way of… I don't know what. I just knew I had to be alone, undisturbed by anyone outside my own little world.'

'And now?'

'And now I have more questions than answers about the way she died. I mean why? What really happened?'

'We don't know,' Mandy says. She is the exact opposite in looks to her friend Agneta, short, dark and hunched.

'I know you don't. I'm really not looking for answers, just clues. As a mother, the way I see Ria, the person she was, is not going to be the same as you see her. We all knew her in part. I'm searching for enough of those parts to make my daughter whole and then perhaps I'll know why…'

'It was an accident!' Green, the youngest, lashes out. My instinct is to hit back with, 'How do you know that?' But something stops me, and instead I say, 'Tell me what you know.'

Green stands up, pushing her chair away with the backs of her thighs. 'When you see Ria as Alex in *The Way to Catch a Swan,* and she's next to that river with her hair blowing away from her…' Green tosses her hair away from her face. 'You can see it in her eyes, it's like she's saying, "Whatever happens to me, no matter how hard it gets, I will never give up, I will never give in, never"' – and the fist of a champion hits the air.

I'm reminded of the photo I took on the beach, the one I kiss every morning and hold onto as if it's the only one I have of her. The way she stood in that millisecond, half mocking, half defiant, woman-child marking her territory. It is the same stance that twelve years later helped to win her an Oscar.

'That was in a film, dimwit. She was acting,' Tulip says.

'Maybe she was acting, but she made me feel strong like I could overcome anything,' Agneta says.

'What else did she make you feel?' I ask.

'Like because she's in the world I'm never alone.'

Wow!

'And now?'

Agneta shrugs. It becomes apparent that Green never sat down again. The long hand on the wall-clock lurches a second forwards. Green has her head bowed. It's uncomfortable. We all feel it. They thank me sheepishly, follow me like ducklings to the front door. I don't open it, but in a sudden change of heart turn around and say, 'I don't want you guys to go.' I can see they're nervous. 'I want to know what else you know.'

They all look to each other.

'We didn't really know her, not in the real world,' Agneta says.

'I understand that but how about you Mandy, what do you think?'

'Do you have any of her things?'

'No, she didn't live here.'

'Can we see the room she stayed in?'

'No, I'm sorry, I'm not ready for you to do that.'

Agneta opens the door.

'Bye then,' they all mumble, one by one, as they leave. Green is the only one that looks at me. I imagine what she sees: a ghostly flagging woman who is a little strange.

★★★

There's a junk room, full of boxes, at one end of the house. I look through them for the ones containing childhood photos of Ria. Not for the first time, I wonder why we've kept so much stuff. What demons tether us to these stowed-away possessions?

I find a box that's big and heavy, full to the brim with albums that chronicle, in pictures, Ria's formative years. I pick it up and stagger onto the landing where I kneel next to it and delve into the top volume, marked, 'RIA 6–10 months'.

The first photo is a large black and white print. Ria's wearing a white dress, sitting in a high chair, lifting a spoon. I remember that day. She hurled that spoon across the kitchen. It hit Perry, our cat. I found him later, eyes startled, hackles up, hiding in the airing cupboard.

At that age, Ria was free of politesse. Her dislikes were expressed by throwing things, spitting, screaming, upturning the whole world if she had to, any attempt to get her own way. Yes, she really was feisty. If she was a reincarnate, what earthly soul had I been given to re-rear? Cleopatra? Catherine the Great? Marie Antoinette? I never thought about it back then. Too busy, sitting before Bechs, with Ria tied to me in a sling, trying to eke out a tune. I wonder now, was it that characteristic that made her succeed in becoming the iconic-female-warrior her fans perceive her to have been?

I used to pride myself on the way I brought her up. The difference between Ria and Katie, who was too materialistically spoiled, in my opinion, with designer gifts descending on her from above like confetti. Ria didn't go to a private school and so I can tell you first hand that even those kids whose parents were out of work, received an abundance of expensive gifts: mobile phones, jeans and T-shirts, all with designer names worn like a coat of arms won in a battle with a parent.

I made Ria do a paper round before school. At fifteen, she worked in a bakery on a Saturday and put on weight with all that stodge she ate on the job. When finished for the day, she brought the leftovers home for us all to get fat on. It paid for taxi fares to and from town on a Saturday night, wearing short skirts, sagging necklines and high heels. I needed to let her know that an innate sense of entitlement was wrong. I thought, I can't just protect her to the hilt and throw luxury items at her one after the other on demand, then expect her to survive as an adult in the world without my help. I was certain I was doing the right thing at the time but now, huh, I'm not so sure.

I turn to the next photo in which she was learning to walk, staggering along the promenade in Brighton, wearing a Puppy-in-My-Pocket pink T-shirt and white cotton jeans. She's holding on to her biological father's hand. She's looking up at him with an expression of sheer conquest on her face. I stare at this photo for quite some time. Then I stare at the wall and see a superimposed image of Ria standing by a river. All around her is green: grass, trees, water. I hear a trickling, light-hearted phrase. I see her in fighting spirit to the sound of harsh chords. Now she's crouching inside a transparent box. She feels crushed, can't find her way out and I can't find my way into the melody, but there's a seed of a song there. I trip over the box and slide on a heap of plastic album covers. I pick myself up, rush from room to room on the lookout for a pen. When I find one, I write on the back of my hand: Ria, green world, transparent box, spirit hunter.

4

Harvey comes home and I'm absent. As he passes me by on the stairs, he's looking at me out of the corner of his eye. He doesn't peer over his shoulder. He doesn't say anything. He just goes directly into the ensuite. I muscle my way in after him. He locks the door and my aching heart steps up a beat as I wonder why he does this: there's no one else in the house apart from us.

Sitting on the edge of the bath, clasping my hands in my lap, I wait for him to roll and light a spliff for us to share. Standing between two sinks, one hip bruising the marble countertop, he's dragging deeply on the joint, dampening his pain. When he's good and ready and calm he says, 'I'm worried about you, Al.'

'I'm fine,' I reply, but in the mirror opposite I can see my smile is crooked.

He goes on, 'I think you should seek help.'

'Help with what? Ria's passing? Maybe take some pills? Pretend this' – I'm waving my arms around and doing the mad thing – 'shit isn't happening?'

'You're eating yourself up,' he says, eventually.

'Uh, hello, and what about you, eating yourself up?'

He's puffing, and staring at me, his eyelids a little

41

screwed to avoid the smoke. I stare right back at him, and I'm thinking, I'm right. I'm not always right but this time I'm right. He goes over to the door, unbolts it, walks out, leaving me alone and I immediately flip into the land of self-doubt. Maybe I'm not right. Maybe he knows better than me about love and grief and what to do about it.

An hour later, we're picking at an Indian takeaway in front of the television, watching *Levison Wood* on his latest expedition across an inhospitable terrain. I take vicarious courage from this intrepid adventurer, and when the adverts come on I pick up the remote and turn down the volume.

'Do you remember Joshua?' I say.

'Al!'

'What's that meant to mean? Al!'

'It's hard enough to come to terms with what's happened without you doing this.'

'Doing what?'

'Concocting a great big conspiracy theory.'

'Is that what you think I'm doing?'

He doesn't answer but his pained expression continues and it's the first time since I've known him that I question being with him and get the idea that maybe, for all these years, I have misinterpreted our closeness and the person that he is.

We go to bed separately. It's getting to be the norm. I don't like it. I doubt if Harvey likes it either, but there it is, the invisible wall that's rising up between us. How did this happen, when we have always taken comfort from each other's warmth?

He eventually comes to bed. We lie as crescent moons turned away from each other. I know that he's not sleeping either, but I'm finding it hard to know what to do. It's so fucking lonely in this bed, and I need him more than ever now. I need him to hold me, stroke my hair, tell me it's going to be all right because we are together and we will always be together, and Ria is just out of reach, waiting for us in her new dimension. I need to hear those words from him – even if I know them to be untrue, I still need to hear them.

The night rides on. I'm hot, then cold, then hot again, ad infinitum. Covers thrown back then pulled up to my throat. I have dark visions that conjure up horrible feelings. My pillow is crumpled. I flip it over, pat it down and look to Harvey. He lies as still as the Dead Sea, but I know he's awake.

'Harvey?'

He doesn't move.

When the ash light seeps in and I'm hungover on too little sleep, I ramp myself up. The bed pulls me down again. Harvey opens his eyes. 'Perhaps we both need to go and see someone,' he says.

That evening, we go out for dinner to discuss. He takes me to a restaurant round the corner from his office; abstract art hangs on grey walls, white tablecloths, pink and white flowers around a flickering candle flame, weighty cutlery in brushed steel, creative food on stark white plates. Harvey orders a very expensive bottle of wine.

'What's the occasion?'

'Us,' he says. 'The occasion is us. We still have each other, isn't that something to celebrate?'

Not sure how to respond, I attempt a smile.

'But we need to sort this out.' He's shifting uncomfortably. 'Couples counselling, I think.'

'And what do you think that will do for us? Help you to adjust to the idea that I'm me? Or do you think this person will make me realise I am not what I am and don't need to do what I need to do? Because that's not going to happen.'

I realise I'm being provocative, but I can't help myself. I seriously don't believe that anyone in this country – this fabricated First World country that we live in – has the insight to help us mend our broken spirits and bring us closer together. You can be as practical as you like. You can talk about heartache and how death affects you but you can't change it. It is what it is and you feel as you feel. I seriously believe that.

'I think it could happen.'

'Which way round, Harvey?'

He shrugs.

I'm stunned that he thinks some outside force can wave a magic wand and everything will be all right for us. Every woman I know who has a problem with her life partner has begged him to go to counselling with her. More often than not, he refuses, or goes along reluctantly, but either way she always leaves him in the end, at least in spirit. Is that what's going to happen to me?

'There's nothing wrong with us. It's just a rough patch because…look, if Ria was here we'd be fine. I just have to deal with the loss in my own way.'

'You're being unreasonable.'

I lower my voice. 'I'm not being unreasonable, you're being unreasonable.'

The waiter comes over and takes our first course away. When he's gone, 'You really mean this?' I say, visualising Harvey leaving me, walking out the front door with a couple of suitcases and never looking back.

I can't stand that thought and agree to see anyone he likes.

★★★

Days pass in a bleak haze. I seem to be spending all my time walking from room to room and in each one forgetting why I'm there. I look out of windows at the world carrying on whilst I take a sabbatical from life. Cut off like an ill person, I see no one, talk to no one. I'm afraid of myself, knowing that I can't keep my promise to Harvey, not in the real sense because, yes, I will go to the counselling sessions but I will not be there in earnest, driven as I am towards finding out about Ria's secrets and why she never shared them with me.

When I can't avoid it any longer, I go to see Bechs. I stroke his glossy lid, afraid that if I peel it back and touch him where he speaks from, there will be no spark between us or he'll make me flip. I am compelled to do it anyway. As I lift the lid his joints protest. My hands flow to the places they are called to and my fingers uncover an unwritten lament. I close my eyes and let things happen.

The vision comes, crackled like old film, just a snippet: Harvey's on his way home from identifying her body. I'm sitting in the car at the airport, waiting for his plane to land. I'm hoping for the impossible, that they've made a mistake and it's not Ria that's passed away but some other female who, inexplicably, was staying in her home, bathing in her tub, pretending to be her.

When her agent called and said we don't have to fly out, he'd go along and do the necessary, Harvey insisted on seeing the body for himself. I couldn't do it. I still imagine she's somewhere on this planet, alive. I see her on the street or in a shop and my heart drops like a bomb when the person turns around. It happens all the time.

A riff seems to have discovered itself. Sparks of light turn orange in my mind. I take it down to the heavy side; angry thunderheads, pounding. There's a ringing sound coming from somewhere. The ringing stops. The intensity of my playing calms right down. The ringing starts up again. I stop playing and answer the phone.

'Yes!'

'I'm sorry Alison…it's Katie.'

'No, no, no, I'm sorry. I was just playing the piano and got a bit carried away.'

'Do you want me to call back another time?'

'No, please, I've left that moment behind now and I really want to hear what you've got to say.'

'It's just that when I was with you the other week and we spoke about Ria, the way she was when we were younger… Well, I can't stop thinking about our conversation. Certain memories. Moments. Things are coming back to me and making me feel uncomfortable. I haven't thought about them for years. I never wanted to dwell on them or give them much importance.

'I spoke to my husband about this and he says I'm just being stupid, and I shouldn't be worrying about these things now. He made them seem trivial and maybe they are, but I feel this pressing need to tell you about them. Anyway, so can I come and see you again?'

'Yes, anytime.'

'How about tomorrow?'

'OK.'

'One more thing, I really don't want to raise this subject with my mum again and ask her to babysit; she's only going to ask me a million questions.'

'Bring your baby with you.'

'If I come about twelve, I can feed him whilst we speak?'

'No problem, that will be just fine.'

As soon as the call is cut, the phone rings again.

It's Harvey.

'Al, I went to see Dr Anise this morning.'

People are speaking in the background. I can hear conflicting voices and noises. I wonder if Harvey's on the street or at a station. Then a door closes and it's quiet his end. 'Sorry, we've just finished a meeting. I'm back in my office now. Are you still there?'

'Yes.'

'Well, anyway, we had a long conversation and she agrees that to talk to someone, together, is the way to go. She said this Shirley Witherspoon person is both a grief and a relationship counsellor. She's helped quite a few of Anise's patients to sort out their differences. I've made an appointment for tomorrow at twelve. She's in town, not far from the new Sainsbury's.'

'Wait, wait, wait, H, I can't go tomorrow at twelve.'

'What do you mean?'

'I have Katie coming over, Ria's old friend. I've just put down the phone to her. She said she needed to tell me something.'

Harvey is silent.

'About Ria… it sounds important.'

'Ria isn't here anymore, Alison. Going forward, we – you and me – are what's important.'

'Harvey?'

'No, Alison, it's not good what you're doing, trying to dig up all the mud, looking for any shit you can find. Where do you think it's going to get you? You want to learn that Ria was actually a manic depressive, or a heroin junkie or something? Is that what you want to know? Because I would have known, Alison, I would have known if our daughter was anything other than who we knew her to be.'

Harvey's breathing heavily.

I should tell him, I'll ask Katie to come over another

time. Instead, I hear myself asking, 'How?'

'What?'

'How do you know that if we ask questions, we won't find bleeding wounds and things we didn't know about? And anyway, it's not about that, it's about not being able to live without knowing the truth.'

As I'm waiting for Harvey's answer, I'm trying to convince myself that having this conversation with my husband whilst he's at work is actually the best thing, much better than counselling, until he comes back with, 'Alison.' There's a catch in his throat. A lump appears in mine. 'Our baby isn't alive anymore. You don't need to ask questions about her. We need to ask questions about us. *We* need the attention. *Our* relationship. I want in. I want *us* to survive. I need you back in my life for more than just the odd moment here and there; it's been a long time.'

I swallow.

He sighs and asks, 'Is it even worth me changing the appointment?'

I want to say, 'Oh Harvey, I want to be exactly how you want me to be,' but somehow I only manage, 'Yes'.

5

For the rest of the day, I think about phoning Harvey and telling him I've cancelled Katie, but I'm too aware that the clashing of appointments is just superficial; he wants the Katie meeting not to happen at all and I can't give him that. Neither can I lie to him.

When he comes home, he finds me sitting on the bottom stair with my phone in my lap, torturing myself. I shuffle towards the wall as he passes me on his way upstairs, undoing his tie, saying, 'Hello.'

'Hi.' I stand and run after him.

He shuts the bathroom door with me on the outside.

He calls out, 'Alison, I'm sorry, I just need to think.'

Too crushed to run into the sonic arms of Bechs, I go into the junk room, the storeroom, I'm not sure what to call it and also lock the door. Sitting cross-legged on the floor, it is the first and only time in my life I have ever banged my head in frustration against a wall.

Katie arrives at noon the next day. We go into the kitchen and she makes herself at home, strapping her baby into a box seat that she fastens to a chair. As she feeds him, she tells me nervously that when she was in her early teens she used to cut herself. I ask why and she says it was because she could never match up to her father's expectations and she used to get bullied in school. She speaks matter-of-factly and tells me not to be shocked. 'It wasn't like I was the only one who did it.' When I say nothing, she goes on, 'My mum made me go and see someone five days a week. It changes the way you think. It makes you notice things you didn't notice before.'

She spoons orange puree into her baby's mouth, and wipes the excess food away with the edge of the plastic spoon.

'When we were fourteen, Ria and I were already drifting apart. I found being around her' – she looks up at me – 'hard. I remember sitting on the floor in my bedroom and Ria taking my arm, undoing the cuff of my school shirt and stroking my scars.'

'Go on,' I say.

Katie shrugs.

I sit down opposite her.

'Did she say anything then?'

'No, but she gave me a weird look as if she was complicit.'

'I'd have known if she was cutting herself.'

'She didn't. Ria wasn't the same as me. My therapist explained that covering up shit only invites more shit and more shit and the shit piles up until all you've got is shit. I got stronger when I opened up, but Ria never spoke about her stuff, not to anyone. She admitted there were things, bad things, that haunted her, but she felt it was better to keep them to herself.'

51

My mouth goes dry and I find it hard to speak. I eventually manage, 'What did you imagine those things were?'

'I don't know but she frightened me.'

'Maybe she was acting.'

'Maybe she was; it didn't feel like it at the time.'

I should grab her hand and say, 'I'm grateful that you came. What else? I need to know these things,' but I can't bear to hear anymore of this right now and blurt out, 'Thanks for telling me.'

★★★

Harvey and I sit in the counsellor's waiting room. His hand lies limply in mine. I'm staring straight ahead, trying to think of how to explain myself to our therapist, but waffle clouds my head. I'm nervous. It's almost a relief when we're ushered into the consulting room.

Shirley Witherspoon has short, curly blonde hair. She wears a navy and white horizontal striped T-shirt, navy trousers, gold anklet and white shoes. The usual niceties and introductions occur. Harvey starts by saying, 'Our daughter died just over two years ago; Ria Connaught, the actress.'

Shirley Witherspoon wears a blank expression.

'Anyway, to cut a long story short, it says, "accidental suicide" on her death certificate. Ria's doctor claims she exceeded the prescribed dose and although she didn't mean to kill herself that's what happened. He was able to produce an original copy of the prescription, but it was dated some years previously. Al thinks there might be an updated version somewhere. Well, whether there is or there isn't is beside the point. We've had the conversation several times. She wants to delve further into the cause of Ria's death. I've tried to convince her that whatever happened, whether she took the overdose of her own volition or whether that dosage was prescribed to her latterly, it is not going to change anything. It's not going to bring her back. But Alison doesn't see it that way. She's eating herself up over this and it's coming between us to the point where I don't know my wife anymore.'

Shirley Witherspoon widens her eyes and turns towards me. She makes a little clearing sound at the back of her throat and asks, 'Would you like to say something, Alison?'

'You're going to think this strange, but I really need to write something on the piano in order to express myself.'

'And have you done that?'

'No.'

'Why not?'

'I've been trying… I can't do it right now, I need to know what happened.'

'And if you can't know what happened?'

'I *will* know.'

Shirley Witherspoon tilts her head to one side.

'My daughter had a very high-profile life. We have no idea what went on. What I'm trying to say is, Harvey and I were just satellites; we weren't in her everyday world. We didn't even live in the same country. There are people who knew her in a way we didn't. I need to talk to them. I need to know what went on.'

Harvey says, 'What more do you need to know? We know. We've been told. She was addicted to painkillers.'

'But what for, Harvey? What did she take them for? We don't even know why was she given them in the first place?'

'That's not true, her doctor said they were for "muscle aches". It's written in her notes.'

'She never once mentioned muscle aches to me, nor did she show any sign of muscle aches when she came to visit us. Did she mention muscle aches to you? Our beautiful and talented daughter, found dead in the bath because she was taking extreme, opiate painkillers for muscle aches that she'd had for years, that neither of us knew about, and I can't believe you don't find that just a tiny bit suspicious.'

'Suspicious in what way? Adults don't necessarily tell their parents if they have muscle aches. Do you think someone murdered her? Is that what you think?'

'No, not directly, maybe not even indirectly.'

'Then why are you doing this mad witch-hunt thing? Why can't you just leave things be? You and I go and lie on a beach somewhere in the Caribbean for six months, sipping cocktails and watching the waves roll back into the sunset?'

'I'm her mother and there are things I have to know before I can do something like that.'

I look to Shirley Witherspoon.

'Maybe we can work towards a compromise,' she says.

I try to catch Harvey's eye but he's intent on brushing something invisible off his trousers.

When we get home, I think to tell him about the photo I took of Ria on the beach, but what I need to say is unquantifiable, so I show him the image instead and look at it with him. I can almost hear the sea frothing so powerfully behind her as she stands there braving the first hint of womanhood. Harvey waves the picture around like a flag. His eyes are liquescent. 'She was lovely,' he says.

6

I go and sit on Annie Forager's bench, waiting. I don't know how but she always seems to know when I'm here. So I'm not surprised when, after a short while, I see her in the distance. She's walking with a tall, slim man who veers off in another direction. She's coming without her brood this time, just herself and her stick.

'No animals today?'

She looks over her shoulder.

'I'm so sorry, Annie. Last time I saw you I pushed you to say what was on your mind and I shouldn't have.' I pat the seat next to me and she sits down. 'After you tell me, I might feel the same about what I'm going to ask you right now, but please, tell me anyway. What did you and John think of Ria?'

Argh, it always happens. Tears are threatening the corners of my eyes – like so many other things in life, they come when they come. Annie looks at me, hesitantly.

'It's OK, I need to hear the truth. I may not like it but I need to hear it.'

'We thought she was wonderful.'

'Is that it?'

I fumble with a tissue.

'We thought that even though she smiled and laughed

there was always something sad about her.'

'I guess you mean when she was in her teens?'

'No, she was always like that.'

There are rivers on my cheeks now. I can't look at Annie, can't tell her it's OK and what I'm expressing is not her fault.

'I couldn't see it.'

'That's because she didn't want you to.'

***

I keep Harvey up half the night talking but it doesn't get us anywhere. I walk away from our conversation and find little jobs to do around the house. Coming into the TV room, 'Please don't give up on us, Harvey,' I say. He continually taps the remote against the arm of his chair.

'It's not easy. You're not making this easy,' he says.

I take his hand and try and pull him to standing.

He resists.

'Please?'

'OK,' he says with a sigh.

I take him into Bechs' room and sit on the stool whilst he stands behind me. My music partner and I play an improvised piece that starts with two hands jamming at the high end of the keyboard. Odd words and witchy phrases escape from me, 'I want…want to fly, but hell no… no… NO… can't live, live like, live like this…' I stand up and pound bass keys. Bechs takes it and I'm caught in a whirlwind of screaming whys.

In a brief glance over my shoulder, Harvey has his head bowed looking up at me. I immediately lay off Bechs. The resonance of my yelling and his bashed keys hang in the air. I cup Bechs' chin. Harvey puts a hand on my shoulder and I flinch.

'Come on,' he whispers.

I fold myself into him. He walks me upstairs. Under the covers, he holds me even after I stop shivering. He breathes, 'It's OK,' repeatedly in my ear. His feathery hands are on my back. I squeeze my eyes shut against the possibility that he'll desert me.

I've been left before. So many twists and turns in life; moments that hit you over the head and turn future plans to fiction. And sometimes, a moment comes along that sweeps you up on a magic carpet ride. That happened to me during Ria's third birthday party. She sat cross-legged in front of the entertainer. Every five minutes she put her hand up; the chosen one, on her special day, helping Mr Happy – or whatever his name was – hatch a rabbit out of a hat or pull a never-ending handkerchief through the ring of his thumb and forefinger.

I was young then, just twenty-four. I'd never had a song published. No one had heard of me or my work. I was in love with Ria but I was also in love with making music. I was with my first husband then, not in love with *him*. Actually, in my head, I wasn't even with him. We were hardly intimate – I'm not talking about sex which doesn't have to be intimate. I buried a deep yearning for closeness in the desire to write a hit song. A dream of worldly success, that if I'm honest, was conceived long before Ria was. I was the archetypal hunter, chasing and longing. Even when I didn't realise I was chasing, I was chasing. The idea of composing a better song, a more well-received song, was never far from my mind.

Lost in my own private world with some keyboard or other – I didn't have a Bechs in my life back then – my ambition was always poking me, spurring me on. In those times when too many publishing companies responded to my tapes with only rejections, even when my self-confidence had been pummelled into the ground and I didn't have the emotional stamina to crawl to the keyboard, the flame was never put out, just diminished, waiting to flare again.

During Ria's party, I stood amongst a small crowd of adult family and friends making polite conversation. We watched our children and grandchildren cross-legged on the floor, slapping balloons back and forth, blissfully ignoring the squelch of those that were being twisted into animal shapes by the now glistening Mr Happy. At half-time, we moved from the living room to the dining room where we stood again, this time around a long table set with pink paper cloths, waxed cups and plates bearing cartoon images. There were homemade sandwiches of shop-bought jam, cream-filled cakes, an assortment of biscuits, and jugs of red and orange fruit juice. Kids stood on their chairs and tried to pull down streamers that hung from the lampshade, whilst others ate themselves into oblivion.

At some point, the phone rang. When I answered it,

a stranger's voice told me that Whitney Houston and her producer liked one of my songs. How soon could I come into the office? We made an appointment for the next day and my hands shook for the rest of Ria's party as I buzzed around contemplating a very different future.

When husband number one left for Canada with another woman, I was already 'successful'. With a young child on my hip, I didn't know which way to turn in my private life, and so I forgot about my private life until Harvey arrived. But until then, and even beyond, if I'm honest, I was living on the high of my songs being recorded, one after the other, by some of the world's greatest rock gods and goddesses, produced by maestros and played on radios all over the world.

I'm sure that my ambitious needs informed the way Ria experienced her childhood. Maybe if I hadn't been so off with the fairies, she would have talked to me more, let me in more and felt more secure. Maybe I wouldn't feel so compelled to discover more about her now. Maybe there would be no reason for it.

I roll out of Harvey's arms to the other side of the bed. The full moon holds me in its spotlight as I curl into a clam and screw my fists into my abdomen, believing I killed my daughter through neglect.

The morning sun helps. In daylight, I consider that Ria was Ria too. Fiercely independent from a very young age, and private. She was always private. Shy with strangers but born with a hunger to explore and be immersed in the world.

I've heard it said that before we're even conceived, we choose our life's circumstance and our important people. I don't know if that's true, but I used to think it was a good thing, and once again, now I'm not so sure.

I can't lie here any longer thinking this through. I go downstairs, make a cup of tea and take it into the living room. Propped up on the mantelpiece is a picture of Ria as a baby, on her back in her cot, strands of unruly hair falling over her eyes. I remember watching her for hours squirming peacefully, at one point a hand behind her head as she looked up at me, her body rolling in the opposite direction, Monroe-esque.

I think most of us are led by desire, if we're honest. I haven't always been honest. I hid things I was ashamed of in the far recesses of my mind, like what I did with Karl, a classmate, when I was fifteen, and how that would have made me appear in the eyes of the world back then, when nice girls didn't.

Karl had confidence and charisma and I was the object of his interest for a very short while. I was in the music room trying to work something out on the piano. Happy to stay late whilst all the other students clambered out of the building, exuberant at the end of their classroom confinement for the day. I could hear their merriment through the open window.

He didn't knock. He just came in, swaggering to the opposite side of the room, squashing his arse right up against a desk. Hands in his trouser pockets, he smirked. I've always been good at ignoring company and disappearing into soundscapes of my own creation, but his presence kept pulling me back into the room. Eventually, I banged the lid shut and asked what he wanted.

He said, 'Alison Grass, are you always this spikey?'

'Am I spikey?' I asked.

'Yes, you are spikey,' he said, still smirking.

I went hot and cold with heightened awareness of how he made me feel. My body confused me. I didn't want to be this obvious, this vulnerable.

'I have records that will blow you away,' he said.

I raised my chin.

'There's nothing better than *making* music.'

'Are you sure?'

I wasn't.

I wasn't sure of anything.

'There are other worlds,' he said. They were my words. I had used them that morning in English Literature. I can't remember why but it seemed like a relevant comment at the time, reminding everyone that there was something other than the material world, like the place I experience when I merge with a keyboard.

'Sexy,' he said, pushing himself away from the desk. Standing in front of me, taking my hands in his, impelling me to rise up from the piano stool as if I was to be his partner in some weird exotic dance.

I didn't dare speak but I let him lead me all the way to his house. I crossed the threshold to its emptiness and quiet. All those thousands of moons ago, I experienced for the first time, a magic with someone not made of wood and ivory but flesh and blood. I embraced the moment then felt guilty about it afterwards.

I make a pact with myself, in the here and now, that when I write my next song, all internal censors will be switched off, just like that evening after school.

7

Shirley Witherspoon watches as Harvey and I try to get comfortable. I'm shifting around. He's lifting his bum and flicking the tails of his jacket away from the seat of his trousers. We're limbering up before our next fight.

She asks, 'Did you both have a good week?'

I look over at my man and say, 'Well, good is not exactly the way I would describe it.'

'Better,' he says.

'So, would either one of you like to tell me how it went?'

'I think I'm more aware of what Al's going through now.'

Shirley Witherspoon raises her eyebrows and says, 'That's good. How did that come about?'

'It's strange, I wouldn't have necessarily associated it with our discussion last week, although maybe it is. I seem to be making more of an effort to notice what's going on around me. There seems to be a lot of self-loathing going on everywhere. You know, you read posts on social media where people can be scathing about others and, invariably, what they accuse other people of is what they are themselves. And then, articles appear about privileged kids at university who make excuses for things like what ISIS have been doing, and these are probably the same kids who are anorexic or clinically depressed. So I'm thinking that maybe my wife is just tapping into all of this mass-consciousness thing.'

I can feel myself sitting up straighter, thinking, What the hell! Shirley Witherspoon urges him to go on.

'Mass-consciousness is a seductive thing,' he says.

'You mean I'm a sheep.'

'I didn't say that.'

'You didn't have to. It's perfectly clear that you think being a victim of mass-conscious thinking is a much better excuse for my behaviour than wanting to discover, for my own personal reasons, what happened to my daughter.'

'Your daughter?'

'Yes, my daughter.'

'Aren't you forgetting she was my daughter too?'

I say nothing.

He turns towards Shirley Witherspoon, his face boiling red, and says, 'This is exactly what I mean and why I wanted us to come here. When I met Alison, Ria was only four years old and half an orphan; her dad had disappeared completely from the scene a year earlier. When we started living together, long before Al and I decided to marry, I legally adopted Ria.

I wanted to be her father whether Alison and I stayed together or not and I believed I had it in me to bring something really positive to the table and I think I did that.'

Everything Harvey has just said is absolutely true. He

has been, in my opinion, a wonderful father, and I am very, very grateful for all the love he has shown to both me and Ria over all the years. But I can't help thinking that if he was her real father, her biological father, he would be championing my mission.

'Are you frightened of what I might discover?' I ask.

Shirley Witherspoon catches my eye. She tries to open up the conversation, several times. But for the rest of the session, Harvey and I exchange only curt words between extended silences.

We argue in the car going home. I try to articulate my point of view without offending him further but in the end resort to, 'I have to question why you don't just let me get on with what I feel I must do. And why you had to adopt this whole fictitious reason to explain my psychology. And anyway, when did you get so involved with social media?'

His hands spread and press on the steering wheel, then arms outstretched, his fingers curl and clutch, whitening his grip.

Later, I call Clare. She's someone I've known well for over thirty years. When I tell her what's going on in my life, she is quiet.

'You don't understand?'

I imagine her shrugging.

'Talk to me? Tell me what you think?'

'I have nothing to say, I…it's not my life Al, you have to do whatever it is you need to do.'

'But you don't approve.'

'It's not that I don't approve, it's just that, it's not a

normal thing that you're trying to do. You've already said you don't think you spent enough time with Ria, so maybe it's a guilt thing that's driving you. I mean, what are you hoping to find? That Ria was unhappy; a state of mind initiated at three years old because your worldly success began in the middle of her birthday party? You were a good mum. As good as any of us, and anyway, I knew Ria, she wasn't after that kind of attention.'

PART TWO

I've Been Prey

Trouble got evicted
From the devil's lair
I wager she got betrayed
by her friend Despair
Tori Amos

1

On a plane, finally out of the ditch I was digging for myself in England, I am thirty thousand feet high but sober as stipulated. I found this shaman on the internet whose website spoke to me of storytelling, ritual, learning the rhythms of Mother Earth as she is watched over by ancestors, now stars in the cosmos. And pretty pictures of howling coyotes, full moons, red suns, yellow canyons and a description of healing through Hopi ways.

I signed up for ten days.

I didn't just leave; we had the 'conversation'. Me, slumped on the floor in our bedroom, sitting with my back against the wall whilst Harvey got changed out of his work clothes. He was telling me about a colleague who lectured him on socialist values over the proverbial glass of champagne. Afterwards, on his way to the station, the guy – who shall remain nameless – stepped over a homeless person's legs as if the person didn't exist.

'I couldn't stand it anymore and I picked him up on it,' Harvey said. 'I told him, if he really believed in socialist values, he should do something to help the bloke – who was sitting on the floor with an empty paper cup beside him. So do you know what he did? He took a half-eaten sandwich out of his backpack and tried to give it to the man, who said, "I'm not a fucking dog," and quite rightly. Jesus!'

'Harvey?'

'Yes.'

'I need to talk to you.'

'Go on.'

'It's not working, is it?'

'What do you mean?'

'For me, lots of things: writing songs, coming to terms with what's happened, us. You know, trying to live and be happier.'

Harvey sat on the edge of the bed with his arms dangling between his legs. 'Well, what do you want to do?'

'I think we should take a break. No, let me rephrase that, I think I should take a break. Go away somewhere to immerse myself in nature and ancient wisdom.'

'Like where?'

'Does it matter?'

'Well, yes.'

'I'm going to go and stay with a shaman for a week and then if I'm receptive enough I'll be invited to spend some time on a Hopi reservation.'

He said, 'OK,' but the way his eyes flicked up to the ceiling I knew he thought I was making a stupid decision. I admitted to being lost and knocked off my perch, and said that's why I wanted to go, to get back on it.

So I'm sitting on a plane, with the recent memory of

Harvey seeing me off this morning – not at the airport, I didn't want that – at home, in private, by the front door. He hugged me with feeling, stroked my back and had tears in his eyes. The taxi was waiting outside, engine humming. He told me he was worried about me and asked if I'd text him when I got there. I nodded. He smiled as if he understood something at least, even if it was just his own resignation.

I was very close to losing my nerve. Stepping out into the cold, foggy morning, which was a kind of self-fulfilling prophecy, only, unlike I'd visualised, it turned out to be me, not Harvey, leaving with a suitcase. An owl was hooting and the damp penetrating. I had never felt more alone. It was like slipping out of a womb: naked in a clothed world, fragile and exposed. I don't think that's what is meant when they say born again, but in some odd way, that's also how it felt, and a sense of dread took root inside me.

I can still feel Harvey's arms around me, and I pick up his scent on my sleeve.

I am stone cold sober – as I have been for two weeks now – as per my shaman's instructions. In my suitcase, packed between folds of clothes, I have pictures of Ria. The packet of matches I found in her room is in my wallet. My laptop is in its holdall, enriched with a downloaded keyboard app; just in case the unable-to-compose spell gets broken.

What I do and what I think I'll do are not always the same thing. That discomfort I felt prying amongst Ria's things wasn't there when I went back into her room and

73

on impulse took her very old English phone, unlocked and replete with a whole list of contacts, memos and other stuff; it's in my handbag.

Sipping sparkling water with ice and lemon, I'm toasting the road to discovery even though I feel broken and adrift in an unfathomable sea. Trying to calm myself by taking the pressurised air deep into my lungs, I notice the woman to my left, sitting facing me, is staring. Eventually she asks, 'Do I know you?'

'No, I don't think so,' I say, pulling a blanket from its plastic sheeting.

'Wait, I've got it now; yes. Sorry to disturb.'

The hairs on my arms are standing. Writing songs for high-profile artists hasn't in itself made me famous, but being Ria's mother has, and because I haven't been out of our very small village for over two years, this is my first encounter with the fallout from that.

'That's OK,' I say, hitting the button that draws up the screen between us. I close my eyes and fall asleep. When I wake, I'm a little stronger. I've never taken a trip completely on my own before. I have absolutely no right to claim the title 'brave', but I feel as if I am, a bit. It's coming from that piece of me, the one that believes I'm doing the right thing – no question mark.

Hours pass.

'Sancerre, Rioja, bubbly?'

I shake my head. The tall, blonde attendant can see a tear snaking its way down to my lips. With a smile and an uplift in her voice, she asks, 'Are you sure?'

It's a lie but I tell her that I am.

I have a book on my lap, a gizmo between the seat and my thigh and earphones clamped to my ears. I'm flicking between movies; all categories and songs in the genres of *jazz*, *smooth and easy* and *rock around the clock*. It annoys me that so many of those tracks are in the wrong category but I can't concentrate on anything, anyhow, so I don't know why I care.

Four movies and two meals later and I'm stepping off the plane drunk on nothing, reeling and aching. And OK, so I'm going to have to get used to being stared at. Already, there's the sly smile worn by the passport control officer and the thousand eyes flicking over me by the baggage carousel.

Ria had to put up with this attention, too, but in very different circumstances and for different reasons. Perhaps she didn't find being ogled at disconcerting. Perhaps it was all part of the madness she came home to run away from.

At the car hire desk, I'm getting a little heated.

'This is America, right?'

'Yes, mam.'

'And you speak English?'

'Yes, mam.'

'So why don't you understand what a satnav is?'

'I don't know, mam.'

The manageress comes over and she, too, doesn't understand what I'm saying.

'Look, I want a car that includes a device, where I type

in the address, and it talks me through how to get to my destination whilst I'm driving.'

'Oh, you mean GPS?'

★★★

Thank the Lord! Finally, finally. No stray eyes are settling upon me. No ears are overhearing what I'm saying. No one is misunderstanding me. I am alone and on my way. All the windows, like me, are wound down. A warm breeze is playing with my hair. I like the way the roads have been cut into the landscape in straight lines: fat highways and thin B roads. The GPS speaks to me in a southern drawl. *At the next junction, you turn left now*, and I feel like I'm living in one of Ria's movies, with a trickle of sweat slowly making its way down between my breasts.

Phoenix to Sedona is cowboy country. Red dust plains and desolation. Thirst-making air. With one high-heeled shoe slamming down on the brake, I make a last-minute decision and sweep into the parking lot of a wooden shack with a glass door. I think this might be a store where I can buy a bottle of water, but as I push my way into the interior, I can see it is a dimly lit restaurant. Several tables are occupied – all eyes are upon me – I sit down at an empty one. I'm curious about these people, too. I order refried beans in a taco. The guy at the next table is holding his fork like a dagger and saying, 'Where you from?'

I tell him, London.

He says, 'Across the border?'

76

'No,' I say. 'No, across the pond.'

He chews whilst he thinks about it.

'I live in England, the UK.'

Someone else calls out.

'Why you here?'

'I'm on my way to Sedona.'

'Hmm, Sedona. You been there before?'

'Never.'

'So why you going there now?'

'To study ancient wisdom with a shaman.'

They don't ask me anything else.

When my food arrives, I try to concentrate on eating to the sound of slurping and burping and the scraping of cutlery on plates. Eventually, the guy from behind the till saunters over. With his hands in his pockets, he stands next to my table. He's rolling on his heels, looking down at me. He says, 'Not far from here, it's on your way, just a short detour up those hills on your left, and you've got Jerome. It was an old mining community once, but it's a ghost town now.'

Washing down my meal with gulps from an ice-cold bottle of water, I can't resist the short detour up those hills. When I reach halfway, I get out and stare into the big hole in the ground – the abandoned quarry – whilst the wind and heat slap me around. Up ahead, on the hillside, is the town. It's too steep to walk up there in this heat, so I take the car, pay for parking in the lot and saunter down Main Street. The saloon bar, brothel and hotel are all still standing. A gift shop that could have been a gun shop once sells crushed-velvet scarves, Stetsons, sepia stills from old cowboy movies on the back of postcards and fake golden nuggets attached to brass key rings. On my way out, I watch a bird's nest tumble down a red dirt road.

Jerome is a world like my own; today's pretty offerings are nothing more than nostalgia.

Greg, my shaman, lives in a two-storey house inside a maze of roads, just off the main highway leading into Sedona. He's quite a bit older than me; slim, of medium height with indigenous features, wearing cowboy clothes.

'Alison, it's great that you're here,' he says, extending his warm hand which is dry and slightly calloused on the inside of a firm grip. 'I've been waiting for you to arrive. You must be very tired.'

He takes my bag and leads the way upstairs.

'Your room's up here in the attic. You'll have your privacy; my bedroom's downstairs.' He puts my suitcase on the floor. 'Well, I'll be down in the kitchen when you're ready.'

The first thing I unpack is Ria's phone. It's really old with no internet but there is a notes folder and a calendar. Scrolling through the list of contacts, I find a couple of important phone numbers: Joshua's and someone called Sally who Ria knew from acting classes in England and shared accommodation with when she first moved to LA.

'You all right up there?' Greg calls from the bottom of the stairs.

I throw the phone onto the bed and leave the room.

'I'm coming down,' I call back.

Whilst Greg makes me a cup of herbal something in the open-plan kitchen, I stand by the glass doors leading on to the garden, looking out on Indian totems. My head sizzles with jet lag.

Greg says, 'I'm really only half Hopi, on my mother's side.'

I can't believe what I'm seeing.

'Oh!' I step backwards as if stung.

'What's happened?'

'An eagle's just fallen out of the sky!'

'Probably not an eagle,' Greg says, coming over, sliding the patio doors open and walking over to the bird. 'Yup, it's an eagle, all right,' and turning to me, adds, 'When an animal behaves strangely it's because he's sick or it's a sign for the onlooker.'

'Is this one sick?' I ask.

Greg gets down on one knee and scrutinises the bird.

'It's not alive.'

'So, is it a sign?'

'I think so.'

Milk chocolate feathers ruffle in the breeze, a white hooded head stays perfectly still, a custard beak droops as one pale, yellow eye fixes on me.

'What's the sign?' I ask.

'I don't know,' Greg says, going back inside, whilst I stand there with a cold chill running down my spine. Certainty retreats. That bit of me I was so sure of on the plane shrivels and dies. The question mark appears as I wonder what I've done, travelling thousands and thousands of miles to live and study under the roof of this man, who can't even tell me what I believe he should know.

2

Greg and I eat dinner in town, in a log cabin, overlooking the heart of Sedona, which is one broad street like a film set for a 1950s' cowboy movie. On each side of the road, big stores sell hanging crystals, dreamcatchers, incense and other New Age paraphernalia, together with moccasins, cowboy boots, flutes and Stetsons, paintings of indigenous Americans and suede jackets with fringing. There are hints of Disneyland; it's not exactly the most alluring place to embark on a spiritual quest.

My companion wears a pair of brown and perfectly creased trousers, a beige check shirt and a medallion on a leather thong. He has grey, oiled, perfectly combed and collar-length hair, a crooked nose, and eyes one shade darker than his trousers.

He eats steak with fries. I have a combo salad. We both drink water, of course; no alcohol or any other intoxicating substance will be imbibed whilst I'm with this man. These are his orders.

He takes a sip and looks to the glass as if it holds one of the world's finest champagnes. 'It's good water,' he tells me. 'Crystal clean. Yeah, we're lucky here. In other States they've been drilling down to the Earth's crust and the water is black.'

'Fracking?'

'Yeah, fracking.'

Greg's eyes hold mine as he asks, 'So Alison, what's brought you halfway across the world to seek out shamanic healing?'

He lifts his chin as he waits for my answer. I'm a little taken aback. I don't know why, I should have expected this question. After all, that's exactly why I am here, for healing.

'My daughter died.'

He has his elbows on the table either side of his half-eaten plate, his chin resting on his steepled hands.

'She died in the bath. She was living in LA, working on a film. She was an actress. My husband, Harvey…'

My throat is dry. I gulp down my clean, crystal-clear water and Greg refills my glass.

'Can you get drunk on this?'

His raises his eyes.

I carry on with my tale.

'You know, I'm so grateful that neither one of us turned on the news that night because it's very likely we would have heard it there first and I'm not sure how either one of us would have coped with that. Not that we coped well with it anyway.'

'How long ago did this happen?'

'More than two years.'

'You're still grieving.'

'I'm a bit of a mess, actually.'

Greg's eyes are on mine; I look down at the table and play with a crumb.

'I'm a songwriter, except, I can't write. Harvey and I, we're usually close enough to help each other through stuff but this has come between us.'

Greg fiddles with his dessert spoon.

'On Ria's death certificate it says, "accidental suicide". I think that's unusual. Don't you?'

I look up and his eyes, immediately, find mine.

'Ria was addicted to painkillers. But why? Why was she on them? What was the pain that she was trying to numb? Maybe I wasn't as present in her life as I could have been. At the end of the day, aren't all creatives the same? I mean, you check out whilst you're creating and consequently you're not always aware of things going on in the real world. There are pieces missing. I need to find them inside myself and I need to find out about the Ria I didn't know.'

Greg doesn't answer and I shift, uneasily, one hand on the pepper pot.

'I guess I'm here because I'm like a guitar that's so tightly strung you can't get a tune out of me, but I'm thinking that, maybe if I knew the chords to Ria's song, maybe if I could find a phrase, or even a riff, maybe I could just keep strumming until harmony arrives and my strings give a bit. Do you know what I mean?'

The waitress puts the check on the table and moves away. Greg leans back in his seat. I pick up the bill and pay it. He says he will take me up into the hills tomorrow and introduce me to the ancestors. It's a place where you can experience many things. I'll be sleeping up there alone on the last night of my seminar.

He says, 'You need to make friends with her.'

'Are you personifying the land?'

'Sure am.'

'Ha! I do that with my piano.'

***

I'm awakened at 5 a.m. by an acoustic bell that resonates in my mind long after the sound dissipates, making me imagine that I'm in some sort of a monastery. It's an enchanting thought and I take it with me to a breakfast of toast with local honey, fresh orange juice and camomile tea that Greg has made and left for me on the table. He comes into the room just as I finish eating and soon we are heading off in the watery first light, towards Coffee Pot Rock.

It's a slow, rough climb up a dirt track leading to a plateau. Greg parks his minibus next to a pale, almost-naked bush. From the boot, he takes two folding chairs and places them close to the precipice. We sit overlooking Boynton Canyon. The sun is yet to gather its strength and I pull my cardigan tighter around me. Greg speaks in a low hypnotic voice, saying there's no such thing as ownership. Everything is borrowed, even the body we live in, and when it comes to Mother Earth, we don't possess her either – she possesses us. Messages are carried through the air and received by what's buried beneath our feet, and if we listen closely, we'll hear a conversation, not only with our ears but with our whole being. We need to be open and ready for direction. If we only have eyes for what appears to be of solid form, then we are only living in one dimension. He says, we get depressed because when we don't perceive the magic in things, everything seems dead to us, including ourselves. He closes his eyes and sings in a reedy voice what I imagine to be a traditional Hopi song. I close my eyes, too. When the song reaches its final note, we are locked in a moment. Greg's words and his song have silenced my mind. I'm aware only of the wind slapping my ears.

'Can you hear whispering?' Greg asks, and it's an odd thing, because I do hear an indistinct *wha wha wha* sound.

I nod.

Then he tells me to go and have a look at the old withered tree behind us and try to connect with it. Someone's speaking but it's not Greg. It's an experience that's similar to writing a song that just shows up one day, fully formed and deposited in my mind, and all I have to do is cling to it long enough to transcribe it, and when I play it back, I wonder where the hell it came from. So, this is a similar thing: a voice in my head.

This tree, with its roots in red dust and hardly any foliage left to cover its nakedness, is watching you, listening to the sound of your breath.

It's feeling you.

Nourished only by the wisdom of its years, its thin, arthritic, grey and dry splitting limbs are trying to reach out and touch you, but you only see the falling apart, and you are appalled.

I grow aware of Greg's presence directly behind

me. He takes hold of my arm and leads me over rocky ground to a boulder. He motions me to sit down. Jagged limestone pierces my bum. There's a desert fern next to me and something brilliant white, the shape and size of a guitar pick, resting on the faded brush. To the other side of me, there's a slight scrambling sound. A lizard stops in its tracks, merging with the dirt. I look back to the plant, notice delicate antennae emerging from the white shape. I reach out with one finger, but if I touch, such violence will turn its body to dust. So I leave my finger hovering a few millimetres above. The butterfly shivers and a thrill shoots up my arm.

I look behind, expecting Greg to be watching over me, knowingly, experiencing this with me, but he is back there sitting on his folding chair, looking out over the cliff, towards another canyon.

Either the day has heated up now or I'm having a hot flush. I take off my cardigan, tie it around my waist and walk back towards him. When he feels my presence, he talks to the butte opposite but his words are for me.

'Now do you see? You're being guided, but not by me.'

I wonder if, when I thought Greg was taking my arm and leading me over to the boulder, that really happened? Or was he sitting here the whole time, waiting for my return? I've lost my handle on reality. My whole body feels light and tingles as if I'm just about to faint. I'm awash with emotion. Call it awe. Call it fear. Call it my battle with shadow. Call it anything you like, but I still feel as if I'm being played and I am compelled to make light of it. I put my hands on Greg's shoulders and whisper, 'Boo' in his ear. He turns to look at me and I read disappointment followed by acceptance on his face. My lips spasm instead of smile. My head quivers on its stem.

He nods and says, 'Time to go.' It's an even jerkier ride down the hillside. I'm tossed, juddered and swayed. We don't speak and the air is wool between us. When we get back to Greg's house, I don't go inside. I walk the crisscross streets of this residential district in the suburbs of Sedona.

Sitting on a low front-garden wall, I take Ria's phone out of my bag and dial Harvey. His answerphone picks up. I try calling his work and am told by an automated voice that the office is now closed. I cut the line. The UK is eight hours ahead; seven in the evening. It's 11 a.m. here. There are no high buildings, just natural inclines overseeing the world. All the houses are yellow sandstone blending in with the landscape. The sun burns phosphoric. The heat is stifling, but I like this hot-water bottle for my soul. I open contacts and stare at Sally's details. As I punch the call button my heart skips a beat. A clipped London voice answers.

'Hello.'

'Is that Sally?'

'Yes. Yes, it is. Who's calling from Ria's phone?'

'Alison, her mum.'

There is silence on the other end of the line.

'I hope you don't mind.'

'No, no, of course not. What can I do for you?'

'I'm in Arizona. I'm going to be here for the next week

or so. I would like to go home via Los Angeles and come and see you.'

'Sure. But can I ask why?'

'I find myself wanting to talk to people who knew Ria, and I, um, would like to hear anything you'd like to tell me about her. Any anecdotes, observations, anything really...'

She says nothing.

'Turns out I only really knew one side of her.'

Her voice softens when she says, 'I'm currently living in New York. Text me when you've booked your flight. Let's meet for a drink.'

'That would be perfect, thank you,' I say, but she's already gone.

I weigh the phone in my cupped hand and look up at an eagle surfing the ocean-blue expanse. A young man is getting out of a red truck. He crosses the road and comes towards me. He has dark hair, cut short but not too short, and interesting features.

'Hi!' he says. 'What you doing on my wall?'

'Phoning a friend.'

I show him Ria's phone.

'I've never seen you before. You staying round here?'

'Yes, sorry, I should introduce myself. I'm Alison, staying with Greg, round the corner.'

The young guy looks to the ground with amusement on his face. He says, 'Pleased to meet you Alison' as he walks past me and lets himself into the house at the end of the path.

Right on cue, Ria's phone rings. The number's

withheld. I'm thinking it's Sally and she's changed her mind. I'm nervous to pick up, but I do pick up.

'Al?'

'Harvey.'

'You OK?'

'Yes, I'm fine. How are you? How's everything at home?'

'Busy.'

'Good.'

'What about you? How's things over there?'

'Interesting. Different.'

'Is it what you expected?'

'It's only the first day, I'm not sure yet, but hopefully it's going to be.'

'I'm pleased you called.'

'Me too.'

At his end, another phone rings.

'Do you need to get that?'

'No, it's OK. Did you want to tell me something?'

'No, nothing special.'

'Oh shit, I have to go, Al. Keep in touch.'

And he is gone too.

★★★

Pesky things happen just outside Sedona. The buttes completely overwhelm the landscape. The heat whips around your head and the dust is continually agitated. Day two, early morning, and Greg has sent me to Boynton Canyon.

'To do what?'

'Just be.'

Trekking is not one of my greatest talents, especially on a craggy incline. Fit, suitably kitted-out people keep overtaking me. They call out a good-natured, 'Morning' as I puff, sweat, stumble and stop to drink from an ever depleting bottle of water. I try hard to respond to every single one of them, but this scratchy dryness in my throat doesn't always let me. I'm almost on my hands and knees when I get to the ridge, so high up the cars on the road below are Dinky miniatures. I sit here for a while, staring at the butte opposite, as it slowly changes from yellow to rich gold on its way to the bleeding crimson it aspires to. Up here, I feel small and timorous, frightened that when I stand up, my shaky limbs will have me tumbling all the way down into the valley, hitting base like a rag doll.

When it gets too steamy, I slip and slide my way down, finding shade under the oaks and pines in a gorge at a much safer level. A flutter of butterflies swim through dappled light. They have me transfixed until they disband in the sun-filled clearing.

A butterfly yesterday and so many today; is this also a sign for me? Or is it usual in Arizona for insects to communicate with humans and dance for them in a kaleidoscopic display?

Having found a path, I walk down it aimlessly. The butterflies have filled me with a sense of belonging to these rocks, to this dust, and these parched trees. They've initiated an appreciation for the stark beauty I have found here. It's not like I make a conscious decision to leave. I would be happy to stay, but my legs are taking me back to my hired car.

Driving back through town, I pull over outside a shop with *Spiritual Motifs* painted in rainbow colours on its window. As I walk in, a young guy, short and squat, is tapping a monotonous tattoo on the counter.

'Can I help you?' he says.

'Maybe.'

'What is it that you want?'

'OK, well, I thought I could just look around but I guess… a book about animal symbolism?'

He's amused.

'Sure,' he says. 'Follow me.'

He steps out from behind the counter and leads me down a step, past stacks of books on tables, to the full shelves on the other side of the shop, and stands there, watching me, arms akimbo.

'Are the books in any particular order?'

'Probably.'

'That's helpful.'

'Yeah.'

I find myself staring at him as he shuffles from foot to foot.

'The lady who runs the place, she's out at lunch.'

'Shall I come back?'

His aura sucks the oxygen from this dark low-ceilinged, cabin. The air-con blows freezing. He shrugs and I'm flushing and shivering with discomfort. Through the window, I spy brightness and warmth.

'Look, it's OK, I think I've changed my mind,' I say.

3

Greg's house, mid-afternoon, is sweltering and humid. My hair and clothes stick to me. The French doors are open on to the garden. There's a slight breeze but not enough to cool me down. Greg doesn't like air conditioning and nor do I, but it's really hot in here.

He's sitting very still in the armchair opposite. He's told me to get comfortable and so I'm on the floor, legs outstretched, back against the sofa, hands in my lap. With a leather-skinned drum between his thighs, he has a great rhythm going. I close my eyes and tune in until the music suddenly stops.

'You're in a house,' he tells me, 'with a spiral staircase going down and down and down until you get to the basement. A snake with many heads is there to meet you. He takes you into a room, sits you down before him, and says you are completely free to think and feel whatever comes naturally.'

I'm imagining the space that Greg has created for me. I hear footsteps and see the hydra descend the spiral staircase; he has a man's legs. I'm alone, waiting for him. There's a continuous drip coming from somewhere. There's a whirr inside my head as I become aware of the smell of damp seeping through cavernous, mossy walls. I don't trust the creature that is walking towards me. The desire – to open my eyes and run from this room, from this house, from this world – is overwhelming. It takes all my willpower to stay in the daydream. I latch onto the rhythm of the banging in my chest. See myself with a keyboard on my knees, playing a tune I can't hear. The passing of time seems to have stopped. I have no idea what I'm secretly playing on the keyboard that makes me forget who I am, where I am. I only know that when I open my eyes it is dusk.

Greg and I remain silent for a long while. As I readjust my consciousness, my eyes flit over everything like a mosquito: French doors, kitchen in semi-darkness at the other end of the room, a square of electric light on the carpet spilling in from the entrance hallway.

Greg leans over, snaps on an uplighter, pierces the silence with, 'Did you go where I suggested, today?'

I'm confused.

'Boynton Canyon?'

I nod.

A real mosquito buzzes next to my ear. I wave my hand in a desperate attempt to make it feel unwelcome.

'Any experiences you'd like to share?'

'Well, I'm not really sure what experiences you'd like me to tell you.'

'Your journey? What you felt? What you saw?'

'I climbed. Tried to adhere to your instructions and be aware, take everything in…'

I pause.

Greg urges me to go on.

'It was hotter than I'm used to and even though I was wearing my trekking sandals, my feet kept slipping. I caused more than a few baby landslides. In fact, at one point, I thought I might slip over the side into the valley. So, I found this out-of-the-way place to sit, drink my water, watch the butte opposite and the road below that I'd driven on to get there.'

Greg's looking intently at me.

'I hadn't noticed how high I'd climbed until I saw how small the cars were and how tall the surrounding landscape was in comparison. The sun was lording it over everything, it was very humbling.'

'And?'

'Anyway, I sat there for some time. Finished my water. It felt like it was time to move on, so I did, and climbed down the other way, where I saw this optical illusion made by a flutter of butterflies as they moved through the light and the shade.'

'A butterfly turned up for you yesterday.'

'Yes, it did. What does that mean?'

'You tell me.'

'Ha! I thought you were going to tell me! Isn't there some standard meaning attached to each creature? Isn't that part of what you're going to teach me?'

'There are books written on the subject, and you can find stuff out on the internet, but that's not what I want you to learn here. There is some personal connection between you and these creatures. Their message can only be found inside you. So, how do you find them, these butterflies?'

'What do you mean? They find me. I don't go looking for butterflies.'

'Well, how do they appear to you?'

'Delicate. Fragile. Beautiful. Sensual. Colourful. Quiet. Compelling. You can't touch them. If you touch them, they'll turn to dust.'

'Have you ever touched one?'

'No, I wouldn't dare.'

Greg smiles, exposing his front two teeth that are crossed like a tepee. He motions for me to continue. I don't know what else to say, but I keep talking anyway.

'My heart grieves for them, really. Don't they only live for one day after being cooped up as a caterpillar forever? They must feel such a wonderful sense of freedom, only to have it cut short in their prime and shorter still if they're murdered for their beauty. I hate seeing butterflies snared under glass or pressed into a book.'

I go silent and cold. An unframed photo of Ria propped up on my piano's sheet-music stand comes to mind. Greg leans forward and lights a candle on the coffee table. Several moths are immediately drawn into the room. Outside, crickets stridulate. A full moon spies down on totems that have turned to predators under the darkening sky. Greg is in the kitchen now, shoving drawers. My skin is crawling. I go and stand near him, rubbing and scratching my arms, feeling distant and shivery.

Greg looks my way, says, 'You OK?'

'No, I'm not.'

'You want to go upstairs and lie down?'

'No, I don't want to be alone.'

He leads me back to the sofa.

'You want to say something?'

I shake my head.

'You sure?'

I feel hunched, old, like this could be the aftermath to my hundredth birthday party and say, 'Too much sun, maybe.'

I'm scared. Scared of the way the unexpected hijacks life. The nasty, unknown thing that leaps out of shadows and steals away someone you love more than anything. Death frightens me. Not the prospect of my own death, but Ria's death frightens me. They tell me she's gone to a better place, that she's at peace now, but what if it's like night – a great big black expanse filled with looming spirits – and I still can't do a bloody thing to help her. My own incompetence frightens me but I don't say, can't say, any of this.

He brings me water and urges me to sip, so I sip, and it leaks down the front of my shirt. The wetness against my chest is shocking. He takes the glass out of my hands, puts it on the table and encourages me to lie down. He places a blanket on top of me. The sky is pitch black now. The room full of silhouettes. Greg leans over me to switch off the uplighter.

Quite pathetically, 'I don't like the dark,' I say.

I don't remember falling asleep but when I wake it's morning. I'm still lying on the couch and the light is still on beside me. I turn it off. All the demons have departed. Night seems like an eon away.

Greg appears in the doorway clutching his hands. He says, he's pleased I've slept well. He didn't want to wake me, but breakfast is ready and keeping warm in the oven.

We eat together in silence. Fried eggs, buttered toast, American coffee in large, glazed, green cups, tasting weak and watery and which I drink without milk. Greg looks fresh in his navy trousers, white cotton shirt and bolo tie. He's soap scented and his grey hair is impeccably neat. I, on the other hand, haven't washed or changed my clothes since yesterday. I haven't looked in the mirror either, so I've no idea how I come across, but I feel crumpled, lesser, better than last night but still out of sorts.

'What's the plan for today?'

'I'm keeping you here.'

In my room at the top of the stairs – Greg's room is downstairs, off the small corridor to the left of the front door – I grab Ria's mobile, sit on the bed and start to type.

Hello Joshua, it's Alison, Ria's mum, here.

I'm nervous, not sure what to say next. My hand hovers over the keyboard and I accidentally press send. He replies immediately:

Mrs C, you nearly frightened the life out of me with this message coming out of Ria's, old, old, old phone. J.

I sit on the edge of the bed gazing at the screen and eventually type:

Sorry Joshua, I didn't mean to frighten you. I'm in the States at the moment and not coming home for another ten days or so, but would like to talk to you in the meantime. Bearing in mind the time change – we're 8 hours behind you – when would be a good time to call?

About?

Ria.

Greg calls, 'Alison, we have a visitor.'

You can call me now.

'Hey Greg, I'll be down soon. I just have to make this urgent call. I'm sorry, I hope that's OK?'
　　Greg doesn't respond and I dial Joshua's number.
　　'Mrs C.'
　　'Joshua, thanks for taking my call.'
　　He says nothing.
　　'We haven't always been on the best of terms but I'm hoping we can put all of that behind us now.'
　　Again, nothing.
　　'Ria liked you, a lot, I think. Are you still there?'
　　'You wanted to ask me something.'
　　'Were you still seeing her? Towards the end, I mean.'

'Some.'

'Did you know about the painkillers?'

'Why?'

'Maybe I didn't phrase that right, I mean, do you know why Ria was on such strong and dangerous medication?'

He sighs. 'Headaches,' he says.

'Were they really that bad? I mean, they told me she had aches and pains, but if they were that bad then surely I would have known about them.'

'Why me? Why are you asking me? Why aren't you asking the doctor who prescribed them for her?'

'I'm sorry Joshua, I'm just trying to find out what was going on in her life; trying to understand what happened.'

'The industry, Mrs C…and the people in it.'

'What are you saying?'

'I'm saying that there were a lot of bad influences around Ria that were a whole lot worse than me.'

'What else can you tell me?'

'Nothing. I'm not in that industry and I don't have anything to do with it.'

'Joshua?'

'Yes.'

'Can I come and see you when I come back to England?'

'I don't think…'

'Please?'

'Goodbye, Mrs C.'

'Joshua.'

He's gone.

I stare at the phone for a couple of moments then rush

downstairs, wiping my clammy hands on my jeans. The guy with the red truck is standing in the hall by the front door. He wears a discomfiting expression as if I'm the source of comedic entertainment and says, 'I've just come to give you this.' He hands me an envelope. I'm perplexed and look to Greg.

'Anything else?' Greg asks, opening the front door for him. The man leaves, touching his Stetson like an actor in a 1950s movie. The door closes behind him. I stand there fanning myself with the envelope and Greg says, 'You better decide what you're gonna do with that.'

I'm going over the phone call with Joshua, rephrasing things in my mind, and berating myself for what I said – I have no idea what to do with this bloody letter.

'What shall I do with it?'

'Well, either you're going to read it or I can take it back unopened and tell him that whilst you're taking lessons with me, there's going to be no time for anything else.'

'The latter.'

'OK, good.'

'What do you think it says?' I ask, placing the letter on his outstretched palm.

'Something you don't want to get involved in.' He points through to the garden. 'Go and wait for me under the lady with the big hairdo. I'll take it now.'

The lady with the big hairdo is a juniper tree. I'm sitting on the bench at a rectangular wooden table. There's a jug of water, a royal blue, transparent, plastic glass before me and a sack at my feet that contains remnants of cloth: silks and cottons, some in plain colours, some patterned. I have a large needle and different colour yarns. My job is to sew a hem on my chosen materials before threading them onto a long length of string. The task feels menial at first, then at some point I get into it. When Greg returns, I ask him if he minds if I listen to music through headphones. He says it would be best if I stay listening to nature. 'We can make music later,' he says. 'The young man, Donny, didn't take kindly to having his letter returned. I explained that you're here as my student and the course I'm teaching you is intense and contra to receiving mail from strangers who live around the corner. If he bothers you again, you must tell me straight away.'

He leans back in a reclining chair that is made of the same grey, splitting wood as the bench and the table. He places his Stetson over his face. As I pick, thread and sew, he relates this monologue:

'The ancestors knew that the Earth has feelings. They walked upon her in bare feet and felt the throb of her pulse. Like a mother, she provides and yearns to be respected because if she's not then the love that nourishes everything is withheld. And if that's the case, she grows weary and something beautiful within her withers and dies. Her reaction is mirrored in the hearts of men. These are things that the ancestors didn't have to be told; they witnessed it for themselves. When the Mother is cherished and appreciated, she thrives, and when she feels love, she performs miracles. You will see at least one miracle when you go to the reservation.

'What you're doing now is a kind of creative meditation and a vow of intent. You're making a row of prayer flags that you can hang around the rocks on the night you sleep alone in the canyon. You wrote and told me your intention is to be able to write music again. These flags will be signalling your intention to the Mother. The Mother will inform the Universe and the sky will reflect the message back to you. The ancestors will be your witnesses.'

I spend the best part of the day working on the prayer flags. At dusk, the scent of citronella wafts and the prayer flags are now covering the full length of rope. I ask Greg what he thinks I'm learning.

He says, 'Just being with the moment.'

'I'm not always in the moment,' I confess.

'You don't have to be *in* the moment, but if you are *with* the moment, all you need to do is be aware of the present. Keep coming back to it, and if you do that, even when you're thinking other thoughts, you will still be *with* the moment.'

'Sounds like cheating to me.'

'Not cheating,' he says.

A sense of unease stirs within me again. It's not as bad as the previous evening, but it's there and it's bad enough. Greg's talking and I don't hear what he's saying, I'm just looking through him.

'I've lost you again,' he says.

'I've lost myself.'

'Tell me about it.'

'Well, that's just it, it feels like something terrible is

SONG FOR RIA

going to happen and I can't stop it. I know that something
terrible has already happened but this feels...my heart's
beating so fast, I don't know...'

Greg takes hold of my hands, walks me inside the
house and urges me to sit on the floor. My knees bend and
when I get down there, I'm just glad to be supported by the
wooden planks beneath me. Greg flits around the room
grabbing hold of all manner of percussion instruments and
puts them on the rug before me. 'One more thing.' He
goes back out into the garden and returns with my prayer
flags. Using Blu Tack, he displays them along one wall.
When he's finished, he sits facing me. 'A musician must
make music,' he says.

I take up a drum, play notes on its skin as if it's a
keyboard. The tapping is barely audible, but I carry on
pretending the drum is Bechs. And then things change.
The instrument starts to speak to me in its own language
and I no longer have to pretend I'm with anything but her.
She instructs my fingers to become lighter, like feathers,
whilst she requires the heels of my hands to thump before
giving way to the balls of my palms. I roll my hands back
and forth between raps, drumming now to the rhythm
that's taken me over. Greg has another drum between his
knees. He's following my cadence. We're jamming. I'm
smiling, feeling every beat; doing something I trust.

4

Greg smacks the roof of my hired car and waves. My foot presses down on the accelerator.

'Cathedral Rock,' he calls after me.

I brake and stick my head out the window.

'How long do you want me to stay there?'

'Take the whole day, explore.'

On the way there, I am unnerved by Donny in his red truck almost glued to my back bumper. When I need to go right at a roundabout, I almost go around it the wrong way, then quickly turn the steering wheel in the opposite direction. Donny pulls out into the next lane and continues straight on towards Sedona. I'm a little shaken when I get to the canyon. I would like to explore the caves of the ancient tribe that are set into the cliff face. Apparently, so I've read, you can feel Earth's vibrations shooting up into your body in those caves. People manage to climb into them, but it's too steep for me, and I don't believe I can get in and out without breaking my neck.

I find a stream instead, at Red Rock Crossing, under the shade of a cluster of willow trees. I'm itching to get my feet wet in the rushing water but there's too many spiders hanging from gossamer in the foliage all around. I'm not frightened, I just don't want to disturb them. Instead, I sit inside the dappled light and watch, for hours, whilst those ladies weave their silver threads.

It must be around four o' clock when I get back. Greg welcomes me as I step through the front door. I haven't been wearing sunglasses, so I'm light blind. As he makes me a cup of chamomile tea from yellow buds and fragrant grey stalks, my vision clears.

'What did you experience today?'

'The magic of spiders.'

He looks up at me.

'The way they build their webs.'

'Can you describe them?'

'Ingenious. Instinctive. Innovative. Inventive. It's an art form, what they do, making these silk creations, fine nets that waver in the breeze and shimmer in sunlight. Although really, it's just a trap for insects. They fascinated me today, though.'

'You're starting to understand about creatures.'

I'm hearing a chord progression in my head. I've had these moments before. Waking with a tune or a melody. Standing at a supermarket till and wanting the inspiration to stay until I don't have my hands full anymore. It's not the same as when I improvise, that comes from inside me, whilst this comes to me from somewhere else and insists I take note. My computer's lying on a chair. I rush to pick it up and open the keyboard app.

'I've borrowed an electric keyboard from a friend,' Greg says. 'It's up in your room.'

I'm like a child, rushing upstairs, storming through the door, sitting on a flimsy stool to capture the sounds that have abandoned my head now. Nevertheless, my hands have remembered them and are playing what I heard, over and over and over again. I'm wondering where to take this song because I know it's a song; it has its own atmosphere, lives in its own world. Only I can't see the whole world. I can only see a small part of it, like a painting in progress with the full picture not revealed. I stay with it, become part of it, urging the source of inspiration to trust me with the next phrase, but nothing else comes. So I begin to play with it, but don't hit on anything that makes sense. My friend, Inspiration, has flown. That big bubble of excitement inside me has popped and left me with the same old, same old awful depression.

'Perhaps it's a start,' I say, over my shoulder to Greg who's standing on the threshold. But even if it is, I feel it's too little, too late, as we're almost at the end of my retreat now.

★★★

'It's going to be a fine day, today,' Greg tells me. 'We have a couple of people joining us for a ceremony.'

There's certainly a festive feel in the air. Greg is rushing around doing goodness knows what and on the tray in the kitchen there's a jug of non-alcoholic punch that he has concocted, four tumblers and a plate of homemade cookies.

I'm not sure how I feel about all of this. I'm not ready

for party time and ceremonies. I'm worried about how it's going to appear when I don't go with the flow and storm out or break down.

When they arrive, Greg is carrying the electric keyboard into the garden. He calls out for me to open the door. I do and two people are standing there beaming. They introduce themselves as George and Winnie. He's tall and skinny, a lot younger than her, or at least he looks it. She is curvaceous, with long, thick, wavy white hair.

'Hi, I'm Alison.'

I offer my hand which they shake enthusiastically, one after the other.

'How are you getting on here?' George asks, as we walk through to the garden.

'I don't know yet. I'm not sure,' I mumble.

'Oh well, that's kind of usual for the first time you go on one of Greg's adventures. Adventures of the soul, Winnie calls them, and they take time to get absorbed.'

'They sure do, Winnie says.'

We stand in the garden, eat cookies and drink fruit juice, ice tinkling in our glasses. Greg talks to George about American football.

'Something tells me you're a piano player,' Winnie says to me, nodding towards the electric keyboard that now sits beside a drum and has an orange lead trailing from its underbelly into the kitchen.

'Yeah.'

I bite my bottom lip.

'Greg always gets us to do something we love when

we're the main person for the ceremony. I've stood where you're standing a number of times. The thing that originally brings everyone here is the need to find another way. Greg is good, he helps you find it.'

Very soon, I am improvising on the keyboard whilst Greg plays a set of drums. Winnie is dancing around George and shaking a maraca whilst he is aping a sumo wrestler doing a knee-holding dance. When they're exhausted, we eat a lunch of homemade corn soup spiced with hot peppers and served with cornbread, which the couple have brought with them. I learn that Winnie is a prolific artist and George looks after her gallery. Greg urges me to tell her my stories of butterflies and spiders, which I do, and she thanks me for sharing. She says, 'I paint all manner of insects and your thoughts will inform one of my future paintings, for sure.'

Then Greg orchestrates a ritual ceremony. I sit blindfolded on a chair whilst the others are making circles around me, shaking rattles, banging drums, singing and giving thanks to the powers that be. I see bright lights exploding behind my eyes. I see a crowd of people. Ria is amongst them but the vision is disturbed by a sudden silence. Greg stands before me and slowly peels away my blindfold. He says a prayer for my protection on the night I will spend alone in the wild.

When Winnie and George leave, it's late afternoon, and Greg takes me up into what he calls the Number One Canyon. We sit on those folding chairs of his looking over at a woodpile in the thicket. He asks what I see.

'A pile of wood.'

'Look again.'

'What do *you* see?' I say.

'What I see is different to what you see.'

'Well, what *do* you see?'

He says, 'First you, then I will tell you what I see.'

I say, 'Broken limbs, I can even hear the snap of them.'

He smiles and his face opens like a morning flower. He says, 'I see trees that are growing more branches to replace the ones they've lost. I've brought you up here today because this is where you'll be sleeping tomorrow night and I want you to become friends with her.'

'The landscape?'

'This landscape.'

We stay there for hours, mostly silent, listening to our chairs crack with each tiny movement, the rustling of creatures scuttling around in the foliage, and the odd bird squawk. Sometimes we have our eyes closed. At other times we're just looking around, drinking in the peace, until the sapphire sky is pierced with stars and white taillights race across the dome like rockets. We stay there until our stomachs nag, reminding us we have bodies to feed as well as our souls.

We return there again at five o' clock the next afternoon, my penultimate day with Greg. On our way, in the old people carrier, I tell Greg that I do feel better, in some ways, but not in others. In other ways, I feel a whole lot worse and despite my earlier experiences with nature, I'm not sure I'm ready for this one.

'You're not ready?' he asks.

'No.'

'Because?'

'Because I don't think I've grasped whatever it is you're meant to be teaching me; I haven't learnt enough.'

'Oh, you'll be fine. Now is too early to evaluate what you've learned here.'

He drops me off halfway up the incline with a bag full of homemade good-luck charms, a litre bottle of water, a large piece of tarpaulin and a tiny bit of Hopi wisdom. I won't need a blanket or even a sheet as it doesn't cool down all that much here at night. I'll be fine, as I've been told.

I climb until I reach a part of the canyon that looks flinty with big boulders and small plateaus, no foliage. That's where I make my home for the night. Sitting on a rock, I watch the heat haze disappear. Usually, I love dusk's sense of the unreal, but the blue sky is deepening, the canyon rock is almost indigo, and I can hear animal sounds coming from somewhere way off in the distance; but even way off in the distance is too near for me. The smell of scat is in the air.

Greg will come and get me at 5 a.m. In the meantime, he has armed me with a whistle. My guesstimate is his house is well out of hearing range. But hey, I'm to find a ledge wide enough to sleep on… check. Prepare my personal space by making a large circle out of baby rocks… check. Pee all around the exterior circumference of my circle… check. When my urine is dry, hang my prayer flags over the rocks and dot my artefacts all around… check.

I lay out my tarpaulin, sit cross-legged upon it, gulp my water and pat my whistle down in front of me. My urine will ward off most of the animals in this habitat, such as coyote and wild boar. Scorpions hide under things, so I must be careful when I raise my head in the morning, especially if I've used my shoes, or my bag as a pillow. Because I know these things, I will be safe, so I'm told. Animals only act out of character if they are sick.

As night deepens, I lie on my back. The big black diamante screen above sucks me in. I am enthused and entertained. Stones beneath the tarpaulin dig into my spine. Unseen insects brush against my skin. I am anxiously both sleepy and wired. I slip in and out of consciousness, see things: The dead eye of an eagle staring at me. Someone in shadow outside of my rock circle. I'm on my feet, taking a couple of steps backwards as Ria steps forwards spot-lit by moonlight. She stands on the threshold of a break in my rock circle, beckoning me. I go to her. She takes my hand, leads me through the exit on a jaunt outside the circle. I feel vulnerable and lead her back inside. We sit on the tarpaulin facing each other. The break in the rocks is still there. It disturbs me. Ria has her hands in mine. Her eyes are full of compassion. My eyes keep darting to the break in the rock circle. She is speaking but I can't focus on her words and I haven't a clue what she's saying. I am conscious that there are vultures and lions, snakes and bears out here. There are crackles and spit and unseen demons. I must be vigilant. I mustn't get distracted.

'I'm meant to be alone here,' I say out loud, and Ria is gone before I catch my next breath.

Fully awake now, I'm lying in the foetal position. I don't witness the diamond-studded night give way to a yellow and light-blue morning. I have my head buried in my hands, no longer caring if a scorpion might be hiding under my makeshift pillow. I am open to the disdain of a wild boar. Golden Eagle, come and peck me to pieces. Mountain lion, I am here for you to feed to your cubs. I've thrown the last of my water away in a rebellious act of self-defiance. I am pleased I have this thirst that sticks the back of my throat together like glue. My daughter came to me last night and I didn't embrace her. I didn't smooth her hair and tell her how beautiful she is and how much I love her. No, instead, I sent her away.

Greg sounds the horn, my wake-up call. I don't move. It's too hard to go on with this repeated behaviour. I want to un-manifest. I want to sink down inside the rock and become part of its stratum. To move would invite another betrayal of my better self. I lie there with warm crosswinds cuffing me from all sides. The memory of Greg's horn is persistent and I can't help but stir. Reluctantly, I come to standing, pick up my paraphernalia and throw it all in the bag. I place the stones that form my circle back where I found them. The only trace of myself I leave behind is my smell. Specks of dirt stick to the dried tears on my cheeks. I don't wipe them away; I keep them there like fresh tattoos.

Heavy on my feet, I descend towards Greg's jalopy. I get in in silence, not beside him but in the back, so it's not so easy for him to see my face. We are both jostled around on the rocky trip down. When we reach the road,

Greg looks at me in the rear-view mirror and says, 'Your daughter came to visit you last night.'

'How the hell do you know that?'

'I dreamt it, the same as you.'

I rub down the gooseflesh on my arms and avert my gaze to the side window; a myriad of cars are going the other way.

'Remember the eagle?'

'Yes.'

'Its spirit had flown; that was the message for you.'

'I don't understand.'

***

Over breakfast of pancakes, orange juice and honey, I'm thinking about Ria, I'm thinking about the eagle, and I'm angry. It's my last day with Greg. I came all this way to be under the tuition of this man, this spirit hunter, to learn what? That my last lesson, the pièce de résistance, is just a re-hashed version of Annie Forager's words: I must simply adjust to a life without Ria. I feel as if nothing has been solved, nothing has been resolved, not inside or outside of me. Everyone told me that this would be a wild goose chase, but I didn't believe them. Now I have to accept that my instincts lied to me and I am the idiot who didn't listen.

There's a tension in the room that needs to be snapped.

Greg says, 'When you've finished, I plan for you to paint a picture of your experience last night and then we can do some meditation to learn more.'

'I'm not doing that.'

Greg stares at me. His eyes are still soft, but his lips are pale and taut. He starts clearing away our dishes. I go upstairs to pack my clothes. When I leave the house there is a formal handshake between us. Greg looks as if he's just about to burst into tears. I thank him, although I'm not sure if I mean it.

I drive into town, park outside the motel, and as soon as I step out of my car, fear sets in. Perhaps it has something to do with having been given the tools to defend myself in the wild, amongst nature, but not in an artificial setting like this. Humans are not predictable. Perhaps we're all sick and we've forgotten how we're meant to behave. This place swarms with people, each carrying their own history of resentments that like boils can erupt at any moment. I feel them; their auras are palpable in the heavy collective atmosphere.

My motel room overlooks the canyons. Sick of canyons, the heat haze and blue sky, I shut the curtains. Lying down in the darkness, I intend to stay on that bed for a very long time, but I'm restless. I look at Ria's phone and get the feeling that Harvey won't pick up but I dial him anyway and, as predicted, he doesn't. Staring at the ceiling, I wonder what he's been doing with himself. A torturous vision arrives of him in bed with another woman. They are writhing around, his lips are teasing hers, their bodies are moving as one. I can't lie here any longer. I get up and pace, but actually, I need to get out of this room. The telephone on the bedside table rings several times but as Greg is the only one who could know where I am, I choose to ignore it.

I take a shower, change my clothes, put on make-up and find my way to the nearest bar. It's cool and quiet. Sitting at the counter, I order a glass of wine, best in the house. What gets put before me is a wave of golden liquid inside a huge frosted balloon glass. I make a swirl and transparent legs cling to the glass, then retreat into themselves like stage curtains lifting before a nineteenth-century play. I sniff and sip the lip-kissing, bone dry and aromatic wine. Just one sip and I'm already feeling slightly out of it, wondering why my anxiety is getting worse and not dissipating, although maybe it will if I sip some more. The door opens and blaring sunlight delivers a man in shadow. When he stands next to me, too close, I recognise him as Greg's neighbour, Donny, the one who propositioned me with a letter.

'I see you've finished your retreat,' he says, smiling at me again, in that same sly way. 'Greg gets up to some real shit. I can't believe you people are still paying for it.' He laughs.

'So, I suppose your letter was to warn me.'

He orders a whisky, rests his elbow on the counter, hand clamped to his ear like a phone. He stares at me and says, 'No, it was to ask you if you wanted to have a drink with me. When he brought my letter back, unopened, I was upset. You made me upset.'

'I'm sorry, but I'm not available. I'm married.'

'You're having a drink with me now though. Cheers!' He lifts his glass. 'Your husband should know better than

116

to let his woman out of his sight. Does he know who was teaching you Indian ways?'

I gaze down at my half-empty glass. No alcohol for weeks and now it's turned my head to cotton wool. I pick up my sweating bowl of nectar with a shaky hand and put the drink down again, hoping Donny doesn't notice my fragility. When I look up, he's still staring at me. I stumble off my stool and he grabs my arm.

'Thank you. It's OK. I'm OK, thank you.'

He lets go. Raises his hands in surrender. Looks behind at the barman who is watching us and says, 'What?' The barman immediately averts his gaze to the glass he's polishing.

'That's better,' Donny says, sliding his hands into his back pockets. He reaches across the bar, picks up and finishes his drink before following me out into the street.

The fierce sunlight bleaches everything, but even so, when the person in front of me glances over his shoulder, there's no mistaking it's the guy from *Spiritual Motifs*. Donny pushes past me. They're walking together now, blocking my way. When I step off the curb to get ahead, a car hoots so loud and sudden, I leap back up onto the sidewalk. The duo slow their pace and I tap Donny's arm.

'Look, what do you boys want from me?'

They look to each other.

Donny says, 'What do you think?'

'I think it's a bad idea, a very bad idea,' I say, and try to walk past them into the parking lot of the motel. Donny's friend shoves me, hard, and I'm falling backwards onto my arse. People on the street glance our way before bustling onwards. The friend wipes his mouth.

'Stupid shit!' I say.

'You cursing me?' my assailant says. 'Because that's not very ladylike if you're cursing me.'

Donny comes over. He doesn't say a word as he helps me up and shuffles me away from his friend. The next second, I'm swivelled in the opposite direction, my body rebounding off the back wall of a shop. Hidden from the street, I'm a bundle in their grasp; both of them. I catch a glimpse of someone peeking out the glass door of my motel and sidling away. I try to shout 'help' but the word gets stuck in my burning throat.

I'm on the ground again, flat on my back with a man-boy on top of me holding down my arms. I can't believe this is happening whilst my head is in such a fucking mess. He's inching up my dress, pulling at his fly. Pissed off enough not to care about the consequences, I spit in his face. His head springs backwards and I manage to knee him in the groin really hard, although not hard enough to prevent his fist colliding with my left eye. Slowly, he peels himself off me, sits on his knees at my feet, chin on his chest, holding his crotch. When he stands, he's bent over, swaying as if drunk. He wipes his mouth again. I'm thinking, Donny is going to come for me next, but I can't see past the staggering and blurred silhouette of my would-be-rapist. I turn my head away and fix my eyes on two unlikely blades of grass growing out of the tarmac. One of them has a minuscule red ant-like creature upon it. I stare and stare at the red dot that, like me, doesn't move. When I look back they've gone.

5

It's early morning. I've tried turning onto my other side and pulling the duvet up over my head but the knocking on the door is insistent. Totally uncaring about what might happen to me, I get up, throw a long T-shirt over my nakedness and open the door. It's Greg. I say nothing, walk away and perch on the edge of the bed. I feel his hesitation and call out, 'What are you doing here?'

'I tried to call you, several times.'

He points, first to himself and then to the room.

Reluctantly, I nod.

He walks in, silently closing the door behind him and sits down on the chair facing me. He doesn't inquire about my eye, which judging by the way it feels is a purple bowling ball.

'I've made arrangements to take you to the reservation,' he says.

I should be surprised he's turned up at all, but I'm not surprised about anything anymore. The deal was that if I was a good girl and take on Native ways without question or hiccough, only then would I be allowed to go to the ball.

'And supposing I don't want to go?'

'I think you should. There's someone I want you to meet there: my Hopi sister.'

'Why?'

'Because she can help you to understand.'

'Understand what?'

'Why you're here.'

'I know why I'm here and it was a mistake.'

As he gets up and walks to the door, my heart skips a beat. I can't do it. I can't go to New York and see Sally in this state. I can't go home either. I'm completely fucked. It dawns on me that I'm going to have to take one last shot at finding sanity with this shaman and his North American Indian thing.

I call to him, 'OK, I'll meet this woman.'

'Pack for an overnight stay. I'll wait outside,' he says, and leaves the room with the flimsy door protesting behind him.

Under the dim bathroom light, I spend too much time looking at my caricature in the mirror: a fat zipped-up eye in a haggard face, framed by witchy hair.

I stuff a few things into a backpack. Clothe this wash-bag of a body and tramp down the walkway. Greg follows me down. My heels clack, clack, clacking on the iron stairs. Once installed in the passenger seat of my hired car, he tells me I should change my shoes, 'into those Converse. You'll be more comfortable.' Grudgingly, I do as I'm told.

He wants to chauffeur me in my rental car because he thinks it would be best if he takes me. His people carrier is having some work done in the garage, so we can't go in that.

It's a three-hour journey, yet he doesn't mind dropping me off, driving back alone to attend to some urgent business, then coming to pick me up again tomorrow morning. I don't ask him if he's insured to drive my hired car. I don't ask him anything.

It's a relentless ride. Ragged land, dust and cactus to either side. I want to tell him, I'm vulnerable and he's conned me into his one-customer sham retreat. Instead, I sit quietly with a beast roaring inside me. The windows are down. A hot wind wraps around my ears, muffling the radio. Greg doesn't like air conditioning. I don't like it either but there's a time and a place. My mouth and my eyes are parched like this desert.

He turns off the radio.

'I know what happened,' he says.

I pretend not to hear.

He stops the car, leans across me and presses the button that makes my window go up.

'You could have asked me to do it.'

He closes his own window, initiates the air con; the air freezes and thins.

'I heard about it,' he says.

I don't want him to tell me he dreamt it. I don't want him to say that he heard it from the barman, the prying eyes at the motel or his abusive neighbour. I am desperate for 'it' not to exist, him and this whole trip with it.

I'm starting to feel very cold and shivery. I don't want to embrace myself and show weakness. I don't want to stay inside this car. I have the biggest urge to get out of here, into the warmth and sunlight, free of everything. I stare at him, willing him not to say anything else as I open the car door, undo my safety belt and run.

Further and further from the car, from him and I've tears bulging in my eyes. I'm like a child, laughing, escaping. It's hard to breathe. Looking over my shoulder, he's coming after me. He is fast. For his age, very fast. My laughter dissipates. I'm out of breath now, hating everyone who has done this to me. I'm not sure if it's his shoes crunching the ground and his breath beating the air or my own. It's like I'm on a treadmill but Greg isn't. He's almost upon me and I'm gagging for air now. I have to stop. I turn and face him. My voice is hoarse as I shout, 'Stay away'.

I'm reeling. My hands are out in front of me like a blind woman's. He's just standing there, hands on his hips, head down like a pecking bird. He's panting, raising his eyes.

'This is what happens when you take advantage of people,' I yell at him. I'm bending over now, holding the ache in my belly. He doesn't move. 'With this…this stupid game of cowboys and Indians you're playing.'

'It's not a game, Alison.'

'It is a game.'

'No, it's not,' he says slowly and patiently.

'OK then, it's a trap.'

He's looking around him for answers.

'What do you want me to do?'

'I don't know. Just go.'

'You want me to leave you here? Is that what you want?'

Feeling confined, I'm pecking at my clothes. Am I

tripping out again like on that night in the canyon? He takes a step towards me and I take a step back.

'Look, I want to help you,' he says.

My hands are in my hair now, shoving it back from my face, lifting my dark glasses and rubbing my sore eye.

'Listen Alison, you can't run away from you. You have to make peace with yourself. My Hopi sister can help you.'

He takes another step closer. I back away. I'm swaying. Must be 140 degrees here. Sweat rolls off my face. Black spots take over my vision. I think I'm in Greg's house with the dark settling in. Heat rising. Heart thumping. Greg's helping me sink to the ground. Must be the moon looking down on me, burning like the sun.

Grit enters my puffed eye and pierces my lips. Stones dig at my heart through my clothes. I lick dirt and mutter to the earth. Greg's lifting my shoulders off the ground, twisting me round to lean against a rock. I don't have the will or the strength to stop him. He pours water into my mouth. I spit it out. When I close my eyes, he taps my cheeks. 'Can you stand?' he asks. Taking my hands, he's pulling me up. I stumble. With my arm laced around his neck, he starts to walk then changes his mind and lifts me up into his arms. I am jostled with each step as he carries me back to the car.

Swivelling me into the passenger seat, he asks if I want him to take me to a hospital. I tell him, no. He slams my door. When in the driver's seat, he starts the engine and the air conditioning blasts.

'Where are you taking me?'

'To the reservation.'

I look out the side window at the piece of land I've just run across and can't believe I did that. Can't believe I was so manic. Can't believe I fainted. I want out of all this madness.

'Maybe that's not such a good idea,' I say.

'You need to be taken care of.'

I don't protest. I'm drained and I don't have an alternative. My body's limp, but I'm experiencing a different kind of strength. A strength that comes from not caring. I say to Greg that I want to tell him what happened yesterday. I want him to hear it directly from me.

'I know what happened,' he says. 'You chose to drink alcohol.'

'Your course had ended. If you thought it was dangerous, you should have warned me.'

'You didn't give me a chance. You stormed out of my house. I emailed you. I tracked you down and I phoned you, several times.'

'I was abused by those guys and I can't believe you're blaming me!'

We drive the rest of the way in silence with the windows up and the air conditioning on. I shiver and drink from Greg's gallon bottle of water until my belly bloats. When we arrive at the reservation, I don't realise we're there. There are no gates, just a dirt road leading to a large clearing where cars are parked haphazardly.

Greg's Hopi sister is standing beside a woodshed ready to greet us. She's short, wearing layers of black and purple linen, and well-worn soft shoes with laces. Her thick silver hair falls beyond her waist. She has coffee skin, small features, prominent cheekbones and grey eyes. She could be forty or a hundred and forty. Greg embraces her briefly and says, 'This is Alison.' She bends down, picks up a handful of dust, from the ground and pours it into my curled palm.

'Throw,' she says. 'Towards the sun.'

I stoop and bowl the powder.

'You've made your offering, now you can come in.'

'Thank you.'

'I am Sister.'

'OK,' I say, brushing the land off my hands.

She squeezes my upper arm then raises a forefinger to her temple and says, 'Lift your shades.'

I concur and she looks deep into my beaten face. 'One thing,' she says. 'A woman must keep herself safe at all times, mostly from men, but it can be from women too.'

I'm expecting a sermon on the evils of alcohol and short skirts when she lifts her arms up into the air, makes her hands into claws, opens her eyes very wide and screams. I jump and scream too. Then she spits in my face. I flinch. My heart pulses. My legs have gone weak again. To my shock-horror she laughs as if her little act was perfectly normal. She says, 'For a woman to look after herself she needs the devil's courage and she needs to learn what to do, if necessary. Then she can watch them run away because no one's going to stay and argue with the darkness of a mad-bull-witch.' She holds onto the strap of my shoulder bag and pulls me along. 'Now you come and learn more Hopi ways.'

I glance over my shoulder. Greg has already left. We walk across the arid land along the tyre printed track. To either side of us, random wooden homes dotted around the landscape are distorted by the heat haze.

She says, 'So this is the Hopi reservation. All those miles of barren land you drove through to get here is assigned to the Apache Navajos. Our villages are on three different levels of that big butte over on your left. We call them mesas. I'm going to take you to the First, Second and Third Mesas. Lots of walking. Eventually we'll go right up to the top, but first we have to get to where we climb to the first plateau. I wanted Steve to take us in his truck but he's going to be in the ceremony.'

'What ceremony?'

'Greg didn't tell you? Never mind. The Ceremony of the Kachina doll. You know, like a harvest festival.'

I'm melting. Sister, in her dark, heavy clothing, seems unaffected by the sweltering heat. She walks like a soldier. I trip over a jutting stone trying to keep up with her. She pulls me to the right of the track towards a small brown clapboard house, and says, 'We'll go in here.'

'Is it someone's home?'

'Sure is.'

'They won't mind us going in there?'

She glances at me as if I'm crazy and pulls me towards the front door. She knocks. A tall, overweight man with a ponytail stands on the threshold. He embraces Sister then turns towards me.

'Hi, I'm Chuckie,' he says, his large fleshy hand clasping mine.

'Alison.'

'Chuckie, Alison needs something to drink and something sweet to eat.'

His house is dark, quiet and cool. He invites us to sit and we do, side by side on the sofa. He brings a large jug of water, two glasses and a plate of biscuits and sets them down on the coffee table which has an ancient map of the world underneath its glass. Sister pats my knee encouraging me to eat and drink. The chewy meat of the homemade cookie is a tonic and more water down my gullet forces me to go and pee.

In the toilet, as I crouch down to relieve myself, I realise I'm taking on the role of Sister's obedient child here, and quite honestly, it's a relief.

As I come back into the room, 'Can you give us a lift, Chuckie?' Sister asks. Ria's phone rings. I fumble in my bag. I'm excited by the thought that it might be Harvey, but as I look at the screen the battery dies. I've no time to ponder on who called or why because we're already leaving.

I'm in the back seat of his car and Chuckie is firing questions at me.

Is this the first time I've been to the States?

What do I think of Arizona?

Where do I live in England?

Does it really rain all the time there?

When he drops us off at the foot of the incline, Sister says, 'Now, we climb. This bit is easy. Eventually we will go up, up, up, to the First Mesa. The government is at the top, that's where I live.'

I follow Sister up, up, up, chalky steps under a royal blue sky with its blistering sun. Sister moves in front of me with the ease of a dragonfly. Me, I'm having a hard time of it; my stiff knees jar with each arrhythmic step. We eventually get there, to the first plateau and the Third Mesa. I stand catching my breath, panting, desperate for more water. Half a dozen villagers congregate around us, all leathery faces and dusty clothes. Someone offers a flask, which I gladly accept. The landscape is craggy; white boulders and loose stones at the ready to roll off the chalky cliff face. On the other side of the road from where we're standing, the buildings appear to have grown out of the rock. Some are homes, others are offices and small shops. Sister introduces me to a posse of street vendors who smile and shake my hand enthusiastically. They show me artefacts they've made: hand-painted pottery, woven baskets and carved dolls in painted tribal outfits that are called Kachina dolls. They encourage me to buy the doll that speaks to me, so I do – the one with brown feathers like petals surrounding an Aztec blue face.

As we walk through the village, Sister tells me: 'Hopi means peace. Hopi is spirit. But many Hopi have left the tradition. Those that invaded the land insisted Hopi children were sent to their boarding schools to be indoctrinated by their ways. If you refused to let your children go, then you were put in prison, simple as that. This led to a cultural confusion in generations of people. Today, many are infected with the sicknesses of addiction and depression.' Sister's own son committed suicide.

'I'm so sorry for your loss.'

She stops walking, looks towards the horizon but doesn't say anything. Eventually, she turns towards me and smiles.

'Come, let's go,' she says.

Wanting to say something else, I put my hand on her arm just as she takes a step towards Chuckie. He has just arrived and is waiting for us with the backdoor of his car open. Like a character out of a 1970s movie, he wears a thick denim shirt, blue jeans and aviator sunglasses.

'I thought we were walking?'

'He knew to meet us at this point.'

'How? You didn't say anything.'

She nods at me.

'He read the situation.'

I have to wait until we're both seated, and as Chuckie makes his way around to the driver's side, I ask, 'How do you cope?'

'Alison,' she says, looking me in the eye. 'Listen to your pain. Listen to it. Write it down, sing it, paint it, do anything you want with it but don't turn away from it. Stare it in the face.'

Chuckie gets in the car.

'He will drive us up to the summit,' she says, and this total wimp is very grateful for that.

First Mesa is a stark, jagged crown. It looks like a well-preserved excavation site. The simple dwellings have flint walls whilst others are made of smooth stones. There's a water standpipe and little else. Sister's house is barely two rooms with menial facilities but the light falls through the window with great kindness. I don't see any electric switches on the walls, just a few worn candles on the dresser.

'What happens at night?' I ask.

'What do you mean?'

'Do you have electricity up here?'

'No.'

'But they have electricity on the Third Mesa?'

'Yes, and they have running water in their homes, too.'

'So, if the people up here are running the reservation, don't they deserve to have what everyone else has?'

'The people in our government are chosen for having the least ego and the most sense, man or woman, it doesn't matter. There are only a few of us. We don't need more stuff.'

'Do you make the laws?'

'No, the laws are made for us.'

'By the American government?'

'Of course, we have to abide by their laws, but their laws are not good enough; our laws are much better.'

'Such as?'

'The United States has given us approximately two and a half thousand square miles to live on, but no man can own the land. If the United States wants to hang on to its delusions, we can't stop that. But the land possessing us is one natural law our community mustn't forget.'

Sister lights pungent incense. Sitting on an old chair, drinking sweet tea out of a tin cup. I relax, a bit.

'You and I need to meditate together,' she says, taking the cup away from me. Sitting opposite, she closes her eyes and asks me to close mine. She doesn't talk me through a scenario to conjure something up; she remains silent.

'What shall I focus on?' I ask.

'With your eyes closed, look downwards to your heart and focus on your pain.'

I don't think I can do this. There are voices in my head telling me how stupid, childish, ridiculous this is, dancing with the devil, tempting fate, but I ignore them.

Not having spoken to Harvey in days, I have some very uncomfortable feelings coming up about him, making me feel quite sick, actually.

'Let your pain show what you need to know,' Sister says.

The wind rattles the door. A bird screeches. I hear myself swallow and focus on my breath. I'm six years old, in the school playground. All the girls are huddled around a couple of trees in the corner. The boys are kicking a ball up and down the tarmac. I am on my own; shut out and set apart. I bring fruit for the teachers. They mark my work down, shame me in front of the class, tell me I should concentrate, but I can't concentrate, that's the whole point.

Tears burn through the corners of my lids.

I manage to concentrate hard on the writing of a poem.

It is my masterpiece of self-expression. My mother's doing housework. I walk behind her and read out my words. She utters a distracted, 'Very nice, darling,' and I am destroyed. But she loves music and I am inspired to take my poem to the piano. With one finger, I compose a melody which is perfect for my poem. I sing the words I have written. My mum walks in. She stands there and listens.

She says, 'That's very good darling, but your voice…'

'What's wrong with my voice?'

'Nothing.'

My life's work becomes writing songs for others. But that's OK. Except it wasn't OK, was it? It's left me feeling guilty of retreating into music my whole life, taking my eye off every other ball and showing up only for music, for years and years and years. The emptiness is so vast without Ria and this hanging onto Harvey by a thread is awful. My belly's sinking with the pain and my dealer for the music-making drug has gone away. That bird screeches again, startles me, pricks my thoughts. There comes a moment when my mind is still; numbed. My brain feels like a balloon, my skull is lifting. I listen to my accelerated breath and feel slightly detached from it.

'Don't open your eyes but bring your thoughts back into the room,' she says.

I imagine the paint-chipped dresser to my left, a couple of plates, a few glasses and cups, a half-eaten raisin cake, coffee and longlife milk, several books. I see Sister and feel her aura of calm like arms surrounding me.

'Now you can open them.'

The world looks a little different, a little newer, fully exposed like coming home from a holiday.

'Have you any questions for me?' she asks.

'Yes,' I say. 'Where do you cook?'

She smiles, openly and warmly and when her lips part it's as if she might break into a laugh.

'What?' I ask.

'That shows you have a little extra room in your heart for what goes on around you.'

She contemplates my face and I think about what she's just said.

'Well,' she says. 'What happens next?'

I shrug.

'You have no plans for tomorrow when you leave the reservation?'

'I'm going to see someone in New York; a friend of my daughter's. She overdosed on painkillers and died in the bath. She was twenty-seven years old. I wasn't there enough for her. Oh, I was always there, but in my head I was somewhere else. I need to find answers to why she was on painkillers, why she died. Before I left, my husband wanted me to abandon the mission.'

'Why?'

'He doesn't trust me, I don't know, maybe he's frightened of what I might find.'

'And you've come here to find yourself; it's all part of the same journey.' Sister bangs her fist against her chest. 'You and your daughter are one and the same now. Both living inside you, inside your heart, with every breath.'

When we step outside, everything about this place appears Dali-esque. We are at the highest point of this reservation where the most important people live and work amongst ruins. I spot an eagle and make a shade with my hand to watch it circle the valley a couple of times.

Three Rastafarians are walking towards us. They are so incongruous. I think they are a mirage at first. One of them, the older guy with grey hair, hugs Sister. The other two greet her by knocking their fists against hers.

She says, 'Reggae Trio. Alison Connaught, also a musician.'

In turn, they each give me a high five.

'What kind of music?' one of the trio asks.

'Commercial stuff. Ballads, you know.'

'Hits?'

'A few.'

'It's so great that we are all here together and meeting up with you.' The elder pats me on the back. 'But we're leaving right after the ceremony and catching a red eye back to Grenada. We come here once a year to play for our brothers and sisters on the reservation and they bless us with a ceremony that gives thanks to life.'

We make our way down to the Second Mesa. Flat-roofed, brick homes, dotted haphazardly around a plaza of square houses, each one painted in a different pastel colour. A ladder leans against every back wall. I am told to climb one, which I do, a little warily. Sister has explained that visitors aren't normally invited to these events but we are guests, so they've made an exception for me and Reggae

Trio. People are already sitting up there. I am being urged to sit at the front. 'See better.' I am patted forwards. 'Yes, see better.' Patted forwards again.

What I witness up there from the gods – amongst an audience of indigenous folk on every rooftop, surrounded by plains and other far-off buttes under the big sky – is breath-taking in all its simplicity.

Down in the plaza there is a scene which has been bastardised in countless cowboy films. A circle of men in traditional dress with lots of feathers and tasselled, suede boots skimming the ground to the left, to the right, to the left, to the right. Their bodies follow on like an afterthought. They ululate to the bam bambambam bam bambambam bam bambambam bambambam bambamabam bam bambambam of a dozen Remo drums.

Women with wide skirts and flowers in their hair are flirting with the music, carrying baskets of corn, beans and sweet potatoes; samples of local produce are deposited on every open palm. There's a sense of openness and belonging inside me. Clapping and swaying, I am hypnotised and almost fall off the roof.

After the ceremony, Sister takes me over to the side of the canyon. I look out over lush fields of beans and corn stretching down to the plains, surrounded by yellow dust, cacti and rocks.

'Ancient seeds. No watering. Dry farming,' she says.

'The miracle.'

Sister puts a finger to her lips.

'Don't tell anyone,' she says.

***

My overnight stay is in Kay's, Sister's daughter's house not far from the entrance to the reservation. Her son is thirteen, quiet, very overweight. For hours, he sits on the sofa tucked away in the corner, carving wood with a penknife, surrounded by a puddle of string and little pots of oil paints.

'He's making a bow and arrow,' Kay tells me. 'He is very creative, but he's learned not to value his craft. They say, how can he support himself selling his artistry by the roadside? That's not going to sustain him. He must adopt American ways.' She stands for a moment looking out the window at her husband who is tinkering away beneath the bonnet of his truck. 'He agrees,' she says.

Now it's midnight. I'm lying on the couch where Kay's son, Tim, sat crafting in the afternoon. After a meal of home-grown miracle food, he sat here again, eating a packet of cheap, chemically enhanced biscuits followed by a large tub of ice cream. I toss and turn on the sticky patch and the crumbs. I acknowledge to myself that there is something magical here, but there is also tragedy and a sense of deep disturbance. These people – this Hopi, peace-loving, nature-loving tribe – bear the same wounds as everyone else on this planet.

The eagle's yellow, unseeing eye stares at me whenever I shut mine. I have to keep opening them in an effort to make it go away. Yes, Greg, I was uncomfortable on that night in the canyon, as I am now. And Ria went away, not because I didn't want her to stay, but because I was on night-watch and her presence was distracting me from keeping safe. What a laugh; life is not safe. Safety is what you might think you have but it's just an illusion, and yet I pursued it and lost my daughter on the way.

The eagle's eye gives way to a show of butterflies moving through shadow into light, through shadow into light, again and again. Easy to forget that each one, in its own right, is beautiful, fragile, colourful, sensuous, but only one small part of the whole tribe. If one should go, the whole flutter will never be the same again, but as an onlooker, you would never really know that.

Sister said Ria is inside me now. Perhaps I'm no longer meant to see her as someone separate from myself. So, I'm trying hard to imagine she's the blood pumped by my heart and the moisture in my breath. That this is *our* journey of discovery and if that's true, and we are that close, then why do I still feel like I need to find her?

A spider in spotlight climbs a silken thread, weaving a fine web of perfect architecture. Nourishment comes to *her*; she never has to leave home. She probably also thinks she can be safe, creating away, blind to the fact that at any moment her whole world can be pulled down and puffed out like a candle flame, leaving her in darkness.

These are symbols that have attached themselves to me, making me more vulnerable but also stronger in their presence. They are my friends but it's the spider who is my soulmate. I can feel her wounds. She and I are both caught up inside ourselves. As we weave our own space, we are unaware of our own vulnerability. And yet, our predators are very aware of us, probably laughing amongst themselves right now, saying, 'Who cares, she wasn't young or pretty,' as we lie curled and failing miserably in anaesthetising the rawness of our wounds.

I touch my bruised eye. See myself as I was when leaving Greg's house on our last morning together: an angry rebel kicking out at the man who was meant to be throwing me into a great big, esoteric bear hug. His front door keeps banging away in my mind, hurting my head, frightening me out of my life.

I thought, with my shaman, I'd find whatever it would take to carry me back to Harvey's arms, satisfied with having ancient wisdom poured into me. But nah, that's not how it works.

★★★

Morning has delivered the first hint of light. The family are still asleep in their own rooms and Sister is knocking on the window beside me. I get up and open the door. Her infectious smile and kind eyes make me think, if only they could plant someone like her in the House of Commons. And then I realise what a stupid idea that is. Even though she might understand where I'm at, where everybody's at probably, no one would understand where she's at or what she could do for us. The whole world would have to stop whilst we worked it all out.

'Put out your hand,' she says, and places a feather earring on my palm. 'It signifies, trust, honour, strength, freedom and wisdom. Go on, you wear it.'

I slip its wire through the hole in my left ear.

'Show me.'

I curl a lock of hair behind the lobe.

'Beautiful!'

'You're beautiful,' I tell her.

I want to give her something too, not just words, and ask her to wait a minute whilst I fetch my bag, fumble for the Kachina doll and present it to her. She holds it in both hands with her eyes closed then gives it back to me.

'No,' she says. 'I can't take this.'

'But…' I try to force it on her.

'Come,' she says. 'Come with me.' She drags me by the arm over to the truck where there's a small mound of red earth beside the tyre tread. 'Give me a handful.'

I bend down, take up a whole load in my fist and let it trickle into her cupped palms. When my hand is empty, she turns towards the rising sun and throws. Grains of grit set off in a smoky mass, twinkling like a firework.

'You've just blessed me,' she says.

She goes inside, leaving me to bask in the memory of her aura.

She's sitting at the dining table when I eventually go back in. I get dressed and join her. The two of us are wrapped in a comfortable silence. Kay is the first of her family to come downstairs. She makes strong black coffee. Kay and Sister converse in sign language. They throw warm smiles my way. When Greg arrives, I realise I've been sitting at the table for quite a while, very still, not thinking, not drinking, just being. My head is bowed. He stands before me, waiting. I raise my eyes to meet his.

'I'm sorry, Greg,' I say.

'No need.'

'You must have been driving since halfway through the night.'

'Yeah, but we have to hurry now. Your case is in the trunk. If we leave right now you can just about get to the airport on time.'

'I'm not taking *that* plane.'

He raises his eyebrows.

'I'm not going home. There's someone I have to see in New York.'

He nods.

'I'm very grateful, for everything. I'm still processing…'

He waves his arm as if swatting away a fly.

'A lifetime's work,' he says.

'Yes.'

'You'll be fine.'

'Eventually, maybe.'

He points to his own eye.

'Gone down,' he says.

'A bit'

I fish in my bag for my sunglasses.

'Shall we go?'

He picks up my overnight bag. I carry the blue and white bow and arrow I bought from Tim. It's fragile and

141

needs to be packed in my suitcase, the clothes making a buffer to protect it. Kay and Sister walk out to the car with us. I so want to return the warmth I have for these people, but mere words aren't enough. The money I've paid for this experience doesn't have the power to convey what I feel. We hug and I hope they can sense it.

***

'Harvey?'

'Hi. Where are you?'

'I'm at the airport.'

'Heathrow?'

'No, no, no, I'll tell you about that in a minute. I'm so sorry we haven't spoken. How are you?'

'That's OK. You did warn me that it was going to be intense. Was it good? Did it help? I'm sure you'll tell me all about it when you get back. I'll come and meet you. What time are you arriving?'

'Harv…'

'Yes.'

'It was terrible and wonderful. More wonderful than terrible, I think. Actually, I'm not sure yet. Ha! I don't know how to say this…'

There's dead silence at the other end of the line.

'I'm not coming back straight away.'

He says nothing.

'Harvey, are you still there?'

'I'm not sure.'

'What do you mean?'

'I was hoping something might change, Alison. I was clinging to that hope.'

'I know, so was I, but...'

'Well, I just want you to know that whilst you've been playing away...'

'Playing? I haven't been playing. This is the hardest thing I've ever done, this vehement soul searching, on my own, away from you, away from Bechs and our home, no Ria in the world... It's probably the hardest thing I'll ever do.'

'Al, come home now.'

'I can't.'

'Well, I can't wait any longer.'

'I don't know what you mean.'

'Look, I don't know how to say this any other way, but I'm on the brink of having an affair.'

A strange animal sound is coming out of me. There are lots of people in this departure lounge, some of them are decidedly looking the other way whilst others are staring. As I reach into my bag for my sunglasses, I try to sound emotionless when I say, 'I have to go, they're calling my flight.'

'Where are you going?'

'To see Ria's friend Sally in New York.' Hearing my voice break, I sever our connection and head for the loo. Devastated is not the word. I lock myself in a cubicle and cry it out. I can't even say that I never thought about Harvey having an affair. I did think it, I dreamt it up, but I was too busy learning to cope with myself to do anything about it.

Do I feel guilty? Yes. Do I feel like the one who has precipitated the end of my marital relationship? Yes. Do I think I could save it if I go straight home now? No, I don't. Would it make me a better wife if I did? No, I can't possibly be someone I'm not. I need to carry on with this mission. If I go home now, I can hear the front door slamming, only this time it's Harvey walking out. Yet, I'm walking out too, out of this cubicle, towards gate sixteen, staring straight ahead. I will not retreat or hang out the white flag. I will board the flight to New York. I will face my pain.

PART THREE

Less than Nothing (that's what I know)

Perhaps when we find ourselves wanting everything, we are dangerously close to wanting nothing.
Sylvia Plath

1

There's no one sitting next to me. I'm alone with my thoughts, hearing my mother say that I've always been obstinate. Apples and trees come to mind. Leopards and spots come to mind. Losing Harvey comes to mind. Karma comes to mind.

The flight attendant asks if I'd like a glass of champagne. My eye twitches and I refuse. Looking out the window at the airport staff loading bags into the hold, I try hard to remember if Ria ever mentioned having aches and pains. Days spent missing school, then auditions were all down to acute, visible ailments like chickenpox, temperatures, livid tonsils, the flu. But aches, pains and headaches, or any signs of depression, no, nothing of that nature is stored in my memory. And yet, I ponder on this until the end of the flight when as soon as we're all standing, ready to disembark, I once again become an object to stare at. Two years on and stories of Ria – always mentioning me and what I do for a living – are still appearing in the media. Many of them are accompanied by that picture of Ria sitting next to me at the Oscars. Passengers nudge their companions; there's subtle pointing and whispering, 'Do you recognise who that is?' Heads shake, more staring, more whispering, smiles and nods. With my sunglasses on, I can stare at them too.

I go straight from the airport to Sally's. Even from the back seat of this taxi, the high-towered city of New York feels claustrophobic. I can't allow myself to believe I have already lost Harvey. I'm touching my feather earring, trying to picture a time in the future when we have reconciled our differences and are once again friends and lovers. I pull my coat closer around me. It's a lot colder here than in Arizona.

Standing outside her door, I'm a little breathless. I hold myself together as Sally places her hands lightly on my shoulders, pecks me on both cheeks and invites me in. Her apartment is lofty; high ceilings on the twenty-fifth floor. An estate agent would call it *minimalist chic*. It's open plan, everything's white and there are three walls of floor-to-ceiling windows. Times Square flashes its lights at me.

Sally is tall and slim with shaggy bleached blonde hair, wearing pale-blue silk pyjamas and white high-heeled shoes. I've only ever met her once before, briefly, a long time ago, pre-success and she wasn't anywhere near as sophisticated as she is today. She leads me over to a couple of soft, cream leather sofas and motions for me to sit down.

'Lovely place.'

'Thank you.'

'It's very kind of you to ask me for dinner, especially when meeting you for a drink somewhere would have been just fine.'

'I thought about it after you rang.'

She kicks off her shoes and hands me a glass of wine. I take a sip and promptly abandon it to the silver coaster on the coffee table in front of me. She perches on the edge of the sofa opposite and says, 'I loved Ria. I don't want to shock you, but I also had a crush on her. I have to add, she was *completely* straight, always amicable, but she kept her distance from me, physically I mean. So painful. All of it. Very raw. Even more so now. Hence my reticence on the phone. I didn't want this to come up. Then realised, OK, it has to. Meeting you somewhere else might have been a way of avoiding it, but then I thought, no, if I'm going to get emotional, I'd rather be at home.' She places her hand underneath her nose.

'I'm sorry,' I say.

'Me too, but however hard it is for me, it's got to be a million times worse for you.'

She looks up at me and smiles sadly.

'You shared a house together in Los Angeles,' I say.

'Yes, up in the hills. Two young English actresses lucky enough to be working in that town. I mean, properly working.' She crosses her legs, reaches for her wine. 'We're going to get take-out. I hope that's all right?'

'Anything,' I say, conscious that she's sitting so still and contained and my hands are wafting around like a mad conductor.

'I used to observe her a lot. Not in a spooky, stalking kind of way. As an actress that's what you do, take notice of how people behave and draw on that. Ria was compelling.'

She bites her bottom lip, stands up, takes large strides to the kitchen and comes back tapping her phone.

'Chinese?'

'Fine.'

'Good.'

She offers me the menu.

'I eat everything, you decide.'

She orders the food as if giving a performance, laughing and joking with the person on the other end of the line. When she's finished, she sits down again and tosses the phone onto the cushion beside her.

'Ria,' she says, 'was so strong but also fragile, that was her appeal. She was witty, self-deprecatingly so. Is this the kind of thing you want to know?'

'Yes.'

'It was like she was very close to her emotions and yet, at the same time, she withheld them. Every move she made, everything she said, even in real life, her timing was impeccable. She didn't have to act. She just was. I wanted to hug her the whole time.'

'Do you know why she took painkillers?'

'I know she admired you a lot.'

'Really?'

'Yes.'

'How come?'

'She talked about you.' Sally closes her eyes, and when she opens them again, she says, 'Ah, my mother, she's great. Different. Other worldly. Alice in Wonderland's got nothing on her. I remember, as a kid, sitting on the floor, listening whilst she made these fantastic sounds come out of this creature she calls Bechs – her piano – and I totally forgot about the doll I was meant to be playing with.'

I'm transfixed. The voice. The mannerisms. My daughter's in the room. I have tears in my eyes and my hand over my mouth.

'Ha! I mean, I could have choked on the arm of that doll and she wouldn't have noticed. And yet, at other times, she'd look at me so intently it was like she was crawling into my mind. I've always wanted to be close to her but something catches in my throat and I can never tell her anything, then I console myself with the thought that whatever I was going to tell her, she probably knew it anyway.'

When she stops speaking the silence rings in my ears. I've forgotten everything; why I've come here, where I am, what I need to say.

'I'm going to play Ria in a television series stroke real-life drama. In fact, I'm one of the producers. Sarah Mason, the director is first class, young, very talented; the next Jane Campion.'

I said nothing.

'Alison, look, I'm sorry if you don't approve, but it's the chance of a lifetime to play Ria. She's somewhat of a muse for me and when Sarah Mason mentioned that she wanted us to work together on the project, well, I just couldn't say no and I had to run with it.'

Sally leaves me sitting there numb as she flits between the kitchen and laying the dining table. When the doorbell rings, she stands on the threshold chatting to the delivery person then runs around hunting for her bag so she can 'give the guy a couple of shekels', and I'm thinking that I don't know how I feel about her playing Ria to the whole world in their living rooms. I can imagine Ria saying every single word of Sally's monologue and even if she never actually said any of those words, they are totally believable. One half of me wants her to do it, to resurrect my daughter so I can see, feel and hear her in the almost flesh. The other half of me is scared witless by the prospect.

Sally calls me over and we are opposites again, this time at the dining table. She's watching me mess with my stir-fry vegetables.

'You play Ria brilliantly.'

'Thank you, that's a great compliment, especially coming from you, her mum.'

'But Sally, television?'

'Alison, I promise, the whole series will have great integrity. Do I have your blessing?'

She dabs her lips with a serviette.

'And what about her death, how will you portray…?'

'We need to do more research. I don't feel comfortable talking about the plot structure yet.'

'Your loyalty is to the show, of course, I understand that, but you lived with her…'

'Yes, and so did you.'

I push my plate away and watch my un-drunk wine become disturbed in its balloon glass.

'My daughter died in the bath, Sally, from an overdose of prescribed painkillers and I have no idea why. Will I have to find out watching television with the rest of the world? Where's the integrity in that?'

'Look, I have the names and numbers of Ria's shrink and her doctor in LA.' Sally picks up her phone and starts typing. 'I've just sent you their details, plus the phone number of the last director she was working with. They are *all* of my Ria contacts, so far. Of course I want you to find out everything you need to know about Ria.' She glances at her watch. 'Look, I really do need to be up early for work tomorrow.'

She scrapes her chair backwards and stands beside me. In my one moment of clarity, I ask for Sarah Mason's phone number too. She glances down at her phone and taps. 'You have it now,' she says, putting a hand on my flinching arm and quickly moving it away again. I can feel my eyes harden as I force myself not to look away from her.

'I hope you don't mind if we call it a night. I mean, I'm tired and you look so tired.'

I say nothing.

Looking down at her phone again, she adds, 'I've just ordered you a cab, it will be downstairs by the time you get there. Would you like me to package up some food so you can take it with you?'

'No,' I mouth, stunned by this turn of events.

Back at the hotel I phone Harvey, twice. The first time, I don't even let it ring before I click off the call. I hesitate before phoning the second time. He picks up straight away.

'Harvey?'

'Yes.'

'Did I wake you?'

'It's OK.'

153

'I need to tell you something.'

'What is it?'

'They're making a television drama of Ria's life.'

'Oh Christ! How did you find that one out?'

'I went to see Sally, Ria's old flatmate. She's one of the producers and she's going to star in it.'

He's silent for a moment then he eventually says, 'I wonder what old fop they'll get to play me.'

'If you're in it.'

'If we're both in it.'

'I don't want to be in it.'

'No, nor do I, maybe we won't be. What did you say?'

'She went into character for me, I was spellbound. She's got Ria to a T.'

'How did that make you feel?'

'Disconcerted. I don't want to find out important things about our daughter along with a billion other viewers. She told me to fuck off. No, not in those words but that's what she meant, after sending me the phone numbers of Ria's doctor, her shrink and her last director, so I could do my own research. Harvey, I'm going to go to LA.'

He says nothing.

'How's things at home?'

'The truth is I haven't been home for days,' he eventually says.

I say nothing.

'Alison? Are you still there?'

'Yes,' I whisper.

'I don't want to lie to you.'

'But you did lie to me, Harvey. It was only yesterday when you told me you were on the brink of an affair, when what you really meant was that you were already having one.'

'I wasn't lying. I've been sleeping alone in the hotel near the office. I can't bear to be with the ghosts of you and Ria hanging around at home. You don't own the copyright on running away, you know.'

'Tell me, I need to know, when does an affair begin? The moment you have a connection with someone? When you look into their eyes and notice you're both breathing heavily? The first phone call? Text? Touch? Full-blown sex? When does it start, Harvey?'

'If it means so bloody much to you, why don't you come home now and discuss it with me properly? Instead of shouting at me down the phone from three thousand miles away.'

'I want to.'

'Then why don't you?'

'I've already explained why I can't.'

'Harvey, are *you* still there?'

He is not.

★★★

I should be unconscious by now but instead, I'm awake with a ton weight in my belly. My first night in New York, but the third night in a row that I can't turn off and my earlobe feels sore. I put the light on, take off the feather earring that I didn't realise I was still wearing and drop it into my sterling purse. The book I bought at the airport is sitting on the nightstand. It's won awards and meant to be brilliant. I open it, read the first page a number of times, tell myself to concentrate harder, and end up throwing the fucking thing across the room. A bottle on a tray on the dresser falls over like a defeated heavyweight shattering a glass. I take some perverse satisfaction out of not clearing up the mess. Knowing I still can't sleep, I plump up the pillows, lie on my back and scroll through Ria's phone. It's so old there's hardly anything on it. In the calendar app there's a series of appointments, one for a voiceover and a few days later a check-up with a dentist. The calendar seems to have been abandoned after that.

I go into Notes:

I know Biddy. I've lived with her. For the last two weeks she's been nagging at me from inside my head, even though I know in real life she doesn't do that. She's far more subtle. But in her own way, Christ, she's manipulative! She makes you want to rip off your skin and I can see myself doing that.

That's the only note. It's got to be about an acting part, hasn't it? Or maybe it's about someone she knew, me, the old biddy. Sighing, I put the phone down, take my laptop out of its bag and cry my way through all of Ria's films. As dawn's first light slips in through the plantation blinds the credits roll on the final one.

I ask myself what I've learned about Ria here in the US

of A that I didn't already know. My answer is zilch, niente, nothing, nada. I start booking my flight to LA. Stopping halfway, I shut my computer, thinking I should make my appointments first, but supposing I do that and then can't get a flight?

It feels as if I've reached an impasse. I don't even know what I'm looking for. Maybe I should just go home to try and save my marriage and what's left of my life. But then I will just morph into Baby Jane and Harvey will leave me anyway. So no, just no. Business hours will arrive. I will make my appointments and get a flight. But I can't stay in this hotel room any longer. I get dressed, grab my bag, and on my way out, slam the door too loudly. As I'm waiting for the lift, the man in room 454 sticks his head out and calls, 'What do you think you're doing at six o' clock in the morning?' And the truth is, I don't know what I'm doing. They say insomnia can make you crazy; I accept that could be happening to me.

I might be out of that room but there are walls that don't come down inside me. I feel them rein me in with every step I take out here, on the street, in the drizzling rain. Ria's phone says the temperature is warm, but I'm cold and shivery.

On the other side of the world, Harvey's probably toasty, cuddling up to his newfound love. She is probably purring into his ear to forget me as she strokes his ego with such tenderness it brings livid tears to my eyes. I see it happening; him like a snowman melting to her touch.

The bright fluorescent lights of the diner I'm approaching make my battered eye ache. I decide that *my* warmth has to be found inside there with a hot drink. Its door is heavy, resistant to my push, so I go in harder till it gives, sit myself down on a red plastic banquette at a Formica round table and slip my ever-faithful sunglasses out of their pouch. The waitress comes over. I start to order coffee but because of my insomnia, think of changing my mind; although what the hell does it matter when I'm continually up anyway? I ask for a large Americano with cream.

'Sure,' the waitress says, tapping a screen. 'Coming over right away.'

I catch myself swirling around on my seat as if I'm sitting before Bechs. I need him now, not that in my present state I'd even know what to do with him. In Arizona, I seemed to be learning to reconnect, but the way to do that is not apparent now.

As a child, I once asked my father to buy me an everything box for my birthday.

'What's an everything box?' he asked.

'It's a box with everything in it, so I'll never need to ask anyone for anything ever again.'

I still have impossible wishes: To have my daughter back. My husband. My life as it was before it was hit by tragedy. I need to sing and play. I need clarity and creativity. I still want everything.

My coffee is letting off steam in front of me. This place was deserted when I walked in, now there are people sitting at almost every table, reading menus, ordering breakfast. The smell of fried food has crept into the atmosphere. I notice that the man at the next table is staring at me. He is young, late teens, early twenties, blonde hair, creamy skin, pretty face.

'Hi,' he says.

The last time a young guy said 'hi' it didn't work out too well for me. I want to tell him to get out of my face, but I remind myself not to be rude and I return the greeting.

'Would you look after my rucksack for a moment?' he asks.

'OK.'

He gets up and goes to the men's room. His presumptuousness annoys me. Just the idea that he thinks he can trust a perfect stranger makes me want to punish him for being so naive. I could pick up his bag and leave. Why not? I have nothing left to lose and there's no one to stop me. He returns and standing before me, he comes out with that old chestnut, 'Don't I know you?'

'No,' I say taking off my shades and hoping that's enough to scare him away.

'No, really, you're famous. Hold on a minute,' he says, reaching into the inside pocket of his jacket and bringing out a newspaper, which he unfolds and opens on to a particular page then places it on the table in front of me. It crosses my mind to say, 'Excuse me,' pay my bill and walk. But I'm curious and look down at the crumpled rag. Before me is a large black and white photo of myself, sitting in Phoenix airport, swollen eye, face lined with pain and a trail of tears running down my cheeks. Underneath there's a short article.

The English composer Alison Connaught who has had an illustrious career writing hit songs for the likes of Cher, Celine Dion, and a whole host of other divas besides, is captured here before embarking on a flight to New York. I have been informed that she is flying across country for a meeting with Sally Denoué – who was nominated for an Oscar several years ago, but was pipped to the post by the late, great, Ria Connaught – yes, that's right, Alison's daughter. I also understand that Ms Denoué will be playing Ria in a forthcoming made-for-TV drama and has a hand in writing the script. The plot thickens. All you box set and scandal lovers, watch this space.

'Not me,' I say, re-folding and handing back the paper.

★★★

It's surprisingly bright outside. I don't notice what neon adverts flash in Times Square nor the nature of Saks' window displays. Cars hoot as I glance the wrong way to cross the road. There could be a naked couple making love in the middle of the street and it probably wouldn't register. I'm concentrating only on walking fast and then faster still. Where I'm going is not the issue here, I'm trying to release endorphins to help improve my mood. I'm no longer cold, so perhaps it's working. Then someone shoves me aside as they walk past without even the vaguest hint of an apology. I stop and gaze at the pavement, panting, steadying my breath. When I lift my face to the sky, I catch a glimpse of a bird of prey circling high above the skyscrapers.

When an animal does something unusual it's a sign for the onlooker.

Is it unusual for a bird of prey to be circling the skies in midtown New York at seven in the morning? I decide that it is and make my way back to my hotel room. I pick up my laptop, previously forsaken on the bed, and type *North American Indian animal signs bird of prey* into the browser. Several answers to my question show up:

Eagle:
Symbol of power, strength and wisdom. A sign to trust your instincts in order to move out of the darkness and into the light.

Falcon:
Symbol of rising above a situation.

Kestrel:
If a kestrel is on your radar, use your wits to rise above the situation you are dealing with.

Hawk:
If you see a hawk, stay focused on the task ahead.

The tight spring inside me unwinds. I feel momentarily absolved. I lie on the bed and fall asleep fully clothed.

When I wake it's just after midday – morning in LA – I

call Austin Obermarle, the director who was working with Ria when she died.

'Austin Obermarle?'

'Who is this?'

'Alison Connaught.'

He says nothing.

'Sally Denoué gave me your number. I'm coming to LA. I understand there's going to be a television drama about my daughter and your experience of working with Ria is part of the research.'

'Hey, I'm very, very, very sorry for what happened to Ria. Yah, it was as such a shock to everyone, and for you the absolute worst, oh my God… Hey, I'm sure you can hear all the background noise here. I'm on set at the moment and don't have much time. Can you tell me why you're calling?'

'Because I don't want to learn about events leading up to Ria's death whilst watching a television programme. I would be very grateful if you could make time to see me and help me make sense of things.'

'When are you coming to old LA?'

'I'll be arriving tomorrow, Sunday.'

'Then how about lunch the next day?'

'Where and what time?'

'I'll text you.'

He cuts the call before I can say thank you. I have to take a few breaths before I'm able to dial again. When I do, I call Dr Stuart Draper, Ria's private doctor.

'Hi, it's Alison Connaught.'

There's dead silence on the other end of the line.

'Hello? Are you there?'

'Yeah, I'm here.'

'Do you know who I am?'

'Yeah, for sure, I know who you are.'

'I'm coming to LA tomorrow and whilst I'm there, I'd like to make an appointment to come and see you.'

'That's fine, but you're going to need to talk to my secretary.'

'Can you give me her number?'

'Are you coming to me as a patient?'

'Not exactly, but I'm happy to pay for your time.'

'Oh.'

'Sally Denoué told me to call you.'

'I don't…'

'Dr Draper, I know you were in conversation with my husband just after the tragedy, but my child is dead because she took an overdose of painkillers and I have to live with that. But the thing is, I don't understand why she was on them and I need to find out for my own peace of mind.'

I can feel his discomfort in the silence.

'Dr Draper, one way or another, I will find out.'

'Tuesday, 5 p.m., my surgery.'

'OK, I'll be there, and thank you.'

'You're most welcome.'

Last but not least is Fay Moth, psychotherapist.

'Ms Moth, it's Alison Connaught.'

'Ria's mom?'

'Yes. I'm coming to LA and wish to book an appointment with you.'

'Good, I'll go and get my diary.' When she returns, she says, 'I'm not being rude, or anything, but I'll ask you how you are when you come in. When would be a good time for you?'

'Wednesday.'

'How long you here for?'

'Not long, hopefully.'

'But, till when?'

'Thursday, I think.'

'Look, I'm fully booked for quite a few weeks but I do want to make time for you. Can you make seven in the morning?'

'Yes.'

'Alrighty, Wednesday it is, I will see you then.'

I have just called, arguably, three of the most important people in Hollywood and all of them answered after the first ring. I put Ria's phone on charge and snap open a bottle of sparkling water from the minibar. Not bothering with a glass, I make a toast in the mirror to their morbid curiosity.

2

I've arrived, in LA, that sprawling mass, so different from the hemmed-in feeling of New York where people can be rude, but you expect that, and at least you know where you stand. Here in LA, the air is tainted with fake theatrical charm, not difficult to choke on. It might even be illegal to turn your back in this city. And no one goes for a walk here. In certain places, at certain times, cars cruise, but otherwise there's no loitering in this town.

There are posters on hoardings for a re-run of *The Way to Catch a Swan*. As I pass one, I catch a whiff of Ria's orange blossom scent from a London perfumery. She's wearing the same fear and defiance as captured in my beach photo: chin down, looking up, spirit hatching. I can hear her whispering, 'I'm going to do it, Mum, and there's nothing you can do to stop me.'

I call Sarah Mason, the director of the docu-soap, but it goes straight to voicemail. I also haven't heard back from Austin Obermarle about our lunch date, so I text him as soon as I get to my hotel.

Hi Austin, what time are we going to meet tomorrow and where?

Hey Alison, I'm so sorry, I completely forgot. Can we meet up another day? How long will you be staying in town?

Oh, I have a couple of other appointments but other than that I can meet up any time this week – the sooner the better.

I've just sent a message to my PA, she'll book us a table at noon on Thursday at the South Beverley Grill. Don't worry, I won't let you down again.

OK.

Great. See you then.

Dammit! I now have to stay longer in this tricky town.

★★★

After one whole completely wasted day – most of it spent pacing up and down in the room trying to contact Sarah Mason – I pull into the parking lot of a duck-egg blue clapboard one-storey building. Slamming the car door, I feel bereft and lonely and not really up to this.

The door to the doctor's practice is open and squeaks when I push it. Dr Draper is on the sofa, spectacles on, looking down at some loose papers in his lap. He looks up as I enter, takes off his glasses, puts them in his breast pocket, leans forward and places the papers on top of a load of magazines on the coffee table in front of him. He crosses his long legs and drapes an arm over the cushion beside him as if waiting for a lover to fill the space. He's wearing navy trousers and a white collarless shirt with the top button undone. His hair is unfashionably long, jet black and straight, his skin is too tightly pulled across his face.

'Mrs Connaught,' he says, not standing to greet me but extending his other hand. As soon as my palm brushes against his, he pulls his hand away and leans his head towards the empty space beside him. I sit on the edge.

'How can I help?'

His half-smile is both disconcerting and alluring.

'Well,' I say, looking around for inspiration. 'Basically, I'd like to know why Ria was on those painkillers.'

'I especially cancelled my one o' clock and took out Ria's notes. She was suffering from constant headaches, plus aches and pains all over her body that sometimes had her – he makes speech marks in the air with his fingers – bending double in agony like an old woman, on some mornings when getting out of bed.'

'What did you think it was?'

'I prescribed painkillers, Mrs Connaught.'

'Didn't you send her for tests to see if it might have been something more serious?'

'Alison… May I call you Alison?'

'Uh-huh.'

'And may I be honest with you?'

'I would like that.'

'The way I see it, Hollywood is an entertainment factory. The people that work here have difficult relationships. They are only as good as the last project they worked on. My job is helping those workers facilitate their lives. I am only one cog in a long chain of others here. Your daughter was brave and very, very talented. Brave and talented people win prizes in this town but there's a price to pay for that, as there is for everything in life.'

I study this man, this good looking, suave and eloquent man, and ask, 'Did you even ask about other symptoms? Try and detect what was going wrong in her body so you could try and fix it?'

'Her symptoms were part and parcel of the Hollywood stress syndrome. I've seen it a million times and, unfortunately, medicine is not advanced enough to cure it. Latterly, the fact that she was doing all her own stunts, also didn't help.'

'Can you explain more about the stress, please?'

'I'm afraid not. I referred Ria to my associate, Dr James Drew. He's a psychiatrist, but I understand Ria never made contact with him.'

He gazes down at his wristwatch. I think, shit, he's going to start ushering me out of here, then he hesitates and there is a slight twitch in his left cheek.

'Tell me more about the prescription.'

He puts his glasses back on, picks up his pile of papers and shuffles through them. I look at the adverts for pharmaceuticals covering all the walls. Draper catches my eye and as if to convince me of his righteousness, he says,

'I used to see Ria in her own home but a couple of times a week I hold a drop-in clinic here and for those that aren't lucky enough to be gainfully employed, I don't charge.'

He hands me a copy of Ria's repeat prescription for OxyContin.

'Your husband has already seen this,' he says.

'It's dated five years ago.'

'Her treatment was on-going,' he says.

When I get back to my hotel room, I phone Harvey. He picks up straight away. I steam in like the first battalion.

'I went to see Ria's doctor this afternoon. He gave me a copy of her prescription. She'd been on that shit for three years!'

'You already knew that. Why are you torturing yourself?'

'It's the same drug that Heath Ledger was on. Were you aware of that?'

'Calm down.'

'Well, were you?'

'No!'

'What did he say to *you* when you went to see him?'

'I can't remember exactly, nothing suspicious.'

'I can't believe someone didn't make us aware of this.'

'We already knew she was taking opioids.'

'It's just that...' my voice breaks.

'Are you OK?'

I intend to say, 'Yes, of course,' but, 'No, not really,' pops out instead.

'I think you should come home.'

'I can't believe you still want me to.'

'It didn't work.'

'What didn't work?'

'Running into the arms of someone else. It was childish. Look, I'm not going to pretend that I agree with what you're doing over there, to me it's just meddling, but I'll get on a plane if you want me to.'

'Yes. And no. I mean, I've only got two more people to see and then I'll come straight home.'

'I don't understand. Do you want me to come or don't you?'

This reminds me of my night in the canyon – Ria sitting before me and my eyes fixing on a break in my rock circle. I wasn't able to deal with the distraction of her company and keep safe at the same time. It was an untenable conflict of interests and it broke my heart, but that's why she disappeared. The message from the keen eagle eye is getting clearer as I face a similar scenario once again.

'No, don't, it would be best if I'm alone.'

'Alison, for Christ's sake, will you please tell me what's going on?'

'Trust me, nothing's going on.'

Is nothing going on? I've been sitting here for a long while, on the edge of the bed, accompanied by Disbelief. She wants to show me something. I have asked her to go away but she won't leave me alone. I want to have faith in the thought that Ria and I will meet up again somewhere in hyperspace. Part of me would like to say, What the hell do you think you were doing leaving us and dying from painkillers in the fucking bath? Didn't you realise how insane that was? How selfish? How destructive for everything and everyone you've left behind? I would also like to believe that if I ever got the chance, I would never say that. I would hold her, suffocatingly close, until she begs me to let go. But Disbelief is telling me that I've already proved I'm a loose cannon, and never mind my fantasies, meeting Ria again is not going to happen. She has me standing by the window, looking down on people in the forecourt of the hotel steeped in Californian sunshine and carrying on with their everyday lives. I feel a great divide between me and the rest of the world. I get a sense that the world has no meaning. Not these walls. Not this ceiling. Not even my own body and the person inside it.

Disbelief wants me to man up to some knowledge about Harvey and our fucked-up relationship, something I would rather not see. She lets me know it's all tied up with why I'm angry with him and I can't ignore her anymore because she's screaming at me, *There's something he's not telling you!* She makes me question that Harvey was the best stepfather ever, even though he was always the first one of us to pitch up at parent meetings and school plays. He was the one who taught her backgammon, counselled her on her finances and bought her way out of a student debt. He was the one who understood her, laughed with her, and even occasionally took her side when the joke was on me. But nevertheless, Disbelief is making me focus on those nights he never stayed up worrying when Ria had childhood ailments, or at two or three in the morning when she was in her teens and not home yet. He wasn't concerned when she tore through the house like a tornado, in hysterics, and I would be thinking something terrible has happened that she's not telling us. As cool as a winter's day, he'd always counter, 'She'll get over it. She'll be OK.'

PART FOUR

All the Heroes

It doesn't matter who my father was.
It matters who I remember he was.
Anne Sexton

1

Two a.m. I'm awake again. I check my emails. There are a lot of them, all trying to seduce me with their little blue dots. I have to wade through confessions of undying love, promises of everlasting erections and new friends in the Third World who want to put millions of dollars in my bank account. I almost think Phil Hammond's message is one of them. In a hurry to get the job finished, I bin it, but then when I realise what I've done, return it to my inbox and open it. He asks how I'm getting on and when I'll be back in the country. I type, *I'm in the country, just someone else's country*, wait a moment, delete, and re-write, *Soon*. Katie's is another I almost miss amongst the junk. It's a long one. I skim over the beginning and arrive here:

> *Even though I know you wanted to hear it, I don't feel comfortable about all the stuff I've already insinuated about Ria. I've spoken to Carl, my husband, about this. He thinks I'm just being oversensitive. Nevertheless, I've been at war with myself over whether to tell you this or not. You might be asking yourself why it's taken me this long to come out with it, well the answer is, because I don't want to hurt you. You're Ria's mum and you've been hurt enough.*

This is so difficult to say but I also think it's something you would want to know. It's about Joshua. There's something dark about him. At school, I used to think he was in love with Ria, but was it love? He followed her everywhere. When she told him once, to leave her alone, he physically pushed her in a corner and wouldn't let her go until he'd talked her into forgiving him for seeing other girls, which he never stopped doing. I think he came from a really bad home. His younger sister, Kay, was in our year. Kay was always nervous and hiding at the back of the class. Once I caught her crying in the cloakroom. Kay didn't want to talk about it, but what she did say was her stepdad used to do worse to her mum, whatever that was supposed to mean…

I shut the laptop. Have a shower, get dressed, and find my way into the hotel bar: a dark room with a pale blue, neon lit, pseudo block of ice for a counter and behind it a gold light beaming down on glass shelves and bottles in silhouette. The cleaner tells me the bar is closed. I spot a baby grand by the window and ask if he minds if I play whilst he cleans. He looks around as if trying to find someone else to consult, then realising there is no one, smiles broadly and says, 'I don't see why not,' before rushing over to lock the door.

'Play as loud as you like, honey. You won't disturb anyone, not in this hotel. This bar is soundproofed just in case they ever host an Oscar party.'

He laughs and looks skyward.

I make my way over to the piano, stroke his lacquered

finish as if he is a horse I'm about to gallop away on. Sitting before him, I lay my fingers on top of his silken keys and play him softly, at first. He sings back to me. His tone is rich and resonant, full of confidence and my body responds, shifting to our rhythm. We play faster. Me, standing, then sitting, at one point arching and throwing back my head.

> *There is nothing*
> *Nothing*
> *That I can come to terms with*
> *No new information*
> *No piece of you*
> *No rambling inside my head.*
> *As much as they tell me*
> *As much as they teach me*
> *As much as the days roll on*
> *As much as the nights are cold*
> *Less than nothing is what I know.*

This keyboard guy has unbolted doors for me. He encourages my hands to try out his bass notes and we get lost down there in a frenzy of chords complete with lightning bolts inside my head.

It's been so long. Too long since I've felt any kind of harmony with a keyboard. I've been tied up in the agony of frustrated love for my daughter and nowhere to spend it. I give it away here, on this improv, more potent than alcohol.

My new friend and I are getting along just fine until Ria's face pops up and I stop playing. The last note doesn't hang but disappears immediately as if the room is stung by it. The piano before me has reverted to a collection of brass pedals, tight strings, spruce and ebony. I play another few notes, but he has zipped up and taken away his soul. That moment of passion was just a quick fuck up against a wall. The cleaner has his coat on and is waiting by the door. I stumble over, suddenly deciding I just might have conceived.

'Have you got a pen?'

He looks at me strangely.

'Or a pencil will do.'

'No, I, um…' He pats his pockets. 'Is it imperative?' he asks, looking at his watch.

'Yes,' I say. 'It really is.'

Huffily, he leads me out to the front of the hotel. Lest I forget the sequence and the chords, a band starts up in my head. My friend goes behind the reception desk, shuffling papers and things.

'I'm not really meant to be behind here. I could lose my job,' he says, handing me a ballpoint.

I thank him.

When he leaves the building, I roll up my sleeve and transcribe the verse all the way up one arm.

★★★

When I turn up at Fay Moth's practice at seven, I'm a cocktail of thoughts, both shaken and stirred. She works in a block where all the other space is taken up by commercial enterprises; not what I was expecting, at all.

She's tall, either in her late thirties or has had very good work done on her face. Her long fingers that belong to a slim, well-manicured hand brush against mine.

In her overly large consulting room, I take in the wall of windows overlooking the city, the plush Middle Eastern carpet rug, antique leather sofas, decorative brass shisha pipe, and a waft of cinnamon incense. We sit opposite each other. She leans forwards, elbows on her knees, hands in prayer against her lips; she watches me.

A moment later, she sits back. 'How can I help?' she says, and despite having repeated this many times now, I reply, 'I have no idea why Ria was on painkillers. I'm finding it hard to live with wondering if it was something I'd done, as a mother. I've come here to learn about Ria's problems, so at least I'll know something of what happened and why.'

She takes a long time to answer, and when she does, she says, 'I'm having a problem with confidentiality.'

'Ms Moth, whatever you believe, whether it's the finality of death or that the spirit lives on, my daughter is no longer on this planet, but I am.'

'It's a moot point, the idea of confidentiality after death. It's mostly left open to each practitioner to decide how they wish to practise. However, as I told you over the phone, I will help you in whatever way I can but I must add to that, "as long as my conscience allows".' Her brown-lipped smile has a slight tremble on one side.

'Dr Draper...'

'Ed.'

'You know him?'

'Of course, everyone knows everyone in this town.'

'He said he gave Ria OxyContin because she was having general aches and pains and headaches. He intimated that this might be something to do with Ria's work?'

'Yes, I would agree with that analysis.'

'How was Ria dealing with the stress, I mean emotionally?'

'Mrs Connaught…'

'Alison.'

'Alrighty, Alison, let me help you to understand. It's not just Ria's secrets that I have to keep, it's the secrets of every single one of my clients.'

'You don't have to give me any references or names, but was my daughter treated badly by anyone?'

'Historically yes, and that's all I'm saying. I can't say anything else at this time.'

'But…'

Her hands flag the air.

'Don't even ask me,' she says.

I pick up my handbag which I'd left on the floor and push myself up from the sofa in order to leave.

'No, wait a minute,' Fay Moth says, standing up, leaning over, touching my arm. 'Please sit down again. There is something I want to tell you. I think it might be helpful.'

I perch back down on the edge of the seat.

'Ria spoke to me a lot about her father.'

'You mean Harvey, her stepfather, who brought her up?'

'No, I mean her biological father.'

'But she hadn't seen or heard from him since she was about three years old.'

'Well, that might be true.'

'What do you mean "might be"?'

'I was encouraging her to get in touch with him and if she got the opportunity to go and see him.'

'Why? Shouldn't the desire for that kind of thing have come from her and not you?'

'You asked me if Ria had been treated badly by anyone. I'm going to be honest with you, Alison, there are many, many women, and men, in Hollywood who have been treated badly by people, both male and female, and it goes on everywhere, not only in this town but all over the world. Certain people are drawn to abuse. If you're going to survive you have to learn what it is about yourself, and the things in your past, that attract you to the perpetrators and make you behave in a certain way that allows it to continue. And you can't just bury yourself in a coat of armour – which many people around here try to do – because it's not going to help when the person inside that armour is breaking down. Do you get what I'm saying?'

I notice a crack in the ceiling and nod.

'There's something inside every one of the personalities that end up on those heavy-duty painkillers that makes them not want to deal with something, and it's often triggered by an experience, or lots of experiences that they've had in their past. You may have beaten yourself up about not being a good enough mother but the truth is, the thing that kept Ria in a bad place was inside her and that's what we were working on, together. No mother or father in the whole course of history ever got it completely right. To err is human. So, you see, it wasn't about you. It wasn't about her father either. It was about Ria, and her interpretation of the past informing her present and resulting in a problem that was playing itself out in her life, again and again and again.'

'Her interpretation of what thing in her past?'

'Ria had an abandonment issue.'

'I abandoned her, too. Sometimes I'd be working or thinking about work and I just wasn't there for her.'

'This was a problem that predominantly concerned her relationships with men. I felt, by making an effort to establish communication with her father she would take some of that power away from him and reclaim it for herself, symbolically, of course.'

'And did she do that?'

'She did some research a while back and discovered he was living in Canada and that he had another family.'

'She knew that anyway. I've never kept my first husband's life and whereabouts a secret from Ria.'

'She also cancelled her last three or four sessions with me.'

'Do you think she purposely killed herself?'

'I don't think so, no.'

'Do you think she was capable of it?'

'There were times when she arrived here after spending days in bed with "the flu", or some other acute ailment, which she told me she'd been prone to since she'd been a teenager, and I have wondered about her state of mind during those times, yes. Ria wasn't an open book. But if you're asking me whether she ever talked about suicide or wanting to kill herself, uh-huh you can rest assured that was not the case.'

2

I discover via a leaflet in a stand on her receptionist's desk that *Fenella Mothson, shortened her name to Fay Moth when she first arrived in Los Angeles from her hometown in Montana.* It's no business of mine what she does with her name, when or why she does it, but this information really pisses me off.

So, it's not Ria's 'abandonment issue' that preoccupies me, when a glossy stretch limousine with blacked-out windows goes straight into the back of my hired car as I sit at the traffic lights: it's Fay Moth's name I'm thinking about. The collision makes my head feel like it's lucky to be still attached to my neck.

The chauffeur gets out of his car, comes over to my window, asks if I'm OK and what I'm on, as if the accident is my fault. He says the lights were already changing, I started to go forwards then braked and I can get arrested for that in California. He has a Cockney accent, is aggressive, but he doesn't faze me. If he wants to call the police, fine. If they want to lock me up, fine. He can do anything he likes, I'm well over the cliff when it comes to caring.

Calm as the Dead Sea, I say, 'You're lying. I never suddenly put my foot on the brake. The lights never changed and I'm being extra careful because I'm also a Brit and I'm driving on the wrong side of the road here.'

Something buzzes in his top pocket. He looks put out, says, 'Just one minute, love,' and walks back to his car.

We are stopped in the middle of the road and I'm vaguely aware of hostilities rising, and the scent of burning rubber as other cars veer around us. I tap on the steering wheel and watch the chauffeur in my rear-view mirror. I tell myself my preoccupied state of mind is going to be the death of me, and maybe that's not such a bad thing. Maybe it will skyrocket me to where I really want to be: beside Ria in some heavenly place above all the action, looking down on everyone whilst they screw things up.

Buried deep inside my daydream, I don't register his return, and I quake from surprise when I hear him.

'Can you step outside and come and have a word with my passenger, please?'

'If your passenger wants to talk to me, why don't they step out of their car and come over here?'

'My passenger can't do that, it would cause too much of a stir.'

I'm intrigued now and almost castrate him with the speed in which I open the door. Outside the passenger window of the limo, impatience and sass take over my being as I wait and I wait and I wait. Eventually, the window winds down. I'm expecting the face of someone famous, but the person who reveals herself is unknown, at least to me. She has teased and hair-sprayed dyed red hair, black kohled green eyes, scarlet lipstick; her face is smooth, but she has a turkey neck. I feel like I've just been played, and I

185

want to deal with this problem as quickly as possible.

'Look, I'm really sorry about this but I'm sure we're both insured so why don't we just exchange details and let the insurance companies sort it out.'

'Alison Connaught,' she drawls with her head inclined.

'Excuse me, mam.'

I turn around to see a police officer standing behind me.

'It's OK, officer, we can sort this out amicably between us,' she calls out.

'Are you sure? No one's hurt?'

'No one's been hurt, officer.'

'Well, OK. It seems both cars are good to drive, so please get them moving as quickly as possible.'

'We'll take care of that right away.'

To me she says, 'Alison, I'm inviting you to my house for brunch. We can sort out the necessaries over smoked salmon and Montrachet. Will you come?'

I don't say no.

'Good,' she says, winding up the window halfway and then down again. 'Are you OK to drive? Follow J, he'll show you the way.'

J's driving so slowly you'd think we were part of a funeral cortège. I ask myself what's going on, many times, during this snail's journey. I don't, however, wonder how the woman inside that limo knows who I am. She's probably read the same article as that young guy in New York. I frighten myself with my vivid imagination, conjuring up a scene with J tying me down to a kitchen table at the centre of a whole cast of ugly, excited characters. The woman in the limo is kitted out in black stilettos, fishnet stockings, purple corset, brandishing a whip and licking her rouged lips. The gothic mansion I've been led towards doesn't make me feel any calmer. I sit in my car watching the limo-woman walk towards me. When she arrives, she extends a well-manicured white hand through my driver's window.

'So rude of me, I didn't think to introduce myself earlier. I'm Andy Buckingham. You can just leave the car here, it will be fine. It's just us. I'm not expecting anyone else to come here today.'

Her place is a pseudo mausoleum. Impressive, in an eerie way, with high ceilings, sandstone walls and lofty stained-glass windows. Our footsteps clack on black and white flagstones as she leads me through the hallway to a kitchen the size of Manchester. A wooden table with benches on either side is already laid with heavy silver cutlery and hand-painted crockery. She takes dishes covered with cellophane out of a massive fridge, and a bottle of wine that's sweating with cool.

'Sit, please sit,' she says, in her southern drawl. 'So, I suppose you're wondering how I managed to orchestrate all of this.' She gestures at everything around us. 'Without knowing that we were going to bump into each other in such a rude way. Well, I could tell you my clairvoyant had a premonition and said, "Be prepared, honey," but I'd be lying. The truth is, I've had a few phone calls advising me you've been prowling around town asking personal questions.'

'So you decided to follow me and stage an accident?'

Her face reveals that she'd rather I wasn't so direct.

'Anyway, you're here now.' She pours the wine into big balloon glasses taken from the freezer. 'They tell me you're not supposed to drink white out of red-wine glasses, but I'm a heathen and I like to, and anyway, who are they to tell me what to do?'

I'm shuffling around on the hard wooden bench. She can obviously see I'm getting impatient.

'Just give me a bit of time, honey, and I'll tell you everything you want to know, and please don't worry if you drink too much of this delicious stuff, I can always get J to drive you back in your own car to wherever you're staying.' She sets a glass down before me as she takes a gulp from another. 'Mmm, it's good.' She catches me staring. 'What are you waiting for? This food is the best.'

I watch her short overweight frame waddle out of the room through a different door than the one we entered. She returns inside a halo of light carrying a chair which she places at the head of the table beside me.

'I'm not great with sitting on benches. I agreed with my interior designer that they were the right choice for the kitchen, a more streamlined look, but I need a chair with a cushion to support my back.'

She's putting things on my plate: an open black-bread sandwich, topped with smoked salmon and wearing a tiara of curled cucumber. 'Do you like olives?' she says, putting a spoonful of greasy black ones, smelling of garlic and dotted with red chilli flakes, next to a heap of potato salad.

188

'This is my favourite brunch of all time,' she says.

I sit perfectly still and ask, 'Why have you brought me here?'

'I don't think you know who I am?'

'No, I don't.'

'*Forbes* magazine had me listed, last year, as one of the most successful Hollywood producers of all time.'

'Congratulations.'

'Thanks, honey. I got into this business after my husband died and I thought well, what *am* I going to do with the rest of my time here on this planet? Am I going to take a lover that's going to take *me* for a ride? Am I going to play bridge with a posse of biddies, same time, same place, every week, every year, year in, year out?'

I know Biddy. I've lived with her. For the last two weeks she's been nagging at me from inside my head, even though I know in real life she doesn't do that. She's far more subtle but in her own way, Christ, she's manipulative! She makes you want to rip off your skin and I can see myself doing that.

'No, I chose this,' she says, as she stretches her arms up to the ceiling and looks around as if wallowing in adulation from a non-existent crowd. Turning to me, she says, 'You know, we could have had our brunch under the gazebo, by the pool, but to be honest, I find it so much more pleasurable in here with the air con on. Who wants to watch their lunch partner sweat droplets into their soup. Not that we're having soup, but you know what I mean.'

She folds one of the sandwiches in half and crams it into her mouth. After she's chewed and swallowed, she brushes her palms together and says, 'OK, I can see you're not going to eat or drink anything until I get on with it.' She rises from her seat, closes both doors, sits back down and looks at me for what seems like a very long time.

'I want you to sign a confidentiality agreement.'

'For what?'

'So you don't dish the dirt.'

'Dish the dirt on my own daughter? Are you crazy? And anyway, that's not me, other people are going to do that.'

'Not on your daughter, Alison, on anyone else in this town, that's what I'm worried about.'

My head is jangling. My feet and hands are tingling. I'm in shock from the accident, which I now understand was not actually an accident. I could really do with a huge swig from that glass of enticing blonde wine. I've been caught out before with that craving, but not this time.

'No, I'm not signing anything. No way,' I say.

'I think you might want to change your mind when you're up against a whole industry.'

'Is that what I'm up against?'

She flicks her eyes over the uneaten food on my plate.

'And what's more, you're in danger of disrespecting our American hospitality.'

'Why are you frightened of what I might say?'

She smiles and nods as if she understands something I don't.

I stare her out.

'Well,' she says, 'you might as well go then,' and she

escorts me to the front door insisting J drives me back to the hotel. 'For my own piece of mind, honey, I have to make sure you get back there safely.'

I can hear J being interviewed at some future date, eager to inform whoever of his boss's concern for my wellbeing, as she surreptitiously makes sure I never work in this town or any other town, anywhere in the world, ever again.

Sitting beside him in the passenger seat, it's hard to know what to say to the man, so I don't say anything and nor does he. I'm just grateful when he parks my rental, locks it and spills the keys into my hand.

It's a hot day. I haven't drunk anything since early morning. I think I must be dehydrated. I'm drained of energy and have a headache. I take a bottle of warm water out of my bag and drink the lot. The concierge says my husband took the key and is waiting for me in my room. My heart skips a beat as I think of Harvey holding me, but all I can see in my mind's eye is one of Andy Buckingham's lackeys sitting on the armchair in the corner, playing with a gun. I ask the concierge how he knows it's my husband. He tips his head to one side, then the other, as if relieving a crick. His neck turns red as he types something into his computer and says, 'Harvey Connaught, is that your husband?'

I nod.

He angles the computer screen to face me, to see the scan of Harvey's passport. I nod again, thanking him, and turn away. I'm thinking that the passport could be fake.

The lift takes for ever. Numbers above the metal cage flick from 1 to 5 to 3 and I'm imagining a chloroformed cloth pressed over my nose and mouth. The door opens. The lift is empty. I'm wondering if I should use the stairs or just run out into the street, but then I think, Where would I run to?

The lift fills up with people. There's a mum with a child, both perfectly innocent, but the two men beside me in their casual clothes, smelling of competing aftershaves, are having a conversation with their eyes.

The two men step out of the lift before me. I follow them down the corridor, watch them enter their room as I hesitate outside mine. Without a sound, I turn the key and open the door. The room appears empty. Trying to do it soundlessly, I check the cupboard, behind the curtains, and the balcony, just in case. The armchair is also empty.

I call out, 'Hello!' and the bathroom door swings open. 'Alison, I'm in here.'

I stand on the threshold. Harvey is relieving himself and I am relieved. With one hand on the wall, he turns to face me. His lower lip falls and I can barely see him through my drowning eyes.

What happens next is between him and me, leaving me blissed out for a whole afternoon and night, and right now, I don't want to move, not even open my eyes. I just want to lie here with Harvey's body shielding mine. But I can see light creeping in through the curtains and I'm very aware that I have a lunch date with Austin Obermarle.

I blow at the hairs on Harvey's chest. He doesn't move.

I start to panic not knowing what the time is or how long I've slept. I raise myself up and push on his shoulder.

'Hey,' I say. 'Wake up.'

As he stirs, he lets out a series of concerned whats, then opens his eyes and looks at me with a smile that makes me think I can move mountains, even now. Falling back down again onto his chest, I let him know that I just want to stay like this for ever. He rolls onto his side. Separated, we prop ourselves up on our elbows facing each other.

'Tell me what's been going on,' he says.

'Oh my God, Harv.'

'Well?'

'Can you just check the time?'

He leans back and picks up Ria's phone from the bedside table. He drops it in the space between us.

11.00

'It's going to have to wait,' I say, jumping up. 'I have an appointment to meet Austin Obermarle, the director Ria was working with. Could there ever be a more pretentious name, do you think?'

'I'll come with you.'

'No,' I say, my left hand fiddling with my unadorned ear.

'No? Well, that's totally OK then, because I really only came all the way out here to make love to you and hand you your phone.'

He sits propped up on pillows with his arms folded in front of him.

'Don't think I don't love and respect you. Don't think

193

I'm not pleased that you're here,' I say, climbing back onto the bed and over his body. 'I have to do this alone, but when I get back, I'm going to tell you everything.' I kiss him on the lips, and as intended that's not where it ends, making me so late I have to get dressed without showering and take a taxi to the restaurant.

***

South Beverley Grill is packed. There are people at every table and waiting staff buzzing around. I'm advised that, 'Mr O is already here,' and am shown to a corner table by a tall, shaggy-haired blonde in a pencil skirt.

Austin is around fifteen years younger than me and wearing a loose black T-shirt that doesn't totally hide his food baby. He stands, takes my hand in both of his and kisses me on both cheeks as if we are old friends. When we sit down, he watches appreciatively as our waitress auditions the menu. He says, he'll have his usual, and to bring it quickly as he hasn't got much time. He turns to me and I shrug.

'Do you eat shrimp?'

'Yeah.'

'Have the Louis salad, you'll love it.'

'OK.'

'She'll have the Louis salad and we'll have a half-bottle of that great wine, you know the one.'

She turns and shuffles off.

'I'm sorry, Alison.' There's emotion in his eyes. 'Seems

194

like I'm always apologising to you. The last thing I want to do is let you down again but I have to warn you, I'm going to get called back on set pretty soon. I don't know, there's always some emergency I have to deal with. That's just how it is.'

I feel rushed and can't think of anything to say.

He carries on, 'I can't believe Ria's gone from our lives. Even now. What is it, two years?' Must be impossible for you.' He shakes his head. 'I've thought about it and I'll tell you anything you want to know.'

'Do you know a woman called Andy Buckingham?' I ask.

'Sure I do.'

I raise my eyebrows.

He laughs in a short, non-committal kind of way. Newly emboldened by Harvey's presence back at the hotel and the knowledge that he'd come and get me if at any point I call him, I smile and pick up my very large glass of wine and take it to my lips. Just before I take my first sip, I say, 'Is she going to have you assassinated for talking to me about everything I want to know?'

Austin sits back and looks at me as if he's just detected something interesting about me.

I put my glass down.

'You really are a very beautiful lady, Alison Connaught. Different from Ria, but nevertheless, there's something about you.'

He leans forward, puts a hand on my knee, and captures me with his intense blue eyes. Our food arrives. I try to centre myself as I pick up my knife and fork. Amid the loud chatter and laughter coming from other tables, we eat in silence for an uncomfortable amount of time.

'Why I came here,' I say, eventually, clearing my throat, 'is because I need to know why my daughter took an overdose of painkillers. The not knowing is killing me.'

He puts down his cutlery, and whilst still chewing, brings his napkin to his lips.

'I mean, you were working with her, intensively, on a film. What was she like? How did you find her? Did she have moods? Did she turn up on time?'

He replaces his napkin on his lap.

'You write songs,' he says.

'Yes.'

'I've heard your work. I listened to some of it last night.'

I don't say anything.

'I can phone up the director who's making the docu-soap. You are the perfect composer to write the title song for the series she's working on.'

'Austin, you don't understand.'

Still looking at me, he lowers his chin.

'I feel as if I've been dragged across hot coals and I haven't written a song since Ria was found in the bath.'

He plays with a spoon for a while and I let him procrastinate. Finally, he looks me in the eye again.

'Ria always turned up on time. She was the consummate professional with a wicked sense of humour. If you were to ask anyone who was on that set with us, they would all tell you the same thing.'

'What about the work itself? Was she acting up to the standard you would have expected from an Oscar-winning leading lady? Because there must have been some sign of something going on if she was taking too many painkillers.'

'She was euphoric and her acting skills were exactly as I expected them to be.'

'Euphoric?'

He shrugs.

'And how did she get on with everyone? I mean, how did she get on with you?'

'Everyone, fine, I think, I'm not always kept in the know about little spats people have on set, unless they turn into something, but there was no talk of that. With me, yeah, we had our disagreements.'

'Why? Did she fall in love with you?'

'Me, no,' he laughs.

'What about you with her?'

'Our arguments were over technical and creative issues. Most things we agreed upon, but there were times when we both thought we knew best. Look, if you want to know about her private life, a guy called Joshua something, not an actor, a Brit, always seemed to be coming and going. Come to think of it, when he was around that could often topple her. You might also like to consider the well-known fact that here in Hollywood, there's nothing quite as stressful as winning an Oscar. Those guys are way up high without a safety net.'

He glares at his phone and asks if I want coffee or dessert. I say, no. Throwing his serviette onto the table, he says, 'Nor do I. I'm sorry, I gotta go. This is what my life's like now. Please, Alison, you'll have to excuse me.'

When he's gone, I try calling Sarah Mason again. The call is cut before it even has a chance to ring. I signal our waitress and ask for the bill. She tells me that Mr O has already seen to the cheque. He has a limousine waiting outside, ready to take me wherever I want to go. I sit for a few moments thinking about Mr O. It's a given he likes women. I'm sure something was going on between him and Ria, not just because he was in control of our conversation and a flirt, but mum's instinct.

In the limousine I take out Harvey's iPad and google Austin Obermarle. Oh yeah, he's married all right, to a French actress who hasn't worked for some time. They have three kids, sixteen, fourteen and two, all blonde and smiling in a family photograph. Was the two-year-old an attempt to patch something up? Perhaps Joshua's comings and goings unsettled Austin more than Ria? I google OxyContin: euphoria is a major side effect.

So, you'd think it would be fine now, between Harvey and me, wouldn't you? You'd think that after yesterday and this morning everything would be hunky dory, and we could just forget our differences and what we've put each other through during the most harrowing two years of our lives. Whilst I'm in Austin's limousine, I stupidly think that.

And maybe I should know, whilst going up in the lift, that I'm going to be in a mood when I walk into the room.

But the way I behave comes as a shock to me as well as Harvey. The television is on. Harvey is flushed from the sun. He says, 'Good timing. I've just got back from a swim in the pool and thought I'd change my wet trunks.'

I'm thinking, he's thinking he's on holiday. He's behaving like he's on a holiday. 'This is not a fucking holiday!' I say.

'What else did you expect me to do whilst you're lunching with your director friend.'

'He's not a friend. I'd much rather have spent the time with you.'

'Then why didn't you?'

I suddenly get it in my head that I have to find my feather earring. If I can find my feather earring that Sister gave me, then my mood will calm right down and everything will OK between Harvey and me. But here I am, a banshee, telling Harvey that he doesn't understand, as I throw things about looking for my talisman. I decide it's in a side pocket in of one of my bags. When it's not in any of them, I decide it must be somewhere in the suitcase, probably fallen in the jumble of unwashed clothes. But, no, it's not there either, and I know it's irrational, yet I can't stop searching for it as if my life depends on it. Harvey stands between me and the chest of drawers.

'I'll tell you why you didn't spend the time with me. It's because this vanity quest of yours is more important to you than our marriage.'

I try to step around him but he blocks my way.

'Fuck off, Harvey.'

'Do you really mean that? Because if you really mean that, that's exactly what I'm going to do.'

'No, I don't. I just want you to get out of my way.'

'Fine.'

He throws the towel at me that he was wearing around his midriff and changes his trunks. Pulling a T-shirt over his head, he leaves the room, slamming the door behind him.

And what do I do?

I sit down and cry because I hate Harvey for not understanding me and I hate everyone else on this planet for being alive whilst my daughter is dead. And most especially, I hate myself, this lunatic person who throws a book across a room, shattering glass and wanting to punish the whole world, but in the end only punishes herself. Such crazy behaviour. So destructive. Is this what happened to you Ri? Did you hate yourself so much you didn't want to be alive anymore? My hand pulls at my naked ear and on repeat in my minds-eye, is me, dropping the feather earring into my sterling purse.

***

Dressed for the pool, feather in my ear, I go into the bar. I can't help being distracted by the aftermath of some kind of gathering that was in here earlier. The hotel staff are buzzing around clearing up, and I'm noticing the carpet's geometric design: dark blue background with outlines of red, yellow and green squares and triangles. The bar lights are turned off. It's more conference room than party atmosphere in the daylight. Not exactly inspirational, but even so, this is where I want to be. Sitting at the piano with an ocean view and once again seeking out poetic sound. My fingers touch and press on keys, skin to skin. Latching onto a riff, he's sucking me into a world where everything that's not music doesn't exist. I close my eyes and my body surfs the notes. I'm lost to the pictures in my head. A beach in another country, without sun and heat. It's not too cold but the sky is grey and the wind is butting me from all sides. Ria's here. Hands in trouser pockets, on the cusp of womanhood, she walks towards me from the seashore. I lower my camera. With every few steps she gains a year. At twenty-seven, she stands right there in front of me.

'Hi Mum,' she says sheepishly, playing notes in the air with her fingers.

If this could be real, I would give up the rest of my life for it.

I sing:

> *Hormones.*
> *Serotonin*
> *Our demons*
> *And the need to win*
> *Maybe I've met your queen*
> *When you were a princess*
> *And the people around you*
> *Loved themselves more than anything*

Hunter is the hunted one
The warning lights were too much to take in
We didn't understand what was happening.
Not an acting script
Not OxyContin
All the come-ons
Made you well equipped
To be an actor
To you, the princess
It was everything.

There's a big crash, plates smashing to the floor in a room off this one; must be the kitchen. I stop playing, turn around. Come back to the piano but my muse has run.

Someone comes over to tell me they're going to start vacuuming. It might be better if I come back later. I tell him, that's OK, real life beckons anyway. And it really is OK, because when it works for me, music is my OxyContin and, oh, I think I have another song.

Poolside, there's another bar, a round one with a thatched roof. Harvey sits on a stool with his back to me. Next to him, is what looks like a husband and wife team. I take a moment, then go and join them.

'Hi Alison, come and meet Angela and Derek.'

I play my part.

We all get on.

Later, in the bedroom, I apologise. Harvey lets me know that an apology is not quite enough.

'Will you let me explain?' I ask.

He sits down on the chair in the corner – the one where my imagination conjured a man with a gun – and he waits for me to speak.

I say, 'Studying with a shaman was very spiritual, but it also fucked me up, at first. I know what you're going to say. You're going to say, "Alison you were already fucked up, and the idea was that you were going there to get less fucked up," and I just want to say that I did get less fucked up but it's a process that's on-going and sometimes I'm aware of it and sometimes I'm not and that doesn't mean that I am not still fucked up, I am. I'm just less fucked up. I could never have achieved what I have over the last week if I hadn't gone to the shaman and visited the Hopis on their reservation.'

'So, what have you achieved?'

I tell him everything from touchdown in New York to entering the room when he first arrived.

'I'm still not sure what you've achieved, apart from putting yourself through a wild goose chase.'

'I don't see it like that.'

'And what way do you see it?'

I push my hair away from my ear, exposing my earring.

'You found it.'

'It holds my strength.'

'Bullshit, that's just superstition.'

'No, Harvey, it's not superstition.'

I'm stroking the feather.

'What is it then?'

'You haven't experienced what I've experienced, so

maybe you can't understand.'

'Maybe not. But are you done now? Can we go home?'

'Yes, I've heard what everyone has to say and no, I can't go home yet.'

'Why, Alison?'

'There's somewhere I need to go first.'

'Are you making this up as you go along?'

'I'm following a trail, Harvey.'

He springs out of the chair.

'I've heard enough. All I can say is thank God the weather's good here.'

He leaves the room.

I understand Harvey's frustration, I do, but I don't have the tools to mend it. My heart is beating so fast with the commitment I've just made to myself. To do the thing that deep down I always knew I was going to have to do. I've been running away from it for two years, running and running, and then I just came out with it and dug my stake into the ground. It's good. It is good. It's a good thing. It will help me move on. My chest is heavy and my breath is laboured. I've contemplated not doing it but that's like writing half a song that you never have the courage to complete. Always there, mocking you, those last few bars, niggling and cajoling, and reminding you of what you haven't done yet. I need to follow the nagging instinct in my womb and go to Ria's house.

3

This is the first time Harvey and I have been away from home together since our bereavement. We have agreed that travel is not a luxury we wanted to indulge in, being a kind of betrayal and disrespect for our loss. But everything's different now. There are no rules, no boundaries, only what's left of our lives.

I find him in the bar drinking rum and coke. He's the only person in there. I climb up onto a stool beside him. Nursing his drink, he acknowledges me with a curt nod. He asks me what I want. I say, sparkling water with ice and lemon. He looks at me, eyes askew.

'We have to talk,' I say.

'I thought we had.'

'You haven't talked. You've only questioned, listened and commented.'

'I've got nothing to say.'

'Are you sure?'

'What do you want me to say? I can't live with you. I can't live without you.'

'I don't know why you're taking this so personally; I've never understood.'

'And that's the problem.'

'Will you please explain it to me so I can understand?'

'OK, I will. You're not the same person. Oh, there are times when bits of you come back and that's what's keeping me in this marriage, but most of the time you're lost to me.'

'Harvey, I could say the same thing about you.'

'This thing you feel you've got to do.'

'Yes.'

'What is it?'

'I'm just wondering if any couple who lost a child can ever remain the same two people as they were before.'

'You haven't answered my question.'

'Because I believe you're being unreasonable.'

'What is so unreasonable about getting upset because you're not featuring in your wife's life anymore?'

'Ssshh, calm down.'

I take a sip of my drink and look around.

'You could have come along and done this whole trip with me. But the reason you didn't is because you already clocked out of this marriage, and I have to accept that. I've had to accept that and go on this journey alone to keep myself sane, whilst you had to be with another woman.'

'I was never really with her.'

'Oh, come on!'

Harvey orders another drink. He's looking around now.

'What do you want to do for dinner?' he asks.

'I'm not hungry and I'm surprised you are.' I put my hand on his back, lean over and whisper, 'Look, I love you.

Every time I'm with you, when we're physically intimate, I try and show you how much.'

'That's just sex.'

I pull back.

He turns towards me. His eyes are liquid and his lips are doing strange things.

'Just leave me alone,' he says.

I leave him alone and go and prowl up and down in our bedroom. I can't think about Harvey. I can't think about Sarah Mason and her reason for not wanting to talk to me. I can't think about anything. I must start making arrangements to go and visit Ria's house; our house now. I've never been there before. Whenever Harvey previously brought up the subject, I always told him, 'No, not now, and I don't care if it makes sense or not, it's not the right time to sell.'

I think the right time has come around. If I can arrange to go there tomorrow, maybe after that we can go home and pick up the threads of our lives. Yet, in the mood I'm in, I can't even pick up the phone. I can't gather the gumption to speak to anyone. I can't do anything but pace.

When he comes through the door, I sense his heavy heart, his hurt, his pain that's lived in the shadow of mine but is just as big, and I call out, 'Harv, are you OK?' I want to hug him, but he pushes me away and throws himself down on the bed.

'I'm going to go and see Ria's house,' I blurt out.

'I'm guessing that you won't want me to go with you.'

'I do want you to come with and be with me when I go there, yes.'

He looks at me. 'I can't make you out,' he says.

I sit beside him.

He turns his head the other way but lets me hold his hand.

4

Harvey can't sleep either. I'm starting to count the number of times he turns over. When I ask if he's awake, he says, no, which I find both endearing and hurtful.

We have decided to go to Ria's house, together, tomorrow. We've promised that we'll leave our resentments back at the hotel and be a support for each other, doing something we should have done many moons ago.

Lying in that strange bed, in a holiday hotel but not on holiday, next to the guy I've loved for many years and watching him drift away from me on a cold front is like being in a world where all points of reference are buried under snow. In that surreal twilight zone, I start whispering. Looking at the ceiling and telling the story of my discoveries here in America. Not in the way I told him earlier. Not about what people said and what I thought about what they said at the time, but the real things I've gleaned from those experiences, those conversations. Whether he's listening, or not, I really don't know.

'I know you think I'm an obstinate bitch, Harvey, and maybe I am, but the way our tragedy stopped me in my tracks and forced me to face up to things was like I never had a choice. I had to find a way and this was my way.'

He doesn't tell me to shut up and so I go on.

'I can see it now. Me with my blinkers on, wearing my privileged life like a coat of armour. Ria grown up and living far away, and I only saw her as she appeared. I stripped away all the concerns I'd had for her growing up, it was like I could pretend that everything was just great, but the signs were always there and I chose to ignore them. This is what I've learned here.'

I turn to look at him. He's lying on his back, very still. In a streak of light falling through a crack in the curtains, I can see his eyelids flicker. I return my gaze to the dark ceiling.

'What the indigenous folk gave me is a window on reality. Then talking to these satellite people in her life… there were no warm arms to hold her here, Harvey.'

I hear ringing in my ears.

***

At breakfast, I watch him. Neither of us mentions a word about the rift between us, but we feel it in the atmosphere. I can see it on his face and no doubt he can read it on mine. He can't even look at me.

I don't ask if he was listening to my monologue last night. I know it's perfectly possible to choose not to hear things. I've done that myself many times, all my life. We only hear what we want to hear, see what we want to see. I've lived it. I know all about that way of being and where it leads.

There's something new about me this morning though. Not glossy and shiny new, but tougher and more realistic. Harvey's letting me know it's not a good vibe. Tears prick my eyes. I don't want to lose him.

He puts his fork down over his uneaten fried egg, puncturing it like a vein; yellow blood runs over his cutlery. The coffee quivers in his cup. His orange juice is untouched. He pushes his chair away from the table. 'Come on, let's go,' he says.

He doesn't want to drive the hired car. He doesn't want me to drive it either.

'It's smashed to pieces. I don't understand why you didn't call the rental company to come and take it away.'

'I don't know, I didn't think of it. It's only the boot and Andy Buckingham's chauffeur managed to drive it back here, so I thought it would be OK.'

'I won't say, you think a lot of things are OK that really aren't.'

I don't say, 'You just did.'

In the taxi, he stares out the side window. I look straight ahead. We don't speak. My legs jitter and I keep rubbing my hands up and down the thighs of my old jeans. I'm wearing the kind of things you might put on if you're going to work on the underbelly of a vehicle. The kind of outfit most women in this city would be horrified to own. I don't give a shit. Harvey wears black shorts with yellow and green flashes all over them, a black v-neck T-shirt and sandals, as if he's on his way to a lunch date on the beach.

I know we're going to a house in the Hollywood Hills

but in my head I have a picture of a little chic place. When we pull up outside the big white geometric building, several stories high and surrounded by trees, I am thrown. On the way, we picked up an envelope containing a set of keys from the managing agent but didn't think to ask him what keys opened which doors. If we include the whole circumference of this house, there are quite a few.

Whilst Harvey empties a large jailor's key chain onto the patio table, Ria's phone rings. The number is withheld. I go and sit on one of the poolside layouts and answer the call.

'Hi, is this Alison Connaught?'

A dozen mewing cats mill around my legs. I reach out to stroke them. They intertwine like snakes and caress my hand.

'Yes. Who is this?'

'You don't know me. My name's Charlotte Thomas.'

Harvey goes over to a far door with the heavy bunch of keys.

'I'm one of the actors in the last film Ria was working on. I heard you were in town and I was wondering if, whilst you're here, you'd agree to meet up with me?'

I watch Harvey get frustrated with the keys. He walks round the side towards the front of the house.

'Hi Charlotte, thank you for phoning. Um, can you let me know what this is about?'

'I'd rather just meet with you in person, if that's OK. I was thinking about Grand Park, by the fountain. I don't have a job at the moment so anytime would be good for me.'

'You can't tell me why?'

Charlotte goes quiet.

Harvey comes back. Throws the keychain down onto the table, shakes the envelope and picks up the couple of individual keys that tumble out. He goes over to the nearest door and manages to get inside the house. He'll be back out in a minute, asking what's up.

'OK,' I tell Charlotte. 'We have flights booked to go home tomorrow, so it's going to have to be sometime today. We'll be by the fountain in the park, late afternoon, say between 5.30 and six o' clock. '

'Can you come alone?'

Harvey's walking towards me, head bowed, combing his fingers through his hair.

'I'm here with Ria's father.'

He's standing in front of me gesturing for me to get off the phone. The cats are now wrapping themselves around his legs, looking up at him as if he's their king.

'Alone, please,' she says, and something in her voice urges me to say, 'OK, OK.'

'I'll see you then.'

She clicks off the phone.

'Who was that?'

'Charlotte Thomas, an actress. She said she worked with Ria and wants to see me, alone, this afternoon.'

'Inspector Connaught's still on duty then.'

'I'm pleased you can joke about it.'

He screws up his face, puts one hand on my back and leads me towards the house.

213

'For your information, I did tell her we'd be coming together, but she wanted me to come alone.'

He stops walking and turns towards me. 'Why are you even telling me? Since when has my presence, or lack of it, made any difference to what you do?'

'I could say the same thing about you.'

'Look, Alison, it doesn't matter, OK.'

He ushers me into the annex. To the right is an open-plan kitchen with wooden eau-de-nil cupboards, a range oven with brass accessories, no dining table. To the left are large canvases of eclectic artworks covering a long wall. I home in on a forest of bare trees with a carpet of leaves on the ground which reminds me of our painting above the fireplace at home, and next to it a Cubist work that resembles a Picasso but is actually signed by Braque. There's a silver plaque at the bottom of the frame which reads:

To the best leading lady I've ever had the pleasure of dancing with on screen. Love Danny Boon.

Danny Boon is the actor who starred alongside Ria in the film *Honeyrose*. I'm not sure how to describe this feeling, but it's as if Ria is looking over my shoulder, gazing at the picture with me. I can almost smell her. I am compelled to turn around to the sound of a cats' chorus singing for their supper. I look towards Harvey. He's eyeing up the place as if he's a prospective buyer.

'It looks as if this is some kind of a self-contained granny flat. There's a door here.' He opens it. 'Come on,' he says, walking through to another room.

'Harvey, the cats are hungry.'

'Well, what do you want me to do about it?'

'We need to feed them.'

'Just because Ria always loved strays, doesn't mean I have to cater to them.'

The clutter follows me into the kitchen. Most of the cupboards are bare but there is cat food in the large one under the sink. I find two trough-like bowls and fill them with food and water. They eat, drink, and mess up the floor.

Ria's here. I'm certain of it. She has me frozen in this space. She's seducing me to come over to the other side. If I speak or move I will lose her connection.

'Alison, where are you? Come in here.'

Torn again.

'I'm an adult, don't boss me around,' I shout.

I walk into the other room where Harvey is opening drawers and sniffing around.

'That's something she would have said,' he says.

I shrug and want to cry because just as quickly as it came, her energy has left. I take in the room: Moroccan hanging lamps, candles, shisha, cushions all over the floor, a bed with a grey satin cover that resembles a 1930s curtain and next to it a door that leads to a charcoal shower room.

'Do you think she had someone staying here?' I ask.

'What, you mean rented it out? She earned a fortune. Why would she do that?'

There's an edge to the atmosphere. A certain scent in the air. A will o' the wisp voice whispers in my ear and I know who stayed in this room, who stays in this room.

I walk outside and take a huge breath. Harvey joins me. He puts his arm around my shoulder. Walks me back towards the swimming pool and sits me down in front of the table with the keys, under the pergola with hanging hibiscus and bunches of grapes. The cats are embracing the columns like dancing girls and I'm rubbing my arms because despite the 90-degree heat, I have goosebumps and I am cold.

Looking up at the big sky, I'm thinking, this is a strange place: Millions of dollars spent on a home with a private road and embedded in foliage for optimum privacy, and yet, all day long there are Securitas helicopters spying overhead. And strange too, how my thoughts, like ivy, twist and turn.

'Are you ready to go into the main house?' Harvey asks.

I nod, but I'm not ready. I feel I will never be ready for this. We stand together for a while, looking out at the tops of trees making their way down to the bottom of the hill. When I can't stand the anticipation any longer, I fake punch Harvey on the arm, and say, 'Let's go.'

Opening the sliding doors, I see myself entering another house from a garden where an eagle lay on the ground staring up at me with one dead eye. I falter and Harvey grabs my arm. He keeps me on my feet whilst we go inside. We enter into a huge lounge on different levels with white marble floors and lots of glass. It's austere with no hint of Ria. I can't even imagine her being here.

Sitting down on one of the chamois leather sofas, I contemplate why she would have bought this particular house. Perhaps she was so busy she didn't have time to look around? Or she employed someone to buy this place for her, some kind of personal shopper, and the day she moved in was the first time she saw it herself, with the intention of finding something more homely as soon as she could find a space in her diary…

'What are you thinking?' Harvey asks.

'Why here?'

'Why not here?'

'Because there's nothing of her in it.'

'She never cared much about her surroundings,' he says, picking up an antique silver box from a built-in display unit. He opens it. Closes it. Replaces it on the shelf.

It's true, Ria never bothered to redecorate her bedroom when she came back to live with us, but that was a temporary stopgap and therefore understandable. And yet, Harvey's right, she always seemed to be a stranger wherever she lived as an adult, and she lived in many different places. It was like she never fully moved in anywhere. Nowhere was home.

I get up, walk around a little, try to get a story off the walls. I so regret that I've been employing a professional cleaner on a regular basis over the last two years. There are no tell-tale marks anywhere of anyone having lived here. The whole building is just an impersonal shell. I try and imagine Ria coming home to this house late at night, tired, stressed, unhappy.

Come on, Mum, why so deep? It's just another place to sleep, that's all.

'I'm going upstairs,' I say.

'Don't you want to see the rest of the downstairs? You haven't seen the kitchen yet.'

'You go. I'll see it later.'

I'm already in the entrance hall where columns of sunbeams pile in through telescopic skylights in the high ceiling. It's like a scene from a Star Wars movie. I've never seen anything quite like this in real life before and then I remind myself that this isn't real life, and to most people, nor was any part of the world that Ria inhabited. Walking through one of the columns, I can hear her voice.

This bit is cool, Mum.

I respond out loud, 'Yes, baby, this bit is cool.'

'What?'

Harvey is behind me.

'Nothing.'

'This is really something,' he says, before entering the kitchen. I get a glimpse of a huge rectangular space, black and white tiles on the floor, another range cooker and copper saucepans hanging above a central island.

Did she host parties here? Did she only eat take-outs and never cook a thing? I never asked.

Followed by a small posse of cats – some of them are still wailing outside – I climb the central staircase to the mezzanine floor and open quite a few doors to empty bedrooms and bathrooms. There's one room full of wooden racks of towels and sheets still in their packaging. I stumble into the master suite, two glass walls overlooking the city of Los Angeles and to my right a king size bed. I press a button on the wall by the door and the glass walls disappear into other walls, opening up the room to the elements and a wide L-shaped balcony. On one of the bedside tables there's a pair of 1950s Ray Ban sunglasses, an empty plastic bottle of OxyContin, and a hardback copy of *To Kill a Mockingbird*. I pull back the white dust cover someone has thrown over the bed, lie on the bare mattress and try to smell her.

When I pick myself up, the first thing I do is go over to the walk-in. It would be large enough to hold a party in if it wasn't for all the rails and shelving busting over with clothes and footwear. Items have been neatly placed on hangers or folded politely. That's not like my daughter. Knickers under the bed, regalia strewn or heaped on the floor; that's how she used to treat her clothes. I guess tidying up possessions can be a superficial affair, hiding any hint of something wrong beneath the surface. Although, come to think of it, she probably had someone else tidy up after her, which kind of amounts to the same thing, I would imagine.

I stroke my fingers along the fabrics hanging on the rails, and when I stumble over a switch, I turn on the moody lighting. The cats are all chilled, lying with their faces resting on their paws or licking the underside of their back legs. They must like it in here; a place of indulgence for one's feminine side. There's lots of silk couture dresses and skirts, a whole section of denim jeans, must be about thirty pairs, opposite a row of others in assorted colours.

Love my jeans.

I lift a long, navy chiffon sleeve to my nose that smells

of cleaning fluid and dust. Next to it, the gown she wore to collect her Oscar, under polythene, hanging with its front facing towards me – white opalescent satin, full length, ruched midriff, a décolletage, a broach with ruby droplets still pinned on one side. On the floor are the high heels she wore, silver and sparkling like a million specs of diamonds. Her hair fell in waves that night over her porcelain shoulders. She glided through her standing ovation and up onto the podium.

'I don't want to forget anyone's name, so I'll just say thank you to everyone who made this possible, but I do want to say a particular thank you to my mum who dropped crumbs everywhere along the path for me to find. She showed me, with hard work and determination, a girl can do anything. Cheers Mum!' she said, waving the statuette.

I look away, to my left, at a dozen shoe racks, all empty, and a pyre of shoes before them making me smile; that's more like my girl. But then I remember why I'm here and what I feel I must do. The way I stagger out of that dressing room, you'd think I'd just drunk the whole contents of a wine cellar or been stabbed in the back by a friend. My heart pumps a rapid beat. I could escape over the edge of the balcony before I get there. It's a thought I'm drawn to, so best not to think. I hesitate outside the bathroom, breathe deeply, go in.

The felines follow me. They mew and mew. My ears buzz. I cover my mouth with my hands and tell myself it's just a room. In front of me, captured in the round window is a portrait of the most perfect azure blue, and below it, a bath like a giant cream ceramic bowl with hand-painted glazed cracks, dusty pink roses and leaf tendrils in rich green. I see her beneath the surface of this tub full of water, face bloated, hair floating like seaweed, dead eagle eyes having taken over her own. I don't know what to do. This isn't just a room. This is *the* room… I don't know what to do. My trembling hands persevere with putting the plug in the waste. I need the strength of both arms to run the wide gold tap with both hot and cold. A crystal-clear waterfall spills out. I watch a small puddle become a pool in the bath. I see her. She's in there. Her smoky, transparent form distorted by the movement of water. She's merging with it like a foetus in the womb. I want to hold her. I take off my clothes and climb in. She's gone as soon as my foot hits the surface. I need to steady myself and I put a hand out to the shelf at my side. The perfume bottles rattle in protest. They warn me they can break. My ghostly reflection stares back at me in the mirror. On my knees now, clutching the roll top to either side, I put my head beneath the cascade to wash it all away, wash it all away.

Is this how it felt, Ri?

5

I am descending and descending. Someone is moaning, I think it's me. I open my eyes, not realising where I am, at first. Harvey is carrying me. We move through the opaque columns of light like butterflies in a canyon. We enter the doorway to a sitting room where I'm lowered onto a soft skinned sofa. Harvey leans over me, his face inches from mine.

'I found you out cold and soaking wet with your head and arms hanging over the side of the bath.'

Wrapped in a towel, hair dripping, I'm a shivering numb thing. Harvey leaves the room. Through the wall of glass doors, I watch a mocking glint of sunlight off the surface of the pool. When Harvey returns, he startles me.

'God, I had such a fright when I saw you,' he says, perching on the arm of the sofa, holding a steaming cup of something with both hands. 'Alison, you might think all of this is leading you to enlightenment but where you are right now, from where I'm sitting, just looks like you're torturing yourself and me.' He hands me the cup. 'Neither of us got to choose who we are, or who we became, but we do make choices. You're making yourself sick with yours and I'm not sure how long I can stand by and watch.'

I sip and retreat further inwards.

***

In the taxi, I panic. 'Have we left one of the cats in the house?'

'No.'

'Are you sure?'

'Yes.'

And then I'm inside myself again until I have a meltdown in the hotel room. The rational me – if she ever existed – has bolted. The playful me who would say to Harvey, 'Hey, what shall we do now?' whilst climbing all over him – has bolted too. Those two parts of me have the power to save our marriage, but when *this* me overwhelms, I don't blame the others for not sticking around; it's far too painful and embarrassing.

Harvey and I both sit on the bed, fully clothed, no funny stuff, nothing light-hearted going on here. He's been drinking rum and coke from the minibar. Tears sting my eyes. My nose is blocked and I'm – clutching a handful of tissues – fearful of it dripping.

I used to think I was this emotionally intelligent woman reclaiming herself, but that's not who I am now. The lioness in me has pushed Harvey away and left the ass here to get on with it. I have done this to us. I have done this to me.

'Don't leave me, Harvey.'

I'm pawing at him. He sidles off the bed, moves away, tells me to pull myself together. But Alison can't pull herself together. She's following him off the bed, throwing herself at him, setting off another avalanche of tears.

I have never done this before. I have never been this woman. Not even in front of Greg was I this pathetic. Harvey's shaking me, telling me to sit down in the way you'd talk to a child. He's pushing me into the armchair in the corner. He watches me, waiting for me to do or say something.

'I have nothing to say,' I tell him.

He nods, sits down opposite me on the edge of the bed.

'I think you're having a breakdown,' he says.

The fighter wells up inside me again. She wants to say, 'Because of you. If you would have just accepted me exactly as I am, having to do certain things to sort myself out, then I wouldn't be having this breakdown.' I push the fighter down, and say, 'No, no, really, I'm OK,' as I walk past him into the bathroom.

He stands on the threshold, arms crossed, back against the doorframe, watching me splash cold water onto my face, 'Do you think we can repair us?' I say.

He shrugs. 'We've already tried.'

I grab a towel and try to smile but my lips disobey me and spasm instead.

'Meanwhile, you better get yourself ready for your meeting.'

Despite everything, I manage to make myself look OK. I haven't pulled myself together though, not really. In the taxi, I'm nervous. I don't know whether it's because I'm traumatised from my day, fearful of losing my husband or afraid of what Charlotte Thomas is going to say to me; probably all of those things. I'm trying to shut out snapshots of Ria's bathroom from my mind.

Then in walks Mrs Rational from out of nowhere. She's taken on an African-American persona. I imagine her sitting under a tree, close to a river, smiling, relaxing and saying good day to the spiders, butterflies and birds. She tells me my marriage is being tested – no shit – and puts Harvey in the spotlight.

You swing like a pendulum, girl. You might be in pain but you're completely capable of doing what you have to do, then he turns up and you crumble like a soaked biscuit. Don't think he's blameless in all this just because he says he is. You think he's the picture boy for sanity and wellbeing? Then why is he choosing to addle his brain with alcohol the whole time? At least you're facing your demons.

I wait for Charlotte Thomas on a bench in front of the fountain. I didn't save her number and it seems to have deleted itself from Ria's phone. She's fifteen minutes late. I've no idea what she looks like. I'm picturing her young, Ria's age or thereabouts, petite, pretty, large breasts, blonde. I'm surprised by the woman who shows up in a yellow dress and red shoes. Although youthful, you can tell by her hands and throat that she's not that young. I was right about her curves, but not the colour of her hair; it's dark, like mine.

'Hi Alison, I'm Charlotte,' she says, briefly touching my shoulder.

I smile.

She sits down beside me.

'I phoned because I heard you were in town questioning people about Ria and then someone told me you were using

Ria's English phone and the truth is, I just couldn't let you leave without telling you what I know. I'm not going to be popular for doing this. All the bars and restaurants around here have eyes and ears and that's why I chose to meet you here. I just thought if we're seen together in this open space, it can be coincidental. Do you know what I mean?'

'Yeah, I think I do,' I say.

She looks at the fountain.

'I love it here and come often. The sound of rushing water brings peace to my mind and it's cooling, you know. You leaving tomorrow?'

'Our flight's in the afternoon.'

'To England?'

'Uh-huh.'

'England is home?'

I nod.

'I've never been.'

'You should visit. It's a great place, Americans love it.'

'The home of Shakespeare. All that history and everything.'

'Charlotte, you wanted to tell me something.'

'No, but I feel I have to.'

I look up at the sky waiting for Charlotte to go on. A bat's ragged wings in broad daylight makes me shudder and think of pale skin, fanged teeth and blood dripping down a chin. Another sign for me?

She begins. 'There's always a lot of hanging around time when you're making a movie. During *Archimedes Rising,* Ria and I hung out together a lot of hours, a lot of days. I was

226

playing her mother on screen and she kind of adopted me off screen as well. She was really professional but she was troubled. The tell-tale signs were there; everyone knew. We'd been briefed not to gossip and told that what's seen or heard on set, stays on set.'

'What was wrong with her?'

'Austin Obermarle had his hands all over her. Ria managed it well but Austin's wife was a bigger problem. She's a bunny boiler and an alchie. She set fire to Ria's car, threatened next time it would be her house with Ria in it. Sure, there were whispers but no one dares to talk about this kind of thing openly.'

I'm silent.

'There was something else going on. Something she never told me about but I saw it plain as day, several times: she had bruises on her body and had make-up conceal them. Look, I don't think Ria purposely took her own life, if that's what you're thinking. What I'm saying is, it's not surprising that Ria had headaches and things. She had a lot going on. A lot of stuff she had to deal with and a budding career to nurture. She numbed herself with painkillers and when they weren't strong enough she upped the dose. It happens all the time in Hollywood.'

I look to the fountain and say, 'Accidental suicide.'

'Yeah, an occupational hazard.'

'Did you know they're making a documentary about her life?'

'No one's going to talk about these things I'm telling you.'

'How can you be sure?'

'Andy Buckingham runs Hollywood. She might not have a prick but she can be a real big one. They've worked together for a while and she calls Austin her best boy. She wouldn't want him bad-mouthed.

'If you're wondering why I'm telling you all this, it's because I have a daughter, too, and it doesn't take a lot of imagination to know how you must be feeling. I've never been a Hollywood darling. If they kick me out of town tomorrow, in some ways, it will be a pleasure to go home. There's a part of me that would be grateful for it.'

'Thank you,' I say, and I take her hand in mine, holding it too tightly, the stone in her ring bruising my finger.

Gingerly, I say, 'Can you tell me anything else?'

'No, that's about it really.'

'Are you sure?'

'I've been thinking about it for two years, I'm as sure as I'm ever going to be.'

'I guess I'm never going to get to speak to Sarah Mason.'

'Excuse me?'

'Sarah Mason, the director, of the forthcoming television series they're making about Ria.'

'I suppose not, not with so much to hide. They'll probably cut out the stuff that offends them and dream up the rest. That's what they do.'

I look at the fountain.

'It's time for me to go home.'

'I envy you,' she says, and then, 'I'm sorry, so sorry, you know I meant about going home, just that, just that, just that. I didn't mean…'

'It's OK.'

'It might not be.'

I seek out her eyes, thinking about all the vampires in Hollywood and something that Ria once said to me at the start of her career:

Oh Mum, Lennon got it wrong; love, yes, but we all need luck too!

***

When I get back to the hotel, Harvey and I barely speak. The great unsaid is a continent between us. We sleep back to back, flinching from close proximity and any accidental touch. We both wake early. We are awkward. How can this be when we've lived together for such a long time? And yet, that's how it is now.

'I'm going for a swim,' Harvey announces, swiping his key-card off the bedside table with an accusatory sidelong glance.

By contrast, I slow down my movements and pack my clothes, neatly, as if they aren't insisting to be washed the moment we get home. I check and re-check cupboards and drawers. I bathe and dress, pay close attention to my make-up, lock my case and leave the room.

Instinct takes me to the piano in the bar where we reconnect with my hands on his keys, but the notes and chords we played before seem to have deleted themselves from my memory. My new African-American friend turns up again. She's speaking and singing but I can't quite hear the words or the melody.

'Accompany me,' she says.

I play and hum a jazzy blues riff for her and her voice takes on clarity.

> *He doesn't know*
> *He's in his own space*
> *Thinks he can just wipe me out.*
> *Click his fingers and get over what this is all about.*
> *Can we find it again?*
> *He says, we're too broken down*
> *I say we are*
> *But you leaving me will just make us lonely*
> *From afar.*

She's smiling now, getting up from under that tree, brushing dirt off her skirt, walking away, and I stop because without her, I don't know where this song is going. She's turning her back on me, waving as she shimmies her way into the distance.

'It's down to you now, girl. I ain't coming back. I've already given you what I've never given anyone else.'

I sit with my hands beneath my thighs until someone taps me on the shoulder. I turn around. Some young thing, blonde and beautiful, a lot like the person I was expecting to show up in the park yesterday, says, 'Mrs Cunor?' and I wonder if half of America think my daughter's name was Connor.

'Yes,' I say.

'Excuse me for interrupting, but Mr Cunor's in

reception. His message is, he's got all the bags and will you please come down now or you'll miss your plane.'

'Have you got a piece of paper and a pen?' I reply.

***

I have no idea what time it is or how long it took me to transcribe the bones of that song. At the reception desk on the ground floor, I'm just about to ask if Harvey's still here when he appears by my side.

'You're very late,' he says.

'I'm sorry, I was just…'

'Yada, yada, yada.'

His attitude towards me makes me want to weep. It's like the terrible and the wonderful are juxtaposed. These small pieces of music that have come through me over the last few days are a door that has opened. They are very different from anything I've written before. I have no expectation that they will ever get recorded but they will make me rich in other ways.

'I was composing,' I say, as if this gives Harvey insight into the wonder of my experience, and an indication of exactly how far I've come since being here, where *our* daughter lived, because I won't make that mistake again. Ria was our daughter, not mine and another man's. Harvey was Ria's father, whatever the biology; she was his, she was definitely his.

Without thinking, I take my credit card out my bag. I half expect Harvey to tell me he's already paid. Instead

231

he wears a pained expression as the concierge gives me a handwritten folded letter on hotel headed-notepaper.

Dear Alison,

I want to apologise for messing up your hired car and not serving you a lunch that you actually ate. I know this has been a stressful trip for you and so even though there's not many I would forgive for the lack of appreciation and effort it took to prepare a meal for them, under the circumstances, I consider it a misdemeanour and I, wholeheartedly, forgive you for that.

Look, I'm not known for my niceties, so I'll cut to the chase. I've taken care of your hotel bill and I've arranged for your car rental to be picked up and I'll see to the damages whether you've paid for insurance or not.

Ria was an amazing young woman. I'm trying to arrange for a special award to be given in her honour at the Oscars next year. If I manage to swing it, you will receive an invitation in due course. I hope that you and your husband will be able to attend.

Yours affectionately,
Andy Buckingham

'Alison,' Harvey says, 'our bags are in the taxi.'

It's a relief to be leaving here. I'm actually looking forward to disembarking in the cold, grey and grim weather at Heathrow airport. I get a sudden feeling that I can repair this broken relationship. Smiling at Harvey, I say, 'OK I'm ready now.'

'Praise the Lord.'

'I'm really happy to be going home with you, Harvey.'

'Really?'

'Yes, of course. What did you think?'

PART FIVE

Warrior

All I can do is be me, whatever that is.
Bob Dylan

PART FIVE

1

I'm coping. Sister was right, there is a certain strength that comes from squaring up to pain and not acquiescing to it, but not everything is better for it. For example, my home has taken on an abandoned expression. It's a kind of betrayal, only I'm the one seen as doing the betraying and I know it's because I'm not the same.

Also, Ria's fans have left their shrine; their return to normal life worries the flame that keeps her memory alive. Annie tells me they do come back every so often to pay their respects, but I haven't seen them.

I spend a lot of time with Annie. Our meetings on the bench are subconsciously planned. I speak in a stream of consciousness that helps me to understand things I don't even know I'm contemplating.

'Annie,' I say, 'I've spent my whole life living in a warren. A warm and cosy place I could worm my way into to create a false sense of harmony. I sent artificial messages out into the world about the way love is and the way people are; my songs rained glitter on everything. If you believe in something enough, if you believe in yourself enough, you can sell it. So, everybody bought it, and I profiteered, greatly, that's the scary thing; everyone buying into this dreamscape that has no place in reality.

'At the time, I thought it was safe, but it wasn't safe, it was just a disaster waiting to happen. You have to see things, square up to things in shocking, vivid daylight. That's what you've got to do. They don't teach you that though, do they? They don't tell you that in school. I didn't learn it at home, either. So, disasters happen. People get depressed. They get sucked into being a cog in that great big factitious wheel, thinking that's how you've got to be. You create your coping structure and it really doesn't matter if it's based on a lie. Chin up. Walk tall. Get on with it.

'When I went to Reykjavik in the middle of winter and it was dark all the time. I mean, daybreak happened around eleven and lasted until noon when everything went dark again. Everywhere – in all the shops and restaurants and in the hotel – there was this mood lighting: glowing fires, comfortable chairs, beautiful things. It was like living in a womb. I remember asking someone, "Do you have many suicides here in Iceland?" "Yes," I was told. "We do, but mostly in summer." In summer, Annie. If you've been hiding all your life, the light can shock you to death.'

A comfortable silence.

'You're going to think this sounds really weird but at the same time as feeling estranged from Harvey, sometimes I think that we've never been closer. I mean, there's some kind of an unbreakable bond that happens when you share a tragedy, but that connection sits locked up and gagged like prisoners in our throats. It's like we hate each other for what's happened. I'm jangling with guilt, Annie. I've been halfway around the world trying to discover why Ria had to die, and you know what I've learned? The definition of "accidental suicide".' On and on and on I chat and when I reach the final full stop, I ask, 'How are the goats, Annie?'

'They're fine.'

'And the weather? What was that like whilst I was away?'

'Oh, you know, sometimes it's cold and damp and sometimes it's not.'

'How do you manage? I've often wondered, how you put up with things like being on your own and not having a home where you can lock the door at night?'

'I'm not on my own and I don't need a key; I have animals and wits. And why would anyone invade where I live, when there's a house like yours just up the path?'

I talk shit but she speaks the truth and gives it to me hard.

Harvey phones me from work, something he hasn't done since we returned from the States. I ask him, to what do I owe the honour and he replies, 'I'm asking you out on a date.' I accept, dress up for him and he takes me out for a meal. We go to the hotel in the village where half an avocado with sweet chilli on a bed of wild goat's cheese and lettuce, costs £20. It's very nice. Normally I would tell him that Annie found a puffball that we marinated and cooked over a log fire near our bench and it tasted just as delicious, but of course I don't tell him this now; these are not normal times and he would definitely receive it wrongly. He makes a big deal out of turning off his phone and orders a very expensive bottle of wine.

'Will you drink it with me?'

'Maybe.'

'You used to love wine.'

The sommelier pours potent ruby liquid into two glasses. When he goes away I say, 'I was almost raped in Arizona after drinking wine.'

'Not by your shaman, I hope.'

'Harvey!'

'I'm sorry, I didn't mean to be flippant.'

'It was a big deal at the time…and no, not by Greg, he's far too spiritual, he would never have done that.'

'What happened?'

'Two guys. I went into a bar.'

'What were you doing in a bar?'

'I went there as soon as my seminar with Greg was over. Too much pain had surfaced, I just wanted to get blasted. Forget it all. Everything. One of my attackers was in the bar. He followed me out. The other one was his friend, I think. They were young guys, you know. All of a sudden I was on my back with one of them on top of me.'

'In the street?'

'I can't believe I'm telling you this in a restaurant… behind a building, in the hotel car park.'

'Why didn't you tell me before?'

'I don't really know, there never seemed to be an appropriate moment. You were with…'

'Sarah, and I wasn't with her, not really… You managed to get away from them?'

'I kneed one of them in the groin.'

'I'll drink to that.'

He lifts his glass.

'I got punched in the eye for doing it. You can still see where the skin split.' I point to my scar. 'The raised red bit, just here.'

'I thought that was eczema.'

'I don't have eczema.'

'Anyway, you can drink with me, I'm not going to rape you.'

'I know that,' I say, lifting my glass.

Our food arrives. Mine's a pretty stir fry with coriander and cumin rice. Harvey's is the side of a cow, rare. I can't look at his plate.

'I need to ask you a question,' I say.

'Ask away.'

'Have you forgiven me?'

'Have I forgiven you?'

'I know I've made decisions that you don't agree with and you've felt neglected by me and I've acted out my feelings, but have you forgiven me?'

He puts down his knife and fork and looks over my shoulder.

'I need to tell you something,' he says, and at that moment, Phil Hammond, from the publishing company, comes to stand next to our table with a tall, thin woman.

'Well, hello,' he says, 'fancy seeing you guys here.'

'Hello, Phil. You've met Harvey.'

'Nice to see you again.'

Harvey and Phil shake hands.

'This is my wife, Evelyn. Evelyn this is Harvey and Alison Connaught.'

Evelyn says hello and Phil carries on talking. He's so pleased that I'm home from my trip. 'Welcome back,' he says. 'Did you get the job done?' He doesn't wait for my reply and goes on to tell me I look really well and probably itching to get back on my piano stool.

'So, anyway, it's really good to see you. Fortuitous. There are lots of requests. You know, their people have told our people, they're looking for an Alison Connaught kind of song. Hopefully, you'll find this news inspirational.' His voice ascends in pitch as he finishes that last sentence. He goes on to say that anyway, he won't keep us any longer, our food is getting cold and their table is waiting. He wishes us a lovely evening and he'll be in touch.

I ask Harvey, 'Did you know they were here?'

'No, I had no idea.'

'So what were you going to tell me then?'

'Maybe now's not such a good time,' he says.

'You can't do that to me, Harvey.'

'What do you mean?'

'You know exactly what I mean.'

'This was meant to be a nice romantic dinner.'

'Is that why you wanted to get me drunk, so you could tell me something with impunity?'

'Mellow. I wanted you mellow, so we could have a nice evening.'

'I am mellow.'

'You haven't been mellow since the day Ria... and I

242

can't believe we're arguing again.'

The restaurant's full of couples. Many surreptitious eyes glance our way. Lots of whispering. I take my serviette off my lap and put it on the table beside my plate. 'It might be better if I left?'

'Don't,' he says, grabbing my wrist as I start to rise. 'Sit down.'

He takes a large swig from his wine glass and says, 'We should have talked more about things. The conversation I had with her doctor immediately after, we should have spoken about it in depth.'

'What should you have told me? What should we have said?'

'I don't know. All of it.'

'Why didn't we?'

He takes a big breath.

'I couldn't… I just couldn't.'

He grimaces, puts his hand on his chest and says, 'Heart pain.' His face is white and he tells me his fingers and right arm are numb. I signal the waiter, order the bill, and we leave with my arm around Harvey's back to the kind of attention that's only comfortable when walking down the aisle.

By the time our doctor arrives, Harvey's no longer breathing through pain, although he still looks pale, older and very tired. Dr Tanin tells us it's not a heart attack, a panic attack maybe, or indigestion caused by stress. He administers a tranquilliser. Harvey goes to bed and falls asleep immediately. I, on the other hand, spend half the night stargazing by the window, marvelling at nature's creation of a perfectly round moon, the idea of infinity, the insignificance of me, and in the grand scheme of things, the out-of-proportion concern I have for what Harvey hasn't told me yet.

In the early hours, I receive the call. It's not really a call, not like a voice or a phone ringing; it's more like a feeling that draws me downstairs to the piano room. I'm a little shy, at first. I always am. There's something about Bechs that's like no other piano in the world. The sounds that come out of him resonate so deeply within me. With my hands all over him I have known him to respond with great love and tenderness. And yet, I can't help but recall the more recent dissonance we have made together.

'Hi,' I whisper, cupping his chin with my hand. 'I've missed you and I'm glad to be back.' There's promise in the sure way the stool scrapes forwards with me on it, the confident clap of his lid as I lift it up, and the single singing note we release together. But that's it. I can't even bring myself to play or sing any of the pieces I'm working on. Here in this room, both Bechs and the Muse are continuing to lock me out. There's a tight fist in my solar plexus and if I stay it will only lead to more pain and frustration, so I leave the room and slam the door behind me like a spoilt child.

I fall asleep on Ria's bed and am sad not to find Harvey still in the house when I wake up. So many pieces of me are still missing. Time is not of the essence. Hours slip by as I do inane things like leave dishes soaking in the sink whilst staring out the window. I note the way light changes from phosphorous to pewter and the different shades of browns and greens darkening so early in the day. Birds come and go at the feeder. Squirrels climb and traverse trees. Aeroplanes trail the sky. And here I am, lonely, craving the warmth of a Californian sun and the adrenalin of purpose. Now I've returned, what's happened to my friends? Those beautiful people in their finery who came to our parties. Women draped in expensive fabrics of flattering designs and low necklines, kohled, rouged and lipsticked, hair teased to perfection. Their men with their sun-lamped skin, fluorescent white teeth and soppy smiles. I imagine a conversation:

'Hi Harv, how's Alison doing? Melissa said she hasn't answered any of her phone calls for weeks.'

'She's been away; left her phone at home.'

'Is she back now?'

'Oh yeah, she's back now.'

'And she hasn't turned it on since?'

'To be honest, I really don't know.'

True, I have kept my phone off because in my mind those people were never really my friends. I used to kid myself I don't need them; I have Harv, I have Ri and I have Bechs. Now I avoid them, fearful of conversations over lunch in smart London restaurants.

'How are you doing?

'Well, you know.'

Melissa, Mandy or Angela, looks at me. Strokes my

arm. Says, 'I'm sorry,' with her head tilted to one side, and I want to cry, 'Don't pity me!'

I press the top button on my phone. The screen lights up and tells me I have thirty messages. I haven't the heart for this and press the button again until the screen goes blank.

Looking in the mirror, I ask myself if my trip to the States was just a diversion from a monster thing that has been trying to catch up with me for ever. What is this nebulous anxiety I wake up with most mornings? What is it? The something Harvey was going to remind me of but didn't? That something I should know? That something I still don't know, no matter how hard I search for it?

Sitting corpse-still on a chair in the living room, avoiding the forest painting above the fireplace, I'm thinking maybe Ria had a deep-seated thing born into her genes; a force that took her to the dark side. Perhaps, pursuing stardom, escaping parents and the depressing British winter, was only her conscious objective, when all the while she was subconsciously planning her accidental suicide. I make these stories up. I have a backlog of them. I project them onto the soon-to-be-shown TV series. I try them on for size. Hoping the version that gets aired is one I've thought of already, because I couldn't bear to be amongst the last to know something intrinsic about my daughter. Her fairy-tale success story ending in tragedy will have the public tearful then sighing. They'll take a moment to think about the tragedy, put the kettle on and switch to another channel, whilst I will have to live with it embossed on my heart forever.

I lie in the bath until the water goes tepid. I'm letting out a cascade and refilling from the hot tap until my skin burns. Slipping under the surface and trying not to rise again, I realise drowning is not an easy thing to do. On the merry-go-round of questions seeking answers, I submerge once again.

This is hopeless.

I pour myself a glass of wine, light a joint, pace. It gets late and Harvey's not returned. Drunk and stoned; droned. I pass out on our bed. He comes home, turns on the light, exclaims, 'Oh!' Turns the light off and walks out the room. I turn over.

In the morning, he's gone again before I wake up. This kind of thing goes on for too long. Nothing's changed. Nothing's resolved. Nothing feels any better. My relationship with Bechs has suffered even more. When I'm with him, we go over the same phrase again and again. And the rooms in this house have continual frowns for me.

Hours, days, nights pass. Harvey wafts through our house like a ghost coming and going.

I'm in the kitchen slamming drawers, looking up at the clock, it's six p.m. I have a whole evening and night to get through yet. Harvey's voice catches me by surprise.

'Oh!'

'Don't you ever go out?'

I turn around.

'Just for a walk in the grounds, otherwise no, I do everything online.'

'Avoidance.'

'Both of us.'

'In a way, yes.'

My hands clutch the cold marble edge of the worktop behind me.

'Are you ever going to tell me?'

His eyes plead with mine.

'I don't want to hurt you,' he says.

'This last week has been a joyride, well played.'

'OK then, sit down.'

He pulls out a chair for me from underneath the table. I sit and he stands. It feels like I am the suspect and he is the interrogator.

'You do know that Ria was often on the phone to me, right?'

'Yes, so?'

'She told me things.'

'I know, she always spoke to you about finances and legal issues.'

He's nodding.

'She told me other things too.'

'Like what other things?'

'Things she should have told you.'

All those feelings are resurfacing, the ones I thought I'd dealt with back in Arizona, about not being a good enough mother, not being there for my baby when she needed me the most. Those wimpish tears are welling up in my eyes again, so unattractive, with my nose running and everything.

'Why didn't you tell me, Harvey, about those things?

Why are you only telling me now? Why didn't she?'

'*She* didn't want to hurt you.'

'I know I've always been a bit of a space cadet but all she had to do was trust in me and I would have been there for her.'

'I think she knew that.'

He takes the kettle to the sink and fills it up with water.

'I never ignored her calls to me. If I was busy, I always rang her back. It didn't matter what was going on here, I would have flown to the States if I knew she was in trouble.'

He returns the kettle to its base, flicks the switch. The damn thing growls like a frightened mongrel. An old memory returns. Ria must have been fifteen, sixteen maybe. Whilst she's talking to me, there's a persistent tune in my head. I'm writing it down on the back of my hand. Ria's saying, 'This is important, Mum. Why aren't you listening?' I can see her now, standing before me in white leggings, white collarless shirt, high heels, cascading hair, red lipstick.

'Those shoes are too high and your lipstick's too red.'

'What? Mum? I can't believe you just said that.'

She stamps her feet, carries on talking, but I can't hear her because there are violins, and drums and guitars taking me over. She's crying. She's walking away from me, out through the front door. She's getting into a car and I'm left with an uneasy feeling and the intro to my next hit.

He says, 'She told me about Obermarle propositioning her, and his wife who set her car on fire. She told me about Andy Buckingham, sitting in her living room when she got home from the set one night, suggesting she keep her mouth shut about both those improprieties.'

'And what did you tell her to do about it?'

'I had to leave a meeting to take her call… I told her to phone you.'

'She didn't.'

'I know that now.'

The kettle's done its job despite its protest. Harvey makes an infusion for me and a heavy caffeine-induced brown liquid for himself. He pulls out another chair, sits down in front of me, places a hand on my knee. My eyes smart and my cheeks feel sticky.

'Did you know about her headaches?' I ask.

'Yes, she said she was finding it difficult to work with the pain and over-the-counter drugs weren't helping. I was the one who assured her it was OK to go on OxyContin. That was a long time before she started working with Obermarle, but, oh my God, do I regret that now.'

Silence reigns between us for quite some time. Harvey is studying me with a hard inward gaze as if waiting for me to berate him. I don't say a word.

More days go by, we don't quite touch but we don't avoid each other either. We are in a dance of half forgiveness, half mirroring each other's blame for the most terrible crime.

Harvey's shaving before going to work. When I walk into the bathroom he doesn't turn around.

'Can I tell you something?' I ask.

He's pulling the razor away from his skin midway up his neck. 'Go ahead,' he says, shaking the blades in a sink half-full of foamy water, plop, plop. The little black hairs that escape float to the top like dead tadpoles.

'Ria's psychotherapist told me, she had an abandonment issue, that was all about the men in her life, starting with her father. She didn't mean you.'

'Why didn't you say, her biological father?'

'Because I didn't want to upset you.'

There's a faint clunk as he drops the razor in the sink.

He turns around.

'It seems tiptoeing round each other isn't working,' he says.

'What I wanted to say was, I think she got it wrong. Her father may have left and stayed out of contact, but she never really knew him and you came along soon after, and have always been the best father any girl could have. You were there for her. I'm the one who was preoccupied. That's why she phoned you and not me. It had nothing to do with upsetting me. It's because she'd already got the message that I wasn't available.'

'Is that what you think?'

'Yes,' I say. 'That's exactly what I think.'

'Well, thank you, Alison, for your generosity, but I happen to know that Ria never saw it that way. She didn't want to tell you bad things because she loved you and never wanted to hurt you.'

He turns back to the sink, picks up the razor and continues shaving.

'I'm not being generous, Harvey, I'm confronting my demons.'

He's looking at me in the mirror.

'She cared about your feelings. She fucking loved you. I don't know what else to say.'

'She loved me?'

'Oh, for Christ's sake, yes!'

I'm staring at his reflection.

'And, if she would have come to me instead of you, I would have also told her to go ahead with that prescription. I mean, what did either of us know about opioids back then?'

On his way out of the bathroom he puts his hands on my shoulders. I look to the floor. He lifts my chin. I meet his eyes.

'What?' he whispers, hugging me, his fingers in my hair, his towel dropping from his waist as he pulls away from me. I sink to my knees for him and whatever that makes me, that's what I am.

***

He comes home early in the evenings, pours the wine and chats to me over dinner. We go to bed together. Bechs invites me to his keyboard. We write a song called 'To Love Again'. Lots of bass notes and high notes. My voice shouty at one point, croaky as I bring it down. I never used to sing in such a wild way but this song feels like pure nakedness underneath a waterfall.

Annie turns up at my door with wild garlic, four abandoned quails' eggs and a handful of wild mushrooms. She asks if I've eaten breakfast. I tell her I haven't.

'Why not?' She looks me up and down. 'What's going on?'

'I just wrote a song, straight off, just like that.' I click my fingers in front of her. She blinks, takes a step back, hands me the basket of goodies on a bed of fresh rocket. 'I woke up with it nagging at me to take it to the piano. This day is strange, strange but good,' I say, walking through to the kitchen with Annie trailing behind. 'So what's the occasion? I think this is the very first time you've actually deigned to come inside my house.'

I put the basket on the work surface and note that even though the sky is blanketed by storm clouds, the day feels brighter than it usually does when the sun is blazing down. I hum as I put a skillet on the hob.

'It's good to see you in a good mood,' Annie says.

'Long may it last.'

'Will it?'

'I don't know, Annie. If there's one thing I've learned over the last few years, it's to live in the moment because that's all there is and it's best not to expect anything of the future at all.'

Annie stands beside me, a little awkwardly.

I continue, 'Best not to expect anything of yourself either. I mean, you can't always analyse everything before you do it in life. You just have to play it out and if you fuck things up, well you fuck things up.'

Butter spits and bubbles in the pan. The mushrooms and garlic darken. I put the kettle on and take the red teapot down from the shelf.

'I've been wanting to think of myself as a good mother. But you know what? I wasn't a good mother. I was a shit mother. I am as I am. I can't be someone else. I've had to come to terms with that and it's nearly killed me, but I'm OK with it now. I've also been thinking that there are some people who have wonderful parents, really wonderful parents, who do everything for them and are always attentive, but that doesn't mean that things are going to turn out right for them either. Their kids can also end up on a destructive path. Perhaps, just perhaps, it's a good thing for kids to be let loose at a young age. There are children in India who grow up in slums, they work selling rubbish from a rubbish heap at two years old and then end up with so much street cred, they are able to use it to move up in the world and move their whole family into a house in the suburbs. You know, I read a book like that once.'

I shift the mushrooms and garlic to one side of the pan and crack the eggs on the other side. The kettle steams. I take down two mugs.

'What do you want to drink?'

Annie is staring at me.

'Annie?'

She grabs hold of my wrist and with my free hand, I put out the flame on the hob as she pulls me towards the table. We sit side by side but facing each other.

'I've never told you much about the family I came from.' She flicks her eyes over me. 'That's because I never wanted to remember what I had to go through with my mum out most of the time and when she came home my dad hitting her. Me and my brother never said much, not even to each other. We missed school a lot. The other kids bullied us when we were there. I remember hiding in corners to keep out of sight. One day my father beat my mother so hard she fell and smashed her head against the cooker, denting it. She never got up. I ran, as fast I could with my father yelling after me. He was a big man, a fat man, a slow man and that was the only bit of luck I had. I lived on the streets after that and never went back. I never saw my brother again. I was fourteen.'

'I'm sorry.'

'So am I. Ria's home life was a dream.'

We eat breakfast in silence, and when we finish, Annie tells me she's moving away from her home in the woods. She's met a man, a farmer from across the way, who lost his wife last year. She'd known him forever from his walks in the wood. Whilst I was in the States, he came to the bench to talk to her every day. Like Annie, he has no family he's in touch with. He disappeared when I returned. Yesterday, he turned up again, out of the blue, and asked her to marry him and live in his house. She said, yes.

'But he's not John,' she says.

I take hold of her hand.

2

White feathers. I'm finding them on the mat outside the front door, on the living room carpet and I found one the other day on the roof of my car. It's been over two years, but I think I know why they haven't shown up before. It's because they are also a symbol of peace and I didn't have peace, so they couldn't find me. Am I more at peace now? I guess I must be.

I am drawn back upstairs to the box room in search of photos that encapsulate my little family history. I have no idea what I will disclose up there, if anything.

Standing on a red plastic step, I can't reach the top layer of boxes, so I try to dislodge the one beneath. The higher box, marked RIA, SIX YEARS OLD, slips and hits me on the head, spilling its contents onto the floor: a shower of My Little Ponies in all assorted colours, Cindy dolls with their extensive wardrobes, teddy bears, a dressing-up Princess outfit, video tapes marked 'Annie', 'Cinderella', 'Sleeping Beauty', and a white crumpled, bulging plastic carrier bag that I sit on the floor with and peek into. It's full of loose photographs. A handful of them were of a family holiday in Devon. We stayed in a hotel that hadn't been renovated since the fifties, run by an ex-colonel with white hair, pink face and large belly, together with his wife who wore tight shapeless dresses and a bouffant hairstyle. There's a black and white picture of Harvey taken from down on the beach. He's standing on the cliff edge with his arms open wide as if he's just about to fly. There's a colour shot of me sitting on the sand with Ria standing next to me. I'm looking up at her and holding her hand, an empty bucket is lying in the sand. And here's one where we're having a meal in a pub garden. Ria's sitting on my lap with her arms around my neck, planting a passionate kiss on my cheek, and I'm laughing. That was the year Ria only wanted to be with us, shunning the other kids and refusing to be left in the kids-club in the hotel. Every day, the three of us would climb down over the grassy verge and descend to the cove where we bathed in the freezing cold sea. We'd bury Harvey in sand and he'd break out, marching like Frankenstein as we ran away screaming. Just the three of us for days and days, having left our work lives behind. Harvey and I were totally present for Ria. Yes, fun times, I remember them well.

I sit with my back against the wall and conjure up some of our other family holidays, two or three times a year, every year. I am also reminded of the bedtimes at home, reading stories, family meals, weekend outings…

The doorbell rings. I rush downstairs enthused by my newly excavated memories. I can see who it is by the hazy outline in the obscured glass. I brace myself and open the door.

'Well, hello,' Phil Hammond sings, carrying a huge

bouquet of ivory roses, which he immediately hands over. 'I hope you don't mind. You don't seem to be answering my phone calls and emails, so I thought, I really do need to speak to you, so why not just turn up?'

'No,' I say. 'No, not at all. These are lovely. I'm not sure what the occasion is but thank you. Come through.' I lead him into the kitchen.

He takes off his coat and drapes it over a chair.

'What will you have?'

I place the bouquet on the dresser, put the kettle on and take two mugs and a teapot from the shelf.

'Whatever you're brewing will be fine.'

'Builder's tea, then. Would you like anything with it?'

'No.'

'Sure?'

He walks away, and waits for me to join him at the table in the conservatory. I pour for him. He adds a dash of milk and stirs in a teaspoon of sugar.

He says, 'So, Mrs Connaught, how have you been?'

'I've been fine, thank you, Phil. How have you been?'

'Can't complain, wifey's just found out she's pregnant again.'

'Congratulations.'

'And Hubby? He didn't look too well, when you both left the restaurant a few weeks back.'

'Oh that, yeah, well, he's fine now, thank you.'

'So,' he says, planting his hands on the back of his head, leaning into his chair and stretching. 'I've come to discuss you writing songs for me, well not for me exactly, but you know what I mean: songs that I can put out there and place for you. As I said when we bumped into you, everyone in the industry seems to be craving an Ali Connaught tune at the moment. It's a big opportunity for you to return to the world.' He sits forward and taps the tabletop. 'Now is your time.'

I blow away the clouds coming off my tea.

'Yes, it absolutely could be,' he says, exuding false gaiety.

I take a sip and the liquid scorches the roof of my mouth.

'I think you're right, Phil. Now is my time.'

'Oh good, glad you agree. I'll send you a list of the artists who have requested your unassigned song list, so you know who you're writing for. I can get my secretary to do that straight away, as soon as I get back in the car, but you're going a have to start picking up your emails and answering your phone calls.'

'No, Phil, wait, wait, wait.' I take my mug over to the window and stand with the backs of my legs warming on the radiator. 'I agree that it's my time to go back to work, but writing songs for other people, no, I'm not going to do that.'

'I don't follow.' He screws up his face. 'So, what are you going to do?'

'I'm going to finish what I've already started.'

'Which is?'

'I'm pleased you've asked because it's prompted me to realise what I am doing, what I've been doing for a while now: writing a collection of songs.'

He's wearing an expression of disbelief that I'm going to pretend is wonderment.

'I don't think I'm understanding you. Has someone contacted you directly to write a whole album of material for them? Is that what you're saying?'

'No, no one's been in touch. I'm on a healing mission. These songs are personal, about me, my feelings and experiences. They're not for sale. No one else is going to sing them, initially. I'm writing this collection for myself. To, possibly, include on a singer-songwriter type album.'

'What?'

'You don't think it's possible?'

'No, I bloody don't. I'm sorry to be so abrupt, but there's just no other way to say it: no one's going to invest in a fifty-something-year-old woman making an album, and certainly not one who's never performed her own material before. You might have written songs for the greats, but blimey, Alison, you have no singer-songwriter history at all, not even in your youth. No use kidding yourself, you're not fucking Kate Bush!'

'I know that.'

'So what exactly *are* you trying to do?'

'I can tell you what I'm not trying to do. I'm not trying to do this for acclaim or money, and at this point, I really don't care if I have an audience.'

His voice is steely when he says, 'I see.'

'I can't understand why you're taking this so personally.'

'I'm not taking it personally. I just think you've lost your way, that's all.'

I just smile, there's no use telling him the opposite is true. He makes a big deal out of glancing at his watch.

'I'd better be on my way,' he says. 'I have a meeting in London at twelve.'

'I'm sorry that this has been a wasted journey for you, Phil.'

'I'm getting used to it.'

He's out of his chair, putting on his coat, leaving his tea half drunk. 'It's not what I was expecting to hear, that's all.'

With reference to some of the songs I'd written in the past and how I'd had to persuade him to present them to various artists who he didn't believe would want to sing them, I say, 'So I can still surprise you then.' He flashes cold eyes at me and says, 'Yeah.'

After I shut the door behind him, I go and see Bechs. He's sitting there demurely, a burst of sunlight deflecting off his sleek veneer. I rub his body with my sleeve as if he's an Aladdin's lamp and sit down before him. I'm not sure if it's anger or pure energy that's bouncing off the walls, seeping through my skin and making my spirit rise. 'Well,' I say to Bechs, 'if you want to do it, we're free to spawn whatever we want now. No restrictions, ulterior motive or prescribed direction. We'll just tell it like it is. We don't have to please anyone, except ourselves.'

I glance down at the floor and glinting back at me is the black and white photo of Ria on the beach with its edges now curled. I pick it up, place it on the music stand from where it tumbles and lies with its back on the keyboard; its acoustic bed.

261

She's in on this, I'm sure. The three of us together must out-create ourselves and *that* is the only thing that matters right now.

***

Having made peace with the two men in my life, everything seems easier. Even picking up my emails, which always comes with a huge temptation to 'delete all'. I scroll through the main body of unread messages to an insurance renewal reminder, a demand for information from my accountant so he can fill in my tax return, one from Greg, one from Katie, etcetera.

I open Greg's. It's a round robin. Colour photographs of an eagle circling over a canyon and the sun inching its way over an earthy red horizon. Underneath is the wording:

> *Those that came before still circle our world like eagles, they just no longer exist in physical form. Not having a material body has given them the freedom to see things in a truer perspective. They are aware of the real nature of light and also darkness, and they can influence those of us down here who are open to their wisdom and infinite knowledge.*

Katie's is different. It's in two parts, the top one, sent three days ago.

> *Hi Alison,*
> *Just wondering if you received my last email?*

Sending again, below, just in case.
Best wishes,
Katie

XXXXXXXXXXXXXXX
XXXXXXXXXXXXX

Hi Alison,

I hope you're OK. I'm not sure if you read my last email or the one I sent you several weeks ago, but I just had to let you know that Joshua's been in touch. I hadn't spoken to him since school days. I have no idea how he knew my contact details. I can only surmise that he had access to Ria's computer.

It was really strange, I was expecting a call-back from the plumber. I couldn't believe it when I answered the phone and it was him. He wanted to talk to me about Ria and asked if he could come over. I said no. He sounded so vulnerable, maybe even a bit out of it, but I was feeling sorry for him and agreed to meet him in a pub in the village, one afternoon.

As soon as I put down the phone I immediately had second thoughts and right up to the time I left the house to go, I argued with myself about turning up. In the end, I went along because my mum arrived to look after my baby and because I thought what Joshua was going to say might turn out to be important.

Oh, my God, it was awful. He's... I can't explain how he is. He's still handsome, very, with his dirty blonde hair, massive ice green eyes (in colour, not coldness, although it might be coldness), and that smile as if he knows what's hiding in your soul. His messy clothes and slightly hunched shoulders make him look as if he's still at school. I mean, it's like he hasn't aged. He still looks that young.

I don't think I can write what he told me. I think I'm going to have to see you face to face. I've been leaving messages on your phone. Can you call me when you pick this up...

The date of the email was around the time we'd just got home from the States. I want to call Katie straight away but Harvey is walking in through the front door.

'You OK?' he asks.

'Yeah, I'm fine.'

'You look like you've just seen a ghost.'

His eyes hold mine.

'You sure you're OK?'

'Yes.'

He stands right in front of me, lifts a lock of hair away from my face and whispers, 'It's been a crap day, but you're here, and you smell so nice.' First his lips, then his tongue finds mine. My back's against the wall. My thigh tells me I'm turning him on. A war rages inside me. One half of me wants to break free and grab my phone. The other half is melting. He undoes the top buttons on my blouse. The tips of his fingers brush across the bulging flesh just above my lace bra. Now his mouth is there. I push myself away from the wall. He moves backwards, touching me only with his eyes. I stare back at him, take off my shirt, unhook my bra and throw it on the floor.

***

We are a heap of entangled limbs and Harvey says, 'What do you think about selling the house?'

'I don't know. It's strange, ever since I've come home I've felt the house is shutting me out, like it's not really my home anymore.'

'Maybe that's a reason to move.'

'But there's an energy here that I don't think we could find anywhere else in the world. Why do you ask me that now?'

'Why not now?'

'OK, I understand that, but something must be making you ask me this now?'

He stays quiet, strokes my arm, says nothing. I untangle myself, go upstairs, put on my dressing gown, and set my hair free from inside the neckline. My mind returns to Katie's email and I start searching for my phone. I'm trying to think where I've left it. Harvey comes into the room just as I find it in my bedside table drawer.

I don't want to disturb what Harvey and I have so recently rediscovered and don't tell him about Katie's email.

'Annie Forager's leaving. She's going to marry a widowed farmer up the road,' I say.

'Are you hungry?' he asks.

'Maybe,' I say moving towards him. I lean over and kiss him on the nose. 'But only if you say we don't have to move from here.'

His extended silence drives me mad.

'Harvey?'

'I can't say that.'

'What do you mean?'

'Sit down.'

He pats the edge of the bed beside him.

'I need to make a phone call,' I say.

'OK, that's fine. You can do that later.'

My phone slips from my hand into his.

I sit down.

He laces his fingers with mine.

'We *need* to sell the house,' he says.

'I can't listen to this right now.'

I disentangle my fingers from his and walk out the room.

3

I meet Katie in a coffee bar. We sit side by side on a leather sofa, turned towards each other as if discussing the weather or what we're having for dinner.

'I'm sorry,' she says.

'For what?'

'I'm always telling you horrible things about Ria, but I also feel that I cannot not tell you.'

'It's OK, as far I'm concerned, I want to know whatever it is.' That's what I say, but the truth is I'm feeling like I can't do this anymore.

'Good,' she says, but she doesn't wear 'good' in her expression. She looks troubled and I'm wondering if anyone can tell me anything more troubling about Ria than I already know.

I say, 'I know a bit about Joshua – that he was living in Ria's house in the Hollywood Hills on a come-and-go-as-he-pleased kind of basis. I know Ria had bruises.'

Katie nods. Moves her head in a prehistoric way like a bird. It's a while till she speaks.

'I've already told you that when we were at school Joshua had an emotional hold over Ria. There's not a lot she wouldn't have done for him and he enjoyed lording it over her. It was painful to watch. I can only imagine…' She shakes her head, pulls a tissue from a pocket and wipes her nose. 'He got in touch with me because he was frightened and thought I could help.'

'Why?'

'Someone called him about a television series they're making. They have footage of Ria and Joshua outside her house. They sent him a clip of both of them drinking tequila from litre bottles and looking as if they'd been beaten up. Joshua vaguely remembers that night. He said, Ria was so smashed she fell into the pool and a stranger leapt out of the bushes, dived in and carried her out. "There was a bit of mouth to mouth going on but she was all right," he said. I guess the stranger must have been the person who was taking the video? Anyway, the researcher wanted to know if Joshua wished to make a comment. He told the guy, no, but then he started dumping this whole monologue on me, beginning with "our relationship was so fucked up". He said, they loved each other to pieces but they couldn't live together for one minute and they couldn't live without each other. They argued about everything, the price of meat, the time of day; everything. He said, Ria's success was difficult for him. She had everything and he had nothing. He was like a slave, coming and going at her behest. It made it impossible for him to focus and have inspiration for his own job, so he didn't work a lot of the time. Ria told him the stress of success and Hollywood was a walk in the park compared to dealing with him, but he didn't believe her. He believed, she just said that to hurt him and that they were cool if they took drugs and got drunk together, unless they did too much and then they'd physically hurt each other and that wasn't cool; that's what he said.

'He said she was worse with drugs than he was. He could go for weeks without them but Ria took drugs all the time. She used painkillers to hold down her job as an actor in Hollywood, which she could only do by numbing her pain. When she threw Joshua out the night before she died, she told him he was her headache, that every ache she felt was because of him.

'He slept in the annex and didn't get to see her again. He took a plane back to London the next day and read about her death in newspaper articles the same as everyone else. Now he thinks he's going to be implicated in her demise.

'I told him, but you are implicated, can't you see that? And why have you come to me? I might not have seen her for years but I loved Ria. He then went on to give me this long spiel about how I should help him because we are both part of a family of friends who loved Ria. "We're not mere fans," he said. "We were important to her. Maybe even more important than her blood relations and we should stick together. You need to help me because Ria loved me and that's what she would have wanted."

'Basically, emotional blackmail.

'He wants money, enough to disappear into the depths of South America and live there in comfort for the rest of his life. I told him, "I don't have it to give and anyway, I am not your friend, you have to deserve friends and you clearly don't."

'He slapped a calling card on the table, and told me it was for when I come to my senses and realise refusing him is an act of betrayal to my old, best friend. I was stunned as I watched him walk out. Does he really think I'm going to buy into all of that being a traitor to Ria shit?'

I don't want to have heard this, I want to run away, but even so, I hear myself saying, 'Did you keep the card? Can I see it? Do you have it on you?'

She fumbles in her bag, extracts items one by one and puts them on the low table before us: purse, tissues, keys, iPhone, fold-up umbrella.

'I just shoved it in here,' she says.

Eventually, she pulls out a thick white glossy card with a red flash through its centre, and hands it to me.

Joshua Waters
Computer games developer
Winner of the YGD BAFTA award
US cell: (424) 861 0900
UK mobile: 07959 901 646

I flip the card and find a London address. My heart is beating so fast I think it might kill me but even so, 'Can I keep this?' I say.

'I'd be pleased to get rid of it. Are you going to call him?'

Unable to answer, I make a gesture with my hands.

'Are you going to give him money?'

'I don't know yet,' I say, whilst I see myself punching him in the face in the calm and controlled way that you can only do in an imagining.

When I arrive home, Harvey's there; it's the middle of the day. He runs downstairs in bare feet wearing tracksuit bottoms and a T-shirt, looking worried and mildly stoned.

'We need to talk,' he says, leading the way up into our bathroom where I sit on the edge of the bath and he stands leaning against the sink with his arms crossed. At this point, I believe that if he told me the sun was just about to move close enough to the Earth to scorch us all to death, I wouldn't be surprised.

He says, 'I need to get out of here. We need to get out of here. There are too many memories. It's like the past has overtaken our lives. We're caught up in this net of unhappiness. We need to draw a line under it and move on into the future somewhere else.'

I don't say anything.

'You're not the only one who hasn't been able to function properly. Work's been difficult. Last year I was talked into something which under normal circumstances I would never have entertained. A bit of a gamble but at the time I thought, what the hell… I put the house up as collateral.'

I sit very still trying to make my reaction benign.

'For what?' I ask.

'A movie.'

The confrontational me has a sudden resurrection.

'You invested in the industry that helped end our daughter's life?'

'I didn't think about it like that at the time.'

'How did you think about it at the time?'

'I don't know, it was something upbeat to be involved in. An alternative to real life. A distraction. I was told A listers were going to be the stars and there was no way it could fail. I believed in it because I needed something to believe in at the time.'

'So let me guess, the A listers pulled out and the film bombed.'

'It never even got made.'

'OK, so I have money, I'll just pay back whoever and we can go on living here.'

Harvey looks at the floor.

'Harvey?'

'I don't want to go on living here, it's a living death.'

'Pardon?'

He looks up, opens his palms to the ceiling and says, 'That's it!'

His eyes are sad but I go on.

'Why are you only telling me this now?'

He shakes his head slightly.

I feel his pain.

'You know what, I really don't care anymore. Ria's gone. I'm not working. I've lost everything anyway, so what difference does it make? Just sell the fucking house!'

I stand up and he comes towards me, puts his arms around me, whispers he's sorry into my hair. I pull away and say, 'I'm going back to Arizona.' But I don't go back to Arizona. Despite a temper that keeps erupting like Kilauea, I can't leave him. I stay. As I've said before, whatever my actions make me, that's what I am.

***

Annie Forager is wonderful. The first thing I do, is go out and sit on the bench waiting for her. She comes quickly. She always comes quickly. She has this second sense that knows whenever I need her.

Sitting beside me, holding onto her Moses stick, keeping an eye out for her entourage of various animals milling around, I tell her what's happened and ask, 'What do I do?'

She doesn't blink. She says, 'Talk to him.' Then she just sits there nodding until I slap my thighs and walk off.

So, that's exactly what I do. I go back inside and ask him – no, that's not entirely true – I slam the front door behind me, burst into the kitchen where he's talking on the phone, and hands on my hips, scream, 'So where exactly are we going to live?'

Harvey makes his apologies to the person he's speaking to, ends his call and says, 'I don't really care. Anywhere you like. My flat in London will be available in a couple of weeks, we can go there…'

'OK, I say, slightly relieved that he hasn't suggested Annie Forager's makeshift home in the woods. 'But you have to agree to something, too.'

I tell him what Katie told me about Joshua.

'I need to find the courage to go and see him; you have to help me.'

He holds me and we both cry out our regrets.

4

When I think of phoning Joshua, as I do numerous times a day, my heart flips and my palms sweat. I really don't want to hear what he has to say, but I can't just leave it there. Whatever I think or feel, I know that I must contact him, and yet I tell myself I don't have to do it now, later but not now, and move on to something else.

I find it easier to make radical decisions like selling most of my possessions along with the house. Bechs, of course, will be coming with me. Finally, we are collaborating well.

With candles burning and the scent of Hopi sage, we are making music better than anything I've ever composed before. It's a passionate affair but these brutal songs force their way inside me until I scream or cry them out. Sometimes, I'm so battered by them I can barely whisper their lyrics.

As I step outside the room, exhausted, with one of those soundscapes swirling around in my head, Harvey's standing there. It must be two or three in the morning. Moonlight is spilling in through the obscured glass in the front door.

'What were you just playing?' he asks.

I shrug.

He sits on the stairs, looking away from me towards the front door, but not before I catch an aqueous glint in the corner of his eyes. He reaches out a hand to me, I take it and he pulls me onto his knee. Draping my arm around his neck, somewhat low and croaky, I sing that lament.

***

Annie keeps turning up. I'm not always happy to see her. She interrupts my creativity, prising me away from my piano stool, cajoling me to sift through mountains of things, pack them up, drive into town and give away whatever I'm not taking. She says she doesn't understand this fascination people have with possessions. Don't they understand what slaves they have become? She treats me like a nurse would a grumpy patient. I find it fascinating, the way our relationship has evolved. I always thought I was the one with something vital to give, but on reflection, I was there in my great big house, with my great big life and my songs connecting me up to the world, and feeling great about that. Well, big fucking deal. The Foragers were the ones who continually turned up at our door with offerings of newly laid eggs, wild sorrel and all manner of fresh foods. I was the taker. Me as the giver was just an illusion. I mean, what did I give? Coats and blankets in winter and the wood from the trees, plus permission to live on our land, that's all. I mean, what did any of that cost me? Nothing of myself and that's the hardest thing to give.

We have long and deep discussions about this. We go

over memories and are honest with each other about what we were thinking and feeling at the time. I didn't realise but Annie used to feel sorry for our family when I thought we had everything there was to have in this world. The way she sees it, privilege comes with a false sense of security. She says, the fight to survive, that we are all born with, is like a muscle that if not exercised regularly, loses its tone. Privilege brings weakness. It might feel safe sitting inside a great big house with thick walls, central heating, plenty of food and nice clothes to wear, but when the universe conspires against you, she says, 'It's more tough for you than it is for me. I've been fighting that fight every day of my life, so I'm used to it. But you are like bone china. You broke and had to put yourself back together again and that's really hard, and not something everyone can do.'

Sometimes, I just look at Annie with her aged face and body that in terms of years is no older than mine, and I search her watery eyes for the wisdom she carries in her soul – so undervalued. Most of us are misled, we misconceive what's important and like magpies we stoop to pick up only shiny things.

I tell Annie, I will miss her when I'm living in London. She says, she will miss me too, but I'll have Harvey and she'll have the farmer.

'Will you come and visit?'

'Goats and chickens and the earth will keep me nourished.'

'There are no goats and chickens in a London flat,' I say.

'You have your music.'

'So, will you come and see me?' I ask, probably

sounding a little too desperate, knowing some things don't travel well and fearing that our relationship is one of them.

She stares ahead.

I persist.

'I'll come and visit you on the farm then. You don't have to invite me. I'll just turn up one day because I won't be able to bear not having seen or spoken to you.'

I know she thinks memories are the gifts that should sustain us and we must take what life throws at us, so I understand when she says, 'Sometimes I wonder if life has taught you anything.'

I went all the way to the States to learn from Native Americans about living close to the Earth and how to reconnect with my spirit, when all the time Annie was living only a few hundred yards away, and now I appreciate that I'm losing her too.

★★★

I switch on my phone, as opposed to Ria's. There are hundreds of messages. When I call people back, I seem to be a kind of curiosity person:

Hi Alison, long time no hear.
That's true.
I'm incredibly intrigued, how did you manage to turn your phone off for so long and get away with it?

Hello Alison, I heard you went to the other side.

Well not quite, almost, but not quite.
You didn't go to the other side of the pond and hang out with the Hopi Indians?
Well yes, actually, I did.
We must meet up and you can tell me all about it.

Alison, Alison, Alison, my little space cadet friend.
Really, what makes you say that?
Phil Hammond told me you're now making music you don't want to sell.
I'm making the music I want to make.
How do you do that?
You want to come over and watch me?

I'm aware that with every call I return I'm getting more and more aggressive. I don't mean for my responses to come out that way, they just do. I can't seem to get a grip on it, so in a bit of a frenzy I trash the remaining voicemails. There's only one I don't trash. I centre myself before dialling…

'Katie.'

'Alison.'

'You called?'

'Yes. Can you hold on a minute? I've just got to put my baby down.'

I'm lulled by sweet hushed sounds followed by a cooing response. When she returns, the normal tone of her voice is shocking.

'Thanks for calling back.'

'Is there a problem?'

'No, well, yes, sort of.'

'Go on.'

'Joshua keeps calling. He's not abusive or anything, quite the opposite. He chats to me about his memories of Ria in school. Do I remember the day…? That sort of thing. But he does keep asking if I've changed my mind about the money and I find that a bit of an underlying threat. So, I told Carl, my husband, and Carl got really angry. He insists that Joshua is stalking me and we should phone the police. Are you still intending to get in touch with him, Joshua, I mean?'

'I am but I've been shamefacedly putting it off.'

'Oh!'

'I will phone him.'

'I need to tell you something else. A researcher who's working on a forthcoming television show about Ria has also been in touch with me. She said they'd heard that Ria could have been involved in a cult that started when she was in school and did I know anything about it? I told her, no, absolutely not, I was her best friend and the idea of Ria being in a cult is absurd. She said their contact was rock solid and mentioned something about teenagers self-harming. It might not have been the best thing to do – I've thought about it ever such a lot since – but I ended the call right there. Now, I'm really worried.'

I'm thrown into silence. Katie asks if I'm still there and to convince myself as much as anything, I blurt out, 'If Ria was involved in a cult you would have definitely known about it. As you said, you were her best friend. And sure as hell, if there was any truth in that assertion, I would have known about it too. I mean, a cult isn't something you can belong to secretly, not whilst carrying on a normal life, is it? And the fact that they mentioned self-harming, well, they were just fishing, you know, trying it on. Fuck them. Don't worry about it.'

Now Katie is silent.

'Katie?'

She says, 'Have you ever thought Joshua might be part of a cult?'

PART SIX

That Strange Thing Called Truth

*I believe a total unwillingness to cooperate
is necessary to be an artist.*
Joni Mitchell

1

Sitting on the bed whilst he's getting dressed, I ask Harvey, 'As Ria was in contact with you and you knew about the OxyContin, I suppose you also knew that Joshua was in Ria's life right up until the end?'

'No, I didn't know that.'

'Oh, that's interesting.'

'Why is it interesting?'

'Because I thought you knew everything.'

He looks at me questioningly.

'Do you think Joshua led Ria into a cult?'

'I think you hung out with those strange folk in Hollywood for too long.'

'So you don't think it's possible?'

'No, Alison, I don't think it's possible.'

When I'm alone, I give myself a talking to, face to face, in the bathroom mirror. I tell myself, listen here, this is getting ridiculous. Harvey is right, I'm conjuring up a B movie with a terrible script. Ria was not part of a cult, just as there are no dinosaurs taking massive strides across our front lawn. Get real, and if you can't get real, leave the packing, leave the songwriting, leave everything and go and see this guy Joshua.

I search for the calling card Katie gave me. It's still in my handbag. I have every intention of phoning him. Don't ask me why I decide to sit down on the bed with the card lying benignly in my hands as I stare into space. I'm thinking of Sally Denoué and her Chinese food. I hear her referring to the series she's making as a real-life drama, which means they'll only check things out up to a point then make up the rest.

My mind wanders to a kitchen in Los Angeles where I'm sitting, not eating, next to Andy Buckingham and I can hear her telling me not to make waves for the people in Hollywood. Not in those exact words maybe, but that's what she was saying and I'm starting to turn into a lioness again, because it's OK for her to tell me not to dish the dirt on her people but what about her people dishing the dirt on my family. I bet she thinks that's OK. Only it's not OK as far as I'm concerned. I take Ria's phone out of my bedside table drawer and find myself choosing Sally's number instead.

Strangely, after the way our dinner date ended, she answers straight away.

'Sally, it's Alison Connaught.'

'Hi Alison, yes, I know who it is. How can I help?'

'I was just wondering if this TV series you're making is going to be based on pure fact or if it's going to be part fictionalised?'

'Oh!'

'You seem surprised by my question.'

'No, I'm just thinking how to answer you, that's all.'

284

'Don't you know?'

'OK, look, let's put it this way, at the moment our researchers are looking into different aspects of Ria's life. I don't suppose we're ever going to be one hundred per cent certain about everything, so I imagine we're going to have to speculate about some things but we are going to make sure the script is as accurate as possible.'

'Who are the other producers?'

'There are quite a few of us, actually.'

'Executive producers then?'

'Sally?'

'Andy Buckingham and Catherine Obermarle.'

'That's Austin's wife, right? To be honest, Sally, I'm not happy about the whole thing. I know you can't slander a dead person but have you ever thought about the feelings of the people Ria left behind?'

'Of course! That's what I'm saying.'

'That's not true, what you've just said is you're going to make assumptions and pass them off as fact.'

'This series will be made with the greatest integrity, Alison. I understand that families do get upset about what is broadcast in this kind of production but you have my word, every episode will end with a disclaimer that says it is only *based* on fact.'

'And everyone will be named? Ria and all the people in her life?'

'Look, it's perfectly acceptable to make a series like this, these days. I mean, Christ, there's even been a couple made about the Queen and she's still alive!'

'The thing is, it's not acceptable to me, and if you go ahead with this project, I won't shut up about what I discovered in America, and I'll have no hesitation in telling the world, in my own way, what Andy Buckingham doesn't want me to say.'

She cuts the call.

I jostle Ria's phone in my hands for quite a while then put it down and use one of Greg's meditations to centre myself before phoning Joshua. He answers, too.

'Joshua, this is Alison, Ria's mum. We spoke briefly when I was in America.'

'Mrs C, I'm not feeling well. Can you make it brief?'

'Katie's been in touch. She told me you're desperate to have money so you can disappear.'

It takes a few moments for me to realise he's no longer there.

Harvey walks in. He asks me why I'm so quiet. I tell him about the phone calls and am met with a wall of silence.

'Say something.'

'What would you like me to say?'

'Whatever you want.'

'Then, well done.'

'Are you being sarcastic?'

'You're taking on Hollywood and Ria's boyfriend, but it's not so Ria can rest in peace, is it, Alison? I mean, do we really need this?'

I swallow hard.

'I understand you're still doing this for you. And it's OK, I've decided, it's OK. We made a deal. If you need to do it, do it, you have my blessing, go ahead. But as far as I'm concerned, they can say what they like and that prick, Joshua, he's always been a prick and he can fuck right off.'

2

I've tried calling Joshua again quite a few times but he doesn't pick up. From tomorrow I'll be based in London and I'll think about what to do then. Today, we're moving and I'm sad to be leaving the bench and regular conversations with Annie. Apart from that, I'm not quite sure what I'm feeling.

We've had brilliant times here and those times once created a smile on the face of each room, but those smiles all dropped on the day Ria died, and Harvey's right, we can never get them back here.

I stand, for the last time on the threshold of her bedroom, propping myself up on the doorframe, looking on to a completely empty space that still holds the spirit of a feisty child, an angry teenager, and a loving guest who returned for brief visits during her love affair with Hollywood.

She was sixteen when she received her first acting job. A tender age, only a few years after that day on the beach. And yes, she had a temper. One time throwing a phone at me for I can't remember what and telling me afterwards that it was meant to be a joke. At other times, lashing out with her words. I'm still asking myself questions. Is teenage anger a precursor to painkillers? Was it the need to blame someone else for what was yet to come? Should she have gone to counselling to talk about her issues with me and her biological dad? Or was it simply the presence of Joshua in her life that turned her into the sometimes Naomi Campbell of the British countryside?

None of us knew, of course, that she was on her way to becoming a celebrated actress, who, like so many legends before her, was to live such a short and iconic life. Harvey and I were so incredibly proud of her, right from her first leading role in a school play and for every single performance she was cast in after that. Sitting in the audience of each film premiere or first night on stage, we beamed and we cried. We stood on the sidelines at after parties and got introduced as 'the parents'. We nodded and smiled. We answered questions. We listened to praise and we joked.

'It's such a great honour to meet you both, the people behind – unarguably in my opinion – the greatest female actress of our time. I'm such a huge fan, ever since seeing her first movie Crazy Bitch, Chicken Shit.*'*

'Oh, you remember that? It was a very small part.'

'That doesn't matter, it was a cult masterpiece and she stood out. The scene where she wore that green dress and so perfectly packed that punch. Oh my! There's a gif of her doing it that's become the symbol of fight on every schoolgirl's Facebook page.'

'Yes, I can understand that.'

'Did you know when she was a child that she had such a talent?'

'Anger? Yes. We knew she knew how to do that brilliantly. But other acting talent? We didn't know until tonight, actually.'

'Ha ha ha.'

And when she walked in during those occasions, shaking hands with everyone, looking as natural as pie, as if every eye in the room wasn't focused upon her, that was her best part ever. My champion chameleon, now immortal, captured on celluloid multiple times and stored in vaults inside computers and minds.

I say goodbye to this, her own private room, that still wears her like perfume.

The only things I'm keeping of hers are: A pair of sunglasses, which I'm going to display on the alabaster bust of Venus in the flat. A white T-shirt – with the words, ASK ME ANYTHING YOU LIKE emblazoned across its front – that she wore when she was waitressing a loooong time ago and I now wear to sleep in sometimes. A gold chain with pendants of a bass clef and an Oscar hanging entwined. The painting of the swirl. Photos. A few soft toys that she clung to as a child. The school reports. And that's it. Everything else stays. The new owners have told us they will be applying for a blue plaque.

I text Joshua to let him know that I'm now based in London and think it would be mutually beneficial if we could meet up. He hasn't replied yet. Every time I think about him and what I should do next, I get palpitations. Other than that, the move is easy. Easier than I thought. It's liberating, in a way, to have unburdened myself of most of my possessions. Living in London is a culture shock though. I soon find out how much I'm missing the house and its natural surroundings. It's not the same when you glance out the window and instead of the big sky, all you see is the external wall of an adjacent tall building. Sunlight is missing, so is the space to run without bumping into things. I feel wrong even saying this when there are so many people living on the street here. I find myself stopping to talk to the homeless. Asking them how come they don't have anywhere else to go: Lost jobs. Addiction. Relationship breakups. Breakdowns. Illness. Kids running away from abusive homes. I understand huge loss and give them all money; how they spend it is up to them. This gets discussed at dinner parties where I'm something of an oddity. All of them are hosted by Harvey's work buddies, and now we live in town, I have no excuse not to go.

'You shouldn't give them money, there are charities if you want to help those people,' I am told.

'Maybe,' I respond, 'but I've always found leaving things up to a third party doesn't get the job done. I mean, sometimes it's the middle of winter and they need shelter in that moment, before they freeze to death.'

'But they'll only buy drink and drugs with the money.'

'I don't care.'

'Doesn't it worry you, being taken advantage of and feeding their addiction?'

'To be honest, if I was on the streets I'd also numb myself with drink or drugs – probably both.'

Elbows meet on the table, eyes roll, a disapproving face appears above a bridge of clasped hands.

'Well, I don't agree with it.'

'I'm not asking for your blessing.'

Harvey tackles me in the Uber on the way home.

'You were a bit harsh on Tom.'

'I was only being truthful, and how come everyone has to agree with everyone these days in order to remain friendly?'

'I know but he's a client.'

'What happened to, vive la différence?'

'Did people used to say that?

'You know they used to say that.'

His hand on my knee signals a truce.

Despite what I've said earlier, the flat is lovely. I've always liked it. But it is not my home. Bechs and I still have our own room, which is smaller, boxier, a stranger to all our past songs. We put up pictures: the painting Ria did at school that hung in our previous room; a blown-up version, on canvas, of the black and white photo of Ria on the beach. We light incense and candles. We make our own atmosphere and the acoustics are surprisingly good.

I'm starting to realise I have an awful lot to say. It might not be what others want to hear but that's not the point. The point is to say these things and frame them with their own atmospheric sound. Right now, we're writing the song 'Invisible', and every time I play it – or it plays me, to be more precise – there are musical shifts and word changes and I'm always thrown back to Ria's house in the California hills.

You were there that day, everyday
like a little bird in my ear
whispering things you want me to know

lodged in the hills
up in the sky
inside the walls
inside me
your sign

like the time before you were born
kicking and rolling to be felt, to be heard
everywhere we go, we go together
invisible
never closer

The song goes on… It's not finished yet.

The move also brings us good luck. Harvey arrives home one day, calls out, 'Hello, where are you? Al, you home?' I'm reluctant to answer as I'm so completely lost in the building of sonic architecture. But there's such a positive uplift and an excitement to his voice, I find myself shutting the piano lid and walking out the room. He takes my hand, pulls me along the hallway. 'I need to tell you something,' he says. We commune in the bathroom, as always. Old dogs and new tricks, you know what they say. He's leaning against the sink.

'Al?'

I sit on the toilet, lid down, and nod.

'You know, it's the third thing I was just waiting to go wrong, first Ria, then the movie, but it hasn't happened that way; it's turned out to be something *good*.'

'That's because the movie was the third thing.'

'What?'

'Nearly losing our marriage was the second.'

'But we're still together.'

'Yes, I know, but...' I raise my hands in what might look like surrender, but is actually impatience. One half of me wishing to return swiftly to Bechs. The other half vowing not to let music come between me and the person I love.

'I'm sorry, just tell me the good news. OK?'

He walks out the room and leaves me sitting there, wishing I hadn't said that uppity 'OK'. Wishing I could just sit back and listen to others, wide-eyed and wondering as I take it all in and learn something. Instead, I fill myself up with a bout of self-loathing and regret, until he comes back, carrying two flute glasses and a bottle of champagne. He pops the cork into a tea towel, pours, chinks his glass against mine and says, 'Now, will you bloody well listen?' and in that moment, I love him very much.

He sits on the edge of the bath, right beside me and says, 'I'm just going to say something first, before I tell you what I want to tell you, because I know you're going to interrupt and ask why I didn't fill you in about this as a possibility before, and the answer is because I didn't view it as a possibility. So, if you'll just keep quiet for a few moments, I'm now going to give you the good news.'

First, he takes a gulp of wine, then he says, 'At the same

time as I invested in the movie that went wrong, I also bought shares in an iffy lithium mining company. At that time, the shares were a couple of pence each and I fully expected to lose the few hundred pounds I'd invested, but today, those shares went through the roof and I sold them all. So, I thought, what about we do something in Ria's memory with the money?'

He beams. I take a sip from my glass. The bubbles smart in my nostrils. Tears threaten to burst through the corners of my eyes. I pinch my nose. When the pricking sensation subsides, I say, 'Yes, babe, that would be lovely. Why not?'

★★★

I get an email from Phil Hammond. I sent him a demo of a couple of the pieces I've been working on. To be honest, I never expected to hear back from him. He asks if I will meet him for lunch in The Ivy tomorrow at noon. He says the recording part of the business has expressed an interest in investing in this project but he would need to have a chat with me before setting up an appointment with them. He tells me to bring my business manager. I phone Harvey straight away.

In the morning, I take extra time getting ready, not that I think my appearance will make any difference to what Phil has to say to me, but hoping to make a coat of armour out of tonged hair, natural make-up, thin kohl lines, mascara, white trousers, gold silk blouse – and high heels, of course.

Phil's already at the restaurant when we arrive. He has his arms folded on the table and leans forward, towards us, as he tells Harvey how fond he is of me and how great I'm looking for my age. Then he smirks, tips his head towards Harvey, and says, 'You better watch out.'

'All right I will,' Harvey says, placing his hand on my thigh.

Phil clears his throat, clicks his fingers at the waitress and orders champagne, which I believe is a bit previous. Then he picks up the menu, pushes his glasses further up the bridge of his nose and says, 'Choose anything you like.'

We eat Dover sole with winter leaf salad, and converse only in small talk. After we lay down our knives and forks, Phil says, 'This project you're working on – Alison, I really want to help you find an audience for it. Our recording division likes the concept as I sold it to them.'

'And how did you sell it to them?' I ask.

'Well, that's why we're here. We need to agree on a few things. First, can we agree that even though you are a very successful songwriter, you are not a household name?'

I lean my head to one side.

'I mean, if it wasn't for the sad news about Ria,' he adds.

I put my hand on the table as a precursor to standing up and walking out. Harvey's hand falls off my leg, then shoots up onto it again, pressing down firmly on my thigh bone. I look towards him questioningly. He gives me a hard stare. I succumb and remain seated.

'OK, we agree with that,' Harvey says.

Phil takes a deep breath.

'I've been in touch with a group of highly influential people who have a very impressive list of financial backers and they are in the process of making a television series about Ria.'

'Yeah, we're aware,' Harvey says, his hand still a clamp on my thigh.

'Oh, you are, well that's a good thing.'

'Please, go on,' Harvey says.

'They'd be interested in an album, composed and sung by Alison to, in some way, be associated with the programme.'

'OK, that's it,' I say, this time managing to get up.

'Excuse me,' Harvey says, and follows me to the ladies.

'What's the matter with you?' he asks, catching up with me.

'Nothing.'

'What do you mean, nothing? You're being aggressive.'

'I don't wish to be associated with their television programme.'

'Why not?'

'They can say what they like about Ria. They can edit things. They can twist things. They can make out like she was in a cult. And you want me to get on board with that?'

'Well, maybe if we get involved, we can have an effect on what they put out.'

'Harvey, you're being very naïve.'

'And you're being defeatist.'

I breathe in deep.

'Look,' he says. 'We, you, don't have to sign up to

anything, but when you shut the door on this deal, at least be in receipt of all the available and relevant information.'

I lay my hand on my forehead and say, 'OK,' and we both return to the table.

Harvey urges me to sit next to Phil on one side of the arced banquette, whilst he sits next to him on the other side, forcing Phil to be in the middle. Phil shuffles towards me. He says, 'I've already asked for the bill and I get the picture.'

The bill comes immediately, and as Phil settles it, Harvey says, 'Thank you, Phil, nice lunch.'

Phil digs his fists into the red leather seating to either side of him, but we are blocking him in, so he can't get out.

Harvey turns his whole body towards Phil and says, 'We understand the situation and would like you to arrange a meeting with the record company, and if possible, a representative of the people who are making the documentary.'

'It's not a documentary,' I say.

Phil says, 'Are you serious?'

'Absolutely.'

They lock eyes.

I leave them to it and wait on the pavement looking out for our Uber.

That evening, when Harvey goes off to play backgammon with a friend, I take the car out of the garage and drive. I sit outside the address on the flip side of Joshua Water's calling card. It's a block of flats in Ealing. I sit there for some time, looking up at yellow lights beaming out from the fifth-floor windows, and I imagine what Joshua might be doing up there. I think of confronting him in person, which is something I know I'm going to have to do, but my legs are water just at the thought. Nevertheless, I place another call to him which once again, to my cowardly relief, goes unanswered.

As my imagination goes into overdrive, I realise I know so little about this man who mesmerised my daughter for so many years. Stories of wild behaviour, drugs, cults, abuse, are all such typical fame-ridden tales, I wonder how much of what I've already been told, really happened. How much truth will be embellished to make more interesting television. How much spite will be invested in the plot by the likes of Obermarle's wife. And whilst the whole world waits eagerly for that day and time of the week when the next sensational episode gets shown, it will be dreaded by this particular audience of one, and the someone else who lives in that building over there.

The day Harvey threw that boy out of our house, I was in full agreement with him. Stung by Joshua for doing wrong by our daughter, I wanted him remorseful, I wanted him shamed. We kidded ourselves that that was a good way of dealing with 'the boy' and Ria's ridiculous fascination with him. It didn't deal with anything. It didn't even scratch the surface. So easy in those days to go back to songwriting and lovemaking, and tossing statements at Ria that she wasn't going to abide by.

'I don't want you to see that boy out of school.'

'Don't let him, or anyone else, ever treat you like that again.'

'You tell him, from me, that if he ever attempts to sweet talk you, his life won't be worth living.'

Stupid, empty, phrases. What were we on? As parents we think we have some control over our children but once they are allowed to leave the house alone, we have no authority over them at all; the only thing we can do is delay what they're going to do anyway.

I start the engine and, on the way back to the flat, I realise it's good that we had to sell our home, that symbol of false security that drugged me insane. Would it have been possible to have changed things? Sliding doors? Maybe, if we were different people. But I know if I had my time all over again with the same knowledge I had then, I would have done the same things. It doesn't make me forgive myself for any of my wrongdoings but I'm not allowing myself if-onlys; hindsight is not clever, it's just a tantalising dream.

3

Annie is getting married to the farmer. Harvey and I are amongst a handful of guests sitting in the church waiting for the bride and groom to arrive. The organist is playing 'For the One', a love song I wrote for a boy band back in the late nineties. I'm touched that Annie has chosen it. I wish my heart would sing for this lovely, happy occasion, but there's an excruciating numbness there on the left side of my chest. All I can think of is why, and how come, Annie is walking down the aisle and not Ria. How come my daughter is not alive to do this and others are. I'm not proud of these thoughts. They just come, uninvited, to taunt me.

It's very surreal. Annie's given up her bobbled jumpers and her long flowing skirts for a salmon-pink tailored suit, looking every bit like Jackie O, if you can imagine that with flat shoes, a ruddy complexion and salt and pepper hair pinned up in curls. A young man dressed in black walks her down the aisle. I presume it to be someone who works on the farm. Her intended turns around and I am surprised by his looks, so handsome though also ruddy with a rugby player physique.

The service is short and to the point. I can hear Annie

demanding, 'no airy-fairy nonsense' and there is none. At the end of the service, they give each other a hugely passionate kiss which takes me by surprise. On the way out, the couple stop and talk to two people, both men, sitting in the front pew. Then they come over to us, and Annie introduces her husband. I would have thought the transition from do-it-yourself eco house to brick farmhouse was difficult, but she makes it look effortless and although it seems strange to me, she wears it brilliantly.

'Andy, this is Alison and Harvey Connaught. It was their land I was living on.'

'Yes,' he says, 'I've heard a lot about the two of you.'

'Very big congratulations Andy and nice to meet you,' Harvey says, planting his slim hand in Andy's large, fleshy one.

I'm a little emotional and although Annie's not the kind of girl who likes hugs, I give it a try.

'All the love,' I say, rubbing her back, before she quickly pulls away and smiles her crooked smile.

We make our way to the The Horse and Dragon, our old local, where Harvey and I have only been a few times before, although we always meant to go more often. It hasn't been renovated for what looks like well over a century. Exposed beams, oak bar and uneven floorboards.

The other three guests, all male, are Andy's friends. It's very much an us and them kind of affair. Boys standing over there and girls sitting down. I take Annie's hand in mine, which she allows, only briefly, and we talk as we've always talked.

'Harvey seems to be fitting in nicely over there.'

'Traitor,' I say.

Annie shoves me with her elbow.

'How's it going?' I ask.

'It's not so very different – although I can see myself growing soft with the warmth and the kitchen and everything. We make a good team.'

'I love you, Annie,' I say, and I mean it, although I think I might have drunk too much alcohol on an empty stomach.

'How are you doing?'

'Oh, you know, carrying on.'

She nods, and it's like we've said everything there is to say. Then I think of something else, something important.

'What can I buy you for a wedding present? I'm struggling to think of something you might want.'

'Good enough that Harvey's bought all the drinks.'

'But I want to give you something meaningful.'

'You already have.'

'What's that?'

She looks me in the eye and says, 'It was enough of a job helping you get rid of your stuff, the last thing I want to do is start accumulating my own.'

Outside, it's just starting to snow and there's a cold draught coming through the Georgian window to my right. I pull my coat up over my shoulders and look towards our posse of men.

'Do you think we ought to mingle?'

'Nope. Andy understands I have nothing in common with most people.'

'I'm flattered then.'

She laughs.

My phone rings. I excuse myself and scramble for it in my bag.

'Hi, Katie.'

'Hi Alison, look, um, I'm being hassled by my husband to phone you. He wants to call the police. It's um, Joshua, he's phoned again, about the money. I really don't understand it, I mean, why me? I was just wondering, 'Did you phone him?'

'Yes, of course I did, several times but he doesn't answer. The thing is, right now, I'm at a wedding.'

'Oh, I'm sorry to disturb, but things are getting a bit desperate around here. It's like he's leapt out of the past to haunt me.'

'I understand and I have every intention of dealing with it. Just give me another couple of days.'

'All right,' she says, but she sounds disappointed as if she doesn't believe me. 'Bye then.'

'Bye.'

Annie's staring at me as I return the phone to my bag. I avert my gaze to the window where a squirrel scuttles across the outside sill. She should be stored away somewhere with her nuts, by now. I guess she's trying to tell me that I, too, should come out of hiding and be brave.

'I'm seriously going to have to confront Joshua, although I'm not quite sure how I'm going to go about it.'

Annie sits back and places her hands in her lap.

'Very soon,' I add.

★★★

Days pass and I'm imagining myself storming through Joshua's building and banging with my fists on his front door. I'm feeling guilty about being unsuccessful in getting in touch with him, but in reality what more can I do?

Right now, we're in this office, Harvey and I. It's a cloudy day but there's still enough natural light pouring in through floor to ceiling windows. There's an abandoned desk, and on the other side of the room, a couple of sofas facing each other like a stand-off with the coffee table in between. A bookcase lines one wall and there's three execs scattered, nonchalantly, as if not sitting at a boardroom table makes them look cool.

We're waiting for someone else to arrive. Someone from a film company; a representative of the people who are making the television series.

'I hope he's got the day and time right. He's not answering his phone,' Sammy says. He's the one wearing a navy tweed jacket with short, dark curly hair, leaning up against the bookcase. This is his office. He's an accountant, apparently.

'Maybe he's got lost up a lens.' This comes from a young guy sitting on one of the sofas. He's a junior A and R person from the music company.

'Not funny,' Phil says. He's perched on the arm of the sofa next to Harvey and myself, opposite the young guy.

'I can't understand it, they're the ones who got excited about this project. Apparently, this Lenny, has never been outside America before,' the young guy continues.

'Nevertheless, I hope when he arrives, you'll remember what you learnt in charm school. You did go to charm school?' Phil says, rolling his eyes.

Harvey and I just sit there like two stuffed dolls. I'm thinking, why the hell did I let Harvey talk me into this circus?

Finally, after another half an hour, Lenny turns up. He's very tall, slim, wearing a well-cut dark suit, black T-shirt, and a baseball cap which he immediately takes off, letting his dreads tumble down around his shoulders and hang next to his caramel skin. He has the most startling blue eyes.

Introductions take place. Lenny apologises for being late, and perches on the corner of the desk on the other side of the room. I'm starting to get used to these us and them situations.

There is talk about Lenny's flight, where he's staying and what he thinks of London so far.

Phil says, 'Thank you for coming all this way to discuss Alison's project.'

Lenny says, 'No sweat, man. We think it will be a good idea for Alison's music to be part of the show. We're familiar with her work. We've listened to the great songs she wrote in the past and the dope recordings by cool artists and we've heard the demos, so we're satisfied she can sing. From our end, we're all good to go.'

'But these songs I'm writing now are nothing like the old songs,' I say.

Lenny purses his lips.

'They're very personal.'

He nods.

Harvey gets up and stands next to the accountant. Addressing Lenny, he says, 'Alison is concerned that this television show will be exploitative. What can you offer us in reassurance that that's not going to happen?'

'Well,' Lenny says, shaking his dreads. 'My understanding is that if we sign a deal today those technical issues can be ironed out later.'

'So, what were you sent over here to discuss?' I ask.

'That some of your earlier works should be included in certain scenes. We're hoping to choose one of your current songs as the main title theme for the whole series. We believe the fact that these songs are personal will make whatever one we choose even more pertinent to the show.'

'I'll only do it if I can have creative control over what happens to my music.'

'Maybe we could arrange for some kind of low-level joint decision making,' he says.

'Will I have a say on how my daughter is portrayed?'

'Mmm, my brief is to give you this.' He holds out a brown paper envelope. 'I think you already know Andy Buckingham. She'd like you to come over to the States as her guest. She offers you first class travel and accommodation and all expenses paid so she can explain how your contribution can be a mutual asset.'

I don't take the envelope. The atmosphere in the room

stiffens. The record company boys all look to Phil whose face has turned into a ripe peach.

'Huh, I thought I was going to go back home with smiles and a signed contract,' Lenny says.

The coward inside me has my heart pumping ten to the beat and my legs weakening. I touch the feather at my ear, stand up, walk over to Lenny, look directly into his marvellous eyes, and say, 'It was really nice to meet you, Lenny, and for you to have come all the way across the Atlantic with this offer is something I really do appreciate. But I'm also going to have to apologise because I don't want to waste any more of your time. From what you've already said, I don't think that being involved with this television series is going to work for me. Please extend my apologies to Andy Buckingham.'

There is an expression on his face of, 'I can't believe you've just turned down the only chance an old dame – who has never made a record in her life before – is ever going to get to have a massive hit, but hey, that's exactly what you've just done.'

Sensing an office full of eyes on my back, I turn around.

'Thank you everyone for helping to make this meeting happen. I'm sorry that it didn't work out,' I say.

Harvey follows me out of the office. He puts a hand on my back and ushers me down a sweeping staircase and through the glass front doors.

In the car going home, he's driving. 'That was brave, Al,' he says. 'You were very gracious; it was sexy.'

I'm embarrassed by my smile and look to the passenger's window.

'If I hadn't done that, what would you have done?'

'I would have steamed quietly. Made sure, in the most diplomatic way I know how, that no deals were signed or agreed to there and then. I would have left the whole thing pending, so you and I could discuss it when we got home.'

'Can we discuss it now?'

'All right.'

'Would you consider investing in my album with the money you've earned on your shares?'

'I was thinking of something…'

Ria's phone rings in my bag. I think it might be Katie and I don't want to answer it, but then I change my mind and fish it out.

MISSED CALL

JOSH

I hit call return.

'Joshua, it's Alison Connaught. I saw you just called.'

'Mrs C, why didn't you tell me that Ria's house is being sold?'

He's his own loudspeaker; I have to hold the phone away from my ear. 'Hey Joshua, thanks for phoning me back, although on the subject of Ria's house, that's no business of yours.'

'You knew I had things there.'

'I did?'

'You knew I stayed there. Don't play games with me, Alison.'

Harvey glances over at me.

'Joshua, calm down. There are things I want to talk to

309

you about, too. I think we should meet.'

I can hear him faffing about at the other end.

'Well?'

'Come over here then, I'm in now. I know you've got my address, Katie told me she gave you my card. And Mrs C, I don't want Ria's dad here. I don't trust him. Come alone.'

The screen goes blank.

'Did you hear that?' I say.

'I did. You going?'

'Yes.'

'I don't care what he says, I'm coming with you.'

'No, I don't want you to.'

'You're kidding?'

'No, you'll get all heavy and I need to talk to him.'

He glances at me again.

'Will you take me there, though?'

'Like your chauffeur?'

'Mmm, more like my bodyguard. I'll keep a live call to you in my pocket. If I'm in trouble, I'll press all the buttons.'

'Alison, that's ridiculous. I'll drive you there and drop you off, if that's what you want.'

'You won't wait for me?'

'Of course, I'll bloody wait for you.'

I tap his number on my phone and show him the screen; he accepts the call on his.

'Don't cut me off,' I say.

***

I'm expecting Joshua's flat to be a rundown tip in an ugly block. The kind of modern block that got built in the seventies, a deteriorating tin can with windows. That's how it looks from the outside but not when you enter. There are windows between each layer of thick, shiny metal. Silver-framed paintings hang on those impenetrable walls. Black marble floors. Polished silver lift. A concierge who questions who I am and who I'm visiting, makes a call, then asks if I need some help getting to number fifty-five.

As I make my way through the arteries of that building, I am full of adrenaline and determined to get answers. I believe I will know if he's lying. I find my way without direction, not knowing why plush surroundings should make me feel any easier, although somehow they do, a bit. He answers the door, and yes, Katie is right, he is very beautiful, in the way Kurt Cobain, Michael Hutchence and Jim Morrison were beautiful.

'Hi, come in,' he says, immediately turning around and walking away from me.

He's bare footed, wearing pyjama bottoms and a grey T-shirt. I want to say, 'You really didn't have to dress up for me,' but I hold back and follow him through to the living room that, at first glance, appears to me to be uncannily like a shambolic replica of Sally Denoué's apartment in New York. The view from the stretch of windows is very different though: winter trees, red rooftops, dark clouds.

'Wow,' I say. 'This is a great place.'

Joshua looks at me and grunts, 'Do you want to sit down?'

I don't take my coat off. Neither am I invited to, and when I perch on a large brown footstool, I'm making sure not to sit on my phone and that it doesn't fall out of my pocket onto the floor. Meanwhile, he turns his computer chair away from the wall and sits facing me.

'You want to talk?' he asks.

'I think we both do.'

'You start.'

He tucks a stray lock of hair behind one ear, folds his arms and sits back in his chair.

'I have many questions, but the first thing that comes to mind is with an apartment this grand, you must have money?'

'That's very personal.'

'So are all the distress calls I'm receiving from Katie. She tells me you're pressing her to give you enough funds to run away on.'

'You want to hear my truth, Mrs C? It's all gone.'

'Call me Alison.'

'OK, Alison. I had money. Yeah, maybe I even had more money than Ria. We were equals. Equals.'

'That's interesting, about you being equals.'

'Is it?'

He's nodding at me.

'Yeah, it is, because that's not what I've heard. I've heard you were a bit of a Svengali, a cult master, a fucking girlfriend basher,' is what I don't say, because I haven't come here to speak, I've come to listen.

He's still nodding when he says, 'You want to know why I was upset about you selling the house without telling me? Because I paid for the annex. I have a stake in that property and normally, I wouldn't care, but I haven't worked a day in nearly four years; since a year before she drowned, to be exact.'

That word drowned does something to me and instead of asking what happened that night, it's a while before I say, 'I've also struggled to work.'

'So you know.'

'Yeah, I do.'

He gets up and walks behind me. With a hand on the outside of the coat pocket where my phone lies, I swivel round to face him. I have no idea if my phone call to Harvey is still active, or if he can hear what we're saying.

Joshua picks up a remote that's lying on the floor. He puts it on a side table on his way to the wall of windows where he gazes out upon the sudden burst of orange sunlight that's hauling in the early evening.

'There's a Mercedes down there. Is that your car?'

'Yes.'

'The guy standing next to it, under a streetlamp, with a phone to his ear, must be Ria's dad. He turns to look at me. 'Except he wasn't her dad, was he?'

I keep quiet.

'Anyway, he's old now and I'm still young, relatively. That makes me happy.'

I say nothing.

313

'It's the dad thing. Ria and I both had a dad thing. Ria's real dad slunk away whilst she was sleeping, never to be seen again. Isn't that right, Mrs C?'

I nod.

'She blamed you for kicking him out and replacing him with a doppelganger.'

'Harvey's hardly a doppelganger.'

Joshua puts his hands up.

'I'm just saying what she said.'

He's on the move again. Picking up things that are scattered around and putting them down elsewhere. A key from an ashtray to its place in a window lock; a book with a cartoon cover from a table to a shelf; an empty glass from the floor to his desk.

'My old man wasn't a good guy either and he was also replicated. Ria and I both had issues about our fathers. Nightmares. I'd wake up some nights drenched in sweat and stinking of fear and she'd hold me. Those dreams, I still have them. All grey with a yellow sky, lots of rocks and fog and people with ugly faces and rats in their hair, holding scimitars to my throat.'

He slumps down in an armchair. Picks up the remote from a side table and places it between the cushion and arm of the seat. Switching on a reading lamp, he encases his face in an orb of yellow light.

'Yeah, we became custodians of the night. She used to say that a lot, Custodians of the Night. It's my award-winning game, based on us and our nightmares. To outwit the enemy you also have to outwit yourself.'

314

I raise my eyes and lower my chin.

'Aren't you going to ask me how you can do that? Outwit yourself?'

'No.'

He points the remote at me, screws up his eyes, and says, 'Pow!'

There's a muffled voice coming from my pocket.

Joshua's looking at me fiercely.

I take the phone out, put it to my ear.

He drops the gizmo into his lap.

'Alison, what's going on?'

'I'm OK.'

I look away from Joshua's stare and notice how this flat actually differs greatly from Sally's. There's no open-plan kitchen and the door left ajar at the far end of this room reveals a hallway. I get up and make my way into that hallway.

'What's happening?' Harvey insists.

'Nothing. Everything's fine.'

I put the phone back in my pocket and stand on the threshold of the living room and ask, 'Where's your toilet?'

'Second door on the left.'

I make my way there. Lock the door, put the seat down, pull the phone from my pocket, and ask, 'You still there?'

'This is stupid.'

'You still OK with this line being active?'

'OK, is not exactly the word I would use.'

I put him back in my pocket, return to the living room, lean against the wall, coolly watching the way Joshua

315

moves, sits, stands, walks around like a bee buzzing for pollen.

I'm thinking, how do I engage with this creature and get him to calm down? How do I get him to give me the missing piece of my Ria puzzle? The something, I sense, only he knows.

'I didn't think you'd come here,' he says, searching for something underneath an armchair and looking at me over one arm.

'Maybe I wouldn't have if you hadn't blackmailed Katie. Why Katie? Why not me or someone else?'

He's on the move again and takes down a piece of electrical equipment from a shelf, goes over to his desk and starts taking it apart.

'No,' he says, not looking up at me.

'Why Katie?' I ask again.

'She's a link in the chain of friendship.'

'Don't you know that you don't inherit friends?'

I push myself off the wall and come to sit next to him on the giant footstool.

'Why are you stalking her?'

He doesn't answer.

'She has a baby and a husband and a completely separate life from yours and what was Ria's. You must respect that. We must respect that.'

'We?'

'Yes, we, that's part of why I've come here, to protect the innocent and Katie is innocent in all of this.'

He doesn't look up.

'Were you there the night Ria died?'

'Yes.'

'Was anybody else there?'

He shakes his head.

'Did you murder her, Joshua?'

He doesn't answer.

'Did you murder my daughter?'

'I wasn't in the house when she died. We had a fight. I was in the annexe.'

'Did someone else come there that night?'

'No, I would have heard them arriving.'

'But supposing they were hiding already? Supposing you didn't hear them arrive?'

He says nothing.

'So if you're innocent, why are you so restless and frightened?'

'I never said I was innocent.'

He's staring down at the piece of equipment he's stopped working on. In one shocking moment he gets up off his chair, goes to the other side of the room and sits on the floor, back against the wall, legs out in front of him.

'Well?' I ask.

'You're not my fucking shrink,' he says.

I don't feel like a shrink, more like a parent talking to an indignant teenager.

'Katie told me the television people approached you about the TV series on Ria.'

'They did.'

'They think you led Ria into a cult.'

Joshua lets out a puff of air and widens his eyes as if to say that assumption is ridiculous.

'You think you'll be safe in South America?'

'Yeah.'

I wait in the buzzing silence and eventually, he says, 'You don't know those people.'

'Yeah, I do, actually, I do.'

'They have the means and the power to throw me to the dogs.'

'Not just you.'

He's picking at his jeans.

'You think their prime time TV series is going to be respectful and sensitive to everyone but you?'

'They're not going to blame you though, are they, for Ria's death? And yet you're every bit as guilty.'

I choose to ignore his words and go on, 'I don't know what they're going to do, and nor do you, but I can tell you one thing, they're going to up the anti in every which way they can because the only thing they're going to be faithful to is sensationalism, and if everyone is shocked and talking about us, they'll be smiling all the way to the bank, that's for sure.'

He's nodding.

'And there's nothing we can do about it. We just have to wait and see where that leaves us, all of us, in our own separate ways. And if you were to run away to South America then that's what they'll say about you. It won't make you any safer. The world is a very small place these days.'

I wish I could say that our conversation ended there, that I take his momentary silence and passivity as a cue to walk out and trust that he won't contact Katie anymore; job done. I even see myself stepping out of the lift, walking onto the street with a bracing wind in my face, and receiving a loving heroine's kiss from Harvey – still waiting for me – as I step into our car.

But that's not what happens. Joshua raises his head and I focus on the twitch in his left shoulder as he says, 'You think you know everything.'

He stands up and comes slowly towards me. Peering down on me, he asks. 'Do you know everything, Alison?'

I mouth 'no,' and shake my head.

'Such a clever lady. At the top of your profession for a very long time. Greatly respected, but the way you dealt with things when it came to Ria was not good, was it? You made her feel like she was really small.' He's showing me his thumb and forefinger with little space between them. 'Like so small, I don't think you even saw us from up there on your artistic cloud. You shut her out.' He clicks his fingers in front of my eyes and I flinch. His eyes are half closed now and his head turned slightly, only slightly, to the left. Then he looks to the floor and I can't see his expression because his hair has fallen in curtains on both sides of his face. 'Yeah,' he tells the wooden planks. 'You shut us both out.' He's reeling like a bee drunk on sap now. I've heard enough. I seriously want to get out of there.

'I'm going home.'

I stand up.

'You see,' he says, coming right up close to me, so close I can smell his sweat and see the creases that reveal his youthful looks to be an illusion. 'We were all playing; you, me, Ria, and everyone else. It filled up the nasty time so we didn't have to come face to face with ourselves. Our distractions became real life.

'"You're like my mother," she used to say and do you know why? Because I liked to lose myself too, only I found my music between women's legs, many women, the more the better. And yet. Ha! She'd say, go and I'd go. She'd say come and I'd run to her. When she wanted me to get high with her, I would get high with her. So over the top high we would shout and scream and blame and tear the clothes off each other and fuck without heart or mind and then she would goad, and she would hit and punch me, and when I was defending myself from your daughter's violence, where were you hiding, huh, Mrs C?'

I strike my phone against his cheek bone. He squeezes and twists my wrist until I drop the phone. He stamps on it, hard, crunching technology beneath his bare heel.

'If they ever say I killed her, remember, you're hardly blameless, Alison.'

I widen my eyes so wide and spit on his cheek with all the venom I can muster. His blood and my saliva, everything bleeding into everything else.

I yell back at him, 'No one's perfect. She loved me and I always did the best I could!'

He captures my other wrist and both my hands are in his grasp now. He breathes out and through a half-laugh stares directly into my eyes and calmly says, 'Yeah, me also and she loved me too.' We are stopped, two ravaged people standing together in this room with more in common than we would like to think. My fingers tentatively find his face. I am looking deep into his eyes, seeing not only myself reflected there, but the whole cast of characters in the drama of Ria's life. I break down and Joshua holds me.

In his dishevelled barefoot state, he puts an arm around my shoulders, limps me out of his flat and through the common parts of the building, finally delivering me to Harvey who is still waiting for me outside.

We sit a long time in the car in silence with the engine running, Harvey and me. Eventually, I tell him what happened. He reaches across, puts one hand on my knee, and we both smile. He turns the key in the ignition.

'Where to now?'

'Perhaps…'

I stare through the windscreen ahead.

'Perhaps what?'

I turn to look at Harvey.

'The Caribbean?' I say.

If you enjoyed *Song for Ria*, you may also like
Michelle Shine's debut novel, *Mesmerised*.

Read on for a taster…

January 1863

I buy pure phosphorus from an old alchemist who lives in a slanted house on the hill that leads to Montmartre. His wife, Madame Armand, has a small plot of land where she grows vegetables and flowers to sell at the market. Many of the brown bottles in my collection contain fluids that were distilled from her produce.

In Monsieur Armand's laboratory, in the middle of the afternoon, all shutters remain closed. Thin streams of light trespass and fall in diagonal lines across glass vessels. Tubes lead from one to the other in a world of liquids that bubble and fizz.

'This is a very combustible material.' Leaning on his stick, he licks his lips, wrinkles deepening in concentration under strands of white hair.

'Monsieur Armand, I really appreciate this. I know that you originally acquired the substance for yourself.'

'Shh, say no more,' he says, his free hand at my back. A baby cries. 'That's Madeleine, my grandchild,' he says, eyes lit.

'What are you going to do with the phosphorus?'

'I'm going to make a homeopathic remedy.'

'What's that?' He pulls down a book from a splintery shelf behind him. Dust puffs into the air like face powder in a thespian's dressing room.

'No,' he says, opening the leather-bound and gilt-edged tome. 'It's not mentioned here. And therefore...' He claps the book shut, '... it does not exist.'

Moving Home March 20th

'It is not enough to know your craft –
you have to have feeling.'

Edouard Manet

It is seven o'clock in the evening and deceitfully dark. I sit on a crate in the centre of the main room in my new apartment in rue Faubourg Saint Denis. I face two large windows which look out upon a full moon that throws a white smudge at my feet. Inside, there is no light. The fireplace is silent in its unlit state. My greatcoat hangs on a hook behind the door wearing a lunar streak. I don't feel cold inside although my feet are numb and when I touch my cheek with my fingers they are shockingly cold. The warmth in my chest brings me comfort. This room is embracing me.

There's the clip-clop of horses' hooves, neighing, the closing of carriage doors and the voices of easily affronted Parisians three stories below. My heart lurches with my good fortune, for this is a great room. The walls are high, luminous, practically begging for art to adorn them. My desk, which seemed so large and cumbersome at my last address in rue Montholon, proudly occupies less than one third of the space, and is tucked away at one end. I imagine receiving patients here, putting chairs out in the hallway where they can wait. I will make the alcove into a kitchen/dispensary for my medicine. But not only that, this room is conducive to artistry. The light is good. It is where I shall paint.

I will store my easel and my canvases in the cupboard in the small lobby leading to the bedroom, through the door to the right of the fireplace.

I shall be happy here.

A knock on the door jolts me from my thoughts. Without thinking to light a gas lamp or candle, I jump up.

'Who is it?' I call through the door.

'Victorine Meurent.'

Releasing the shiny new brass chain, I let her in.

'Bonjour Monsieur Docteur, my dear friend Paul,' she greets me.

'It's very dark. I wouldn't have thought you were a man who was into séance,' she says, bounding in and stopping short only a few steps beyond the threshold. She looks back at me.

'Victorine,' I tell her, 'your vivid imagination influences you. I've just moved in. I've been sitting on that crate contemplating my new direction and inwardly celebrating. Let me bring some light to the situation.'

I rub my cold hands on my trouser legs and hunt blindly through packing boxes for matches, which I eventually find. I strike one and the phosphorus glows bright like the sun, dying as I spark up the gas lamps by their brass cords.

'I've come to ask you when it would be a convenient time to call. I knew that it wouldn't be now, but Camille gave me your new address and I'm desperate to see you professionally, so I thought I would stop by in passing just to ask you this question,' she says, her body as composed as Savoldo's *Mary Magdalene*, silver caped and waiting on a hillside wall above the port in Old Jerusalem.

'Forgive me if I don't ask you what the matter is right away,' I say, indicating with my arms the bareness of the space around me.

'It's the usual.'

'Ah!'

Victorine is a city girl who like so many others, lives on her wits, but she has a talent for life and there is very little that she cannot do.

'I'm not unpacked yet. You'll have to come back tomorrow at around eleven. I will have what you want to hand.'

'Paul, you're wonderful,' she tells me with her palms at my shoulders and her red lipstick making imprints on my cheeks, as usual.

She leaves me alone again. Immediately, I extinguish the light and look around, re-focusing. Perhaps Victorine is on the street looking up, finding me odd to desire darkness in this way. I pick up the matches left on the mantel and strike a bulbous head against the grainy stone fireplace. Immediately it flares white gold and blinding. Phosphorescent. What is to be learned? I do this three more times then retire to bed.

Acknowledgements

There is something ambrosial about being the author of *Song for Ria*. The inspiration came in a nanosecond after listening to a Tori Amos interview. Writing the first draft flowed. Then Isobel Leach at Cornerstones Literary Agency matched me with a perfect editor. Helen Bryant and Nick H at Cornerstones gave helpful advice when *Song for Ria* was recommended to their scouting division. My fabulous editor, Vicky Blunden, had wonderful insights that pathed the way to this work reaching its full potential and her constant encouragement whilst seeking publication was the reason why I didn't give up. Clare Christian who, after hearing a Desert Island Discs style podcast about her work, made me feel I really wanted her to be my publisher, and as if by magic, Clare wanted to be my publisher and consequently having the good fortune to work with an amazing team at RedDoor Press; Heather Boisseau, Lizzie Lewis and Nicky Gyopari, as copy editor. I am also very grateful to Sandra Consentino, my shaman and the Hopi tribe in Arizona for welcoming me onto their reservation. Michelle Tomaselli for coming with me on an experience that informed this book. Caroline True for your photographic artistry. Kate Bush and Tori Amos for allowing me to print their amazing and pertinent lyrics. Linda Gray Sexton for allowing me to print her mother's perceptive words. Kari Brownlie for the cool cover design. Jen Parker for typesetting. Nomads Writing Group for your critiques. Sarah Hervey-Bathurst for your enthusiasm in my work. My early readers, Liz Shine, Emily Brown and Elaine Ratner. My dad, David Ratner. All my wonderful friends, you know who you are. My children, Becs, Matt and Dan. Grandchild Lily. Son-in-law Gavin. And Jon, my late husband, whose handsome spirit is always with me. Thank you all.

About the Author

Michelle Shine was born in London in 1956 and lives in Hampstead. She is the author of *Mesmerised*, a historical novel about the Impressionists, narrated by their friend, fellow artist, doctor and homeopath, Paul Gachet, and *The Subtle Art of Healing*, which was long listed for the Cinnamon Press novella award in 2007. Her short stories have appeared in Liars League, Grey Sparrow, Epiphany and several collections. She has an MA in Creative Writing from Birkbeck.

Find out more about RedDoor
Press and sign up to our
newsletter to hear about our
latest releases, **author events**,
exciting **competitions**
and more at

reddoorpress.co.uk

YOU CAN ALSO FOLLOW US:

 @RedDoorBooks

 Facebook.com/RedDoorPress

 @RedDoorBooks